FREELOVE

a novel

SIA FIGIEL

✧✦✧

It is 1985 in Nu'uolemanusa/Village of the Sacred Owl, Western Samoa. Madonna's *Like a Virgin* rules the airwaves. Brilliant and inquisitive high school student and Star Trek fanatic, 17 ½ year old Inosia Alofafua Afatasi, is sent by her mother to the capital, Apia, to buy three giant white threads. While she waits at the bus-stop, Mr. Ioane Viliamu, her teacher of Science and Mathematics and recent graduate of the University of Papua New Guinea and the pastor's eldest son, in turn, her spiritual brother, stops to offer her a ride in his red pick-up truck. Should she wait for the bus? Or should she accept the ride?

ALSO BY SIA FIGIEL

where we once belonged (novel): Winner of the 1997 Commonwealth Writer's Prize, Best First Book, South-East Asia– South Pacific region
The Girl in the Moon Circle (Novel)
They Who Do Not Grieve (Novel)
To A Young Artist in Contemplation (Prose-Poetry)
TERENESIA, performance poetry CD with Teresia Teaiwa
Fagogo o Samoa (Play)

COMING SOON BY SIA FIGIEL

NOVELS
Headless
S/ex: A Personal Matter

POETRY
Songs of the Formerly Fat Brown Woman

OPERA
Pepe, Le Faletua, translation to Samoan of Giacomo Puccini's *Madama Butterfly,* from the English by R.H. Elkin.

MORE PRAISE FOR *FREELOVE* FROM ACROSS OCEANIA

Sexy, hot, romantic, sensual, funny, and above all a novel of ideas, in a new tradition to indigenous Pacific Islander writing.
Dan Taulapapa McMullin, author of *Coconut Milk*. Amerika Samoa.

Powerful, woven tapestry of culture, language, experience. Defies common stereotypes of Samoan (and PI) people and culture. Fierce. Love letter to our cultures and being. Mana Wahine. Brilliant.
Ku'ualoha Ho'omanawanui, author of *Voices of Fire: Reweaving the Literary Lei of Pele and Hi'ika. Hawai'i*.

Unconventional and unsettling. Portrays the Samoan experience with honesty. A welcome shift that depicts young islanders coming into their own without the hangovers of postcolonialty.
Dr. Fata Simanu-Klutz, Assistant Professor at the University of Hawai'i at Mānoa.

Perceptive and groundbreaking. Challenges a very restrictive colonial ideology characterized by notions of dualism, linearity, and stasis which shaped and continues to shape Pacific spirituality. Inosia (or Sia) from the village of Nu'uolemanusa represents an aquatic culture of fluidity, movement, and openness where both courteousness and errantry become tools in creatively discovering new worlds in life. This novel is a timely offering!
Rev. Dr. Upolu Va'ai, Senior Lecturer and Head of Department of Theology and Ethics. Pacific Theological College, Suva, Fiji Islands

Sia Figel has given us the first Pacific Punk Novel. One should read the book listening to Iggy Pop's 'Search and Destroy' while walking to church on a bright Sunday morning.
Dr. Albert L. Refiti, Senior Lecturer / Spatial Design. Auckland University of Technology, New Zealand.

Over and against "free" or "romantic" love, includes a foretaste of enduring pain, makes its own justifications, and refuses the capture arranged for it. With a charged heart and quickened intelligence, Inosia Alofatua Afatasi claims the right to astound and be astounded as a birthright. What passes between her and Ioane Viliamu crosses boundaries and reaches for the skies. One finishes Sia Figiel's *Freelove* calling after Inosia: "You boldly go, girl!"
Paul Lyons, Professor of English, author of *Button Man*. Hawai'i.

Demands openness to other modes of reading—poetic, fantastical and mythic. And significantly, it definitely demands to be read in an erotic mode. It is so good to have Sia Figiel back in such a powerful way, pushing the boundaries of what can be written and explored in Pacific fiction.
Dr. Mandy Treagus, Senior Lecturer in English and Creative Writing, University of Adelaide, Australia.

Treks in the contrapuntal galaxies of transtextuality, where some Samoans have already been through their talking in opposites, and materializes in the blushes of readers. Make love in the words of Figiel and frees the spirit of readers. IMHO, *Freelove* is where we now belong. Fa'afetai, thank you, Sia!
Jione Havea, Senior Lecturer at United theological College & School of Theology, Charles Sturt University, North Parramatta, Australia.

Artfully woven. Authentic; all at once, raw and haunting. *Freelove* is a critical and insightful narrative that whets the appetite. The residue that remains speaks of sadness and dislocation leaving the reader with questions about how the story really ends.

Dr. Cresantia Frances Koya Vaka'uta, Senior Lecturer in Education, University of the South Pacific, Fiji Islands.

In this fine mix of images and words (said and not said) Sia has storied a compelling tale of sexual discovery, curiosity and exploration - with added touches of gender equity pushing through. Inosia's comment that it is the 'small things that matter' are beautifully reinforced time and time again in Figiel's superb attention to the small details in the telling of this story, which then build into really powerful and unforgettable themes.

Tagaloatele Dr. Peggy Fairbairn-Dunlop, Auckland University of Technology, New Zealand.

Perceptive, historically and culturally stimulating. The detailed insights into pre-colonial Samoan beliefs, gods: Nafanua, Saumaeafe, Pili...are all exquisitely woven through the story giving insights and depth, colour, light and dark, as Sia and Ioage explore the Samoan psyche and soul.

Sauma'eafe Dr. Vanya Taule'alo, Artist, Critic. Samoa.

Freelove...is it really? A fascinating story about the fine mats of alofa—unwoven—only to be redone to capture the essence, the beauty, and the audacious ways we can love ourselves.

Dr. David Ga'oupu Pala'ita, Adjunct Professor of Critical Pacific Islands & Oceania Studies at City College of San Francisco & the College of San Mateo.

Sia Figiel's words are hypnotic songs of love and nature, family lore, teachings, and values which she both respects and challenges. Figiel subtly weaves a subtext of politics and spirituality throughout her deeply felt melodic text, even as she extols the value and role of the Voice, Village, the island Nation, and Oceania to support survival and maintain the empowering of identity.
Kathryn Waddell Takara, poet, professor, author of *Love's Seasons*. Hawai'i.

Bold and beautiful. A reminder of the importance of shedding light on the realities of the underbelly of the Pacific and in turn all people.
Kiki, playwright and writer of 'Puzzy.' Hawai'i.

This is not an easy read. It is laced with the nerve endings of taboo sexual practices. It is for new warriors who need to cross that threshold and get that elixir, and for warriors of old who have lived Inosia's words 'They've taught me how to eat fish well. To be mindful of the bones.' Welcome back Sia!
Tuisina Ymania Brown-Gabriel, Human Rights Activist Fa'afafine, Attorney, Mother, Warrior. Sydney, Australia.

With each of her novels, Sia Figiel has turned a page on Margaret Mead and Derek Freeman's competing claims to represent Samoans to the world. With *Freelove*, Figiel has not just turned a page, she has shut the book resolutely on Mead/Freeman by reclaiming some crucial things that got lost in that overheated anthropological debate. Most importantly Figiel has reclaimed Samoan agency over representing Samoan appetites. While Mead fixated on the sexual appetites of teenage girls and Freeman on a generalized appetite for violence among Samoans, Figiel's focus is on a different appetite altogether: an insatiable Samoan appetite for learning;

learning about science, math, literature, history, nature
. . . the self, the other. Indeed, Figiel has reclaimed the
brain as the most crucial organ in sexual desire for Pacific
Islanders and that is the biggest turn-on of this book.
**Dr. Teresia Teaiwa, Senior Lecturer Pacific Studies.
Victoria University, Wellington New Zealand.**

A dangerous beauty that should not be read by those who
are afraid to love freely without fear or shame.
**Dr. Vilsoni Hereniko, literary critic, playwright,
filmmaker and professor at the Academy for Creative
Media at the University of Hawaii. Originally from
Rotuma, Fiji, he has taught Pacific Literature at the
University of the South Pacific and the University of
Hawai'i for several decades. He is also a former editor
of the award-winning journal *The Contemporary
Pacific*.**

Lō'ihi Press
Honolulu

www.loihipress.com
735 Bishop Street, Suite 235
Honolulu, Hawai'i 96813

For Kat Lobendahn,
Fa'afetai tele sis for keepin' it real
With your undying devotion and friendship.
Philip Culbertson,
We'll always have Palm Springs, darling. Thank you and fa'afetai tele.
Subra, who planted the idea, many, many moons ago.
Loloma, Namaste and Alofas.
The Yam Man I am . . . Malo 'aupito.
Craig and Carol Severance,
Much aloha for you both and your support of me in Hilo.
And for my brave and stinky sons
Pounamu Fa'afetai Figiel Toia and Malamalama Jean-Paul Figiel
Who lived and breathed and survived the *Freelove* marathon with
me. I'll hang your medals around my neck forever.
Sr. Vitolia Moa, Captain, my Captain!
To my sister, Manumanuletitiotama Marilyn To'omalatai Figiel-
Griffin a.k.a Moon Face, O le uo i aso uma, a'o le uso i aso vale...fai
aku ai fo'i!

Mark Panek for your bro/pono work on uploading *Freelove* to kindle.
Many, many thanks and mahalo.
& the adamantine and most remarkable Mr. Robert Barclay and
the Lo'ihi crew of one...for the blood and sweat that made *Freelove*
possible. There are truly no words. Fa'afetai tele and much respect
Bob. Alofa atu to Stacy and the ke'iki & puppies.

For Al, a.k.a. Albert Wendt,
With love and respect
For sighting that first black star.
Thank you for showing us the song lines
And other ways of seeing our Oceanic world and beyond her reefs.
Malo lava le fai o le faiva.
Ua malie mata 'e va'ai.
O lau pule lea.

CONTENTS

FOREWORD

In Oceania's literary history when the cultural, artistic renaissance, with its genesis in independence movements of the 1960s and 70's, was coming to gradual stillness, in midst of political turmoil and authoritarian rule, an audacious new talent blazed into the writing scene, Sia Figiel, giving us the prize-winning novel, *where we once belonged* (1997). She was not only an ingenious prose writer, but also a seductive poet and an astounding performer, exactly the sort of free spirit required to rekindle much needed hype around Pacific writing. There is similar buzz once again; her new novel *Freelove* is building an epiphanic connection across borders with island writers and friends of Pacific writing, setting up the conditions of its production and immediate reception. This extra-narrative is a satellite event around the novel in which we are on wings of imagination voyaging with the seventeen-and-half-year-old *Star Trek* fanatic from Nu'uolemanusa, Western Samoa, exploring new empires of life, love, and language, where no one has been before. The locus of the novel is 'the colonizing moment', poetic conflation of time and space, history and memory, in which the protagonist, Sia, raised both extra-terrestrially and with the subaltern kuaback folks, is in a red pick-up truck with her teacher of science, and brother who is her lover, but she cannot be kept captive in relationship, thus drifts in many directions beyond taboos, constraints of 'the moody language', history and gender, riding stream of thought and consciousness, the quest is mostly inner directed towards many riddles of love. Love is the great integer that makes the ocean flow, the visionary energy that reconciles day and night, meeting and separation, and yearning for each other. That love is for the bravest and wisest and resides in the innermost resources of the self and in the moral order of the galaxy. It reveals to the sagacious voyager 'we triumph conquering ourselves, not others'. The instrument of conquest is language that, in the novel, welds together metaphors of scientific spirit and poetic beauty, fa'asamoa and newness, fusing height and depth, serious and hoaxing game, exhaling deluge of love, and ultimately engendering an incorrigible optimism.

Professor Subramani, literary critic, author of *South Pacific Literature: From Myth to Fabulation* and *The Fantasy Eaters*. Fiji National University.

BOOK ONE

INOSIA ALOFAFUA AFATASI

ENGLISH CLASS FORM 6 VOCABULARY LIST

Vehemently, Divulge, Brim, **Trimester, Forbidden,** Intently, **Hymen blood,** Retaliation, Scrutinize, **Conceal,** Monotony, Emphatic, Alacrity, Divergence, Contradiction, Exaltation, **Affair,** Conspiracy, Uncontaminated, Prejudices, Discriminate, Illuminate. Pulsate, **Penile erection,** Aesthetics, **Relationship,** Aeronautics, Retribution, Offender, **Apology,** Perpendicular, Contemplate, **Incestuous,** Splendiferous, Resolve, Critique, Nostalgia, **Subtle,** Lingers, Philosophical, Infinities, Opulent, Refulgent, Philosophical, Lustrous, Intimate, Opulent, Ecosystem, Suppressed, **Sinful,** Innuendo, Transparent, Symbiosis, Photosynthesis, Resemblance, **Reproduction,** Osmosis, Scintillating, Amaranthine, Nonchalantly, Cannibalistic, Resourceful, Alluring, Reasoning, Indulgent, Cacophony, Paradoxical, Irony, Instinct, Governed, Opulent, Wicked, Expanse, Beaut, Empiricism, **Illicit,** Humility, **Deflowering,** Bacteria, Spirituality, Omnipresence, Premonition, Stupendous, Prediction, **Semen, Sperm,** Traumatic, Recede, Gratification, Pleasure, Multitudinous, Precision, Manipulate, Determinant, Vehemently, Indulgence, Syllogism, Pavlovian, Inter-galactic, Nocturnal, Divulge, Interconnectedness, Rhetoric, Perpendicular, Theory of Relativity, Manifestation. Ceremonial, Existence, Perpetually, Meditate, **Orgasm,** Simultaneously, Nuances, Instinctively, Sensation, Constellation, **Peace,** Polymorphic, Polytheistic, Polygon, Polychromatic, Polysyllabic, **Polygamist,** Polytheistic, Polygamist, Polyp.

SAMOAN - ENGLISH VOCABULARY LIST

Inosia. Despised.

Ino. Excrements.

Sia. *pron*. This.

Sia. One passive termination, as *motusia or inosia*.

Alofatunoa/Alofafua. To love unconditionally, to love freely.

Alofa. *s*. **1.** Love, compassion. *'O lona alofa*. **2.** A present, a gift.

Alofa. *v*. **1.** To love, to be compassionate. **2.** To salute; as *Ta alofa*, contracted to *Talofa*, the ordinary salutation; *pl*. Alolofa; *pass*. Alofaina, alofagia; *recip*. Fealofani.

Fua. *Malay*, Buah, *s*. **1.** Fruit, flower. *I fua mai le nau ina utupupu ia*. *'O lona fua*. **2.** Seed. **3.** An egg. *Le fua lupe e tau tasi*. **4.** Spawn of fish. **5.** A good-looking child of a chief. *E le tauilo fua o ali'i*. **6.** A fleet of canoes. **7.** A measure. Fua, a particle suffixed to the units, with *ga* as a connecting particle, in counting breadfruit, shellfish, & c., *e laufua, e tolugafua*; it is prefixed in counting tens, *e fualua*.

Fua. *adv*. **1.** Without cause. *Lau sala e fa'apua fua*. **2.** Without success. **3.** Uselessly, to no purpose.

Fua. *v*. **1.** To produce fruit. **2.** To proceed from, to originate. *Fua mai lava*.

Fua. *s*. Jealousy; only of the sexes; *'O lona fua*.

Fua. *v*. to be jealous. *pass*. Fuatia.

Fua. *a*. Jealous. *'O le fafine fua*.

Afatasi. n.v. Derived from the words afa and tasi.

Afa. v. To be united in action; from afa, a mesh stick. *'Ua afa fa'atasi*. They all use one mesh-stick, and the meshes are equal.

'Afa. s.i. Sinnet, the cord plaited, from the fiber of the coconut, largely used instead of nails for house and boat building. *O la'u 'afa.* **2.** The name of a fish. **3.** An anchor. Syn. and more common term, TAULA.

Tasi. a.i. **1.** One. **2.** Another; *O le tasi teine, po'o le tasi tamaloa.* The one girl or the one man.

Tasi. v. To be unprecedented, to be unique. *E tasi ae afe.* One in a thousand.

Tasi. adv. Very. *E lelei tasi lava.* It is very good.

Afatasi. v. n. **1.** To connect or unite in one action. **2.** To strengthen as one. **3.** n. One that is unique; the unprecedented one. *O tama'ita'i afatasi.* Plural.

Unique women; unprecedented women.

Women who come together to strengthen or to unite as one.

Women who are anchored by one action or event.

AOGA MAUALUGA NU'UOLEMANUSA
NU'UOLEMANUSA HIGH SCHOOL

Ripoti Fa'ai'u o le Tausaga
End of Year School Report

Itumalo Faleolela / Faleolela School District
Malo Tuto'atasi o Samoa I Sisifo /
The Independent State of Western Samoa
E fa'avae i le Atua Samoa / Samoa is founded on God
Tesema 20, 1985 / 20 December 1985

IGOA / NAME: **INOSIA ALOFAFUA AFATASI**
Vasega: 6 / Class: Form 6.
Mata'upu: Vasega o le Fa'asaenisi / Subject: Science
Amio: Maoa'e le Lelei. / Conduct: Excellent.
Tulaga i le Vasega: Sili. Place in Class: 1st Place.
Togi aofa'i: 100% / Total Points: 100%
Fa'amatalaga a le Faiaoga / Teacher's Comments:

Inosia is one of those rare gems of a student that a teacher is blessed with once in a lifetime. Intuitive and mature beyond her years, Sia is able to grasp the fundamental concepts of Science and is able to excite and share her knowledge, particularly with those fellow students who struggle with them.
She is not afraid to ask questions and I have had the privilege of witnessing her academic growth through this last year of high school. Diligent and hard working, I have great faith that whatever she decides to study and put her mind to, she will do so successfully.
It has been an honor to have been her teacher, although at times, she has taught me more than she'll ever know.

O ou mama na, Sia. / Go with my blessings, Sia.
Mr. Ioane Viliamu.
Faiaoga / Teacher

⌐TOP 20 BEST SONGS OF 1985 ON THE 2AP⌐

1. *Like a Virgin* by MADONNA.
2. *E Pa'ia o le Alo o le Atua* by TAMA O LE TIAMA'A.
3. *Sosefina* by TAMA O LE TIAMA'A.
4. *Pule Aoao le Atua* by TAMA O LE TIAMA'A.
5. *Mo'omo'oga* by PUNIALAVA'A.
6. *I Want to Know What Love Is* by FOREIGNER.
7. *I Feel for You* by CHAKA KHAN.
8. *Take On Me* by A-HA.
9. *Malu A'e le Afiafi* by FETU LIMA.
10. *Everytime You Go Away* by PAUL YOUNG.
11. *Careless Whispers* by WHAM.
12. *Sa Ou Nofo ma Va'ava'ai i Fetu o le Lagi* by PENINA O TI'AFAU.
13. *Taualaga a Solomona* by PENINA O TI'AFAU.
14. *Cherish the Love* by COOL & THE GANG.
15. *The Power of Love* by HUEY LEWIS & THE NEWS.
16. *Sina Ea, Sau Se'i Fai Mai* by TAMA O LE TIAMA'A.
17. *Pele Moana* by THE GOLDEN ALI'I'S.
18. *Beyond the Reef* by THE YANDALL SISTERS.
19. *Tupe Siliva* by 'ELEVISI' "ELVIS OF SAMOA" LAUOLEFISO TO'OMALATAI.
20. *Saving All My Love for You* by WHITNEY HOUSTON.

"Space: the final frontier. These are the voyages of the starship Enterprise. Its five-year mission: to explore strange new worlds, to seek out new life and new civilizations, to boldly go where no man has gone before."

This brave and compelling introductory speech to *Star Trek* echoed and echoed throughout Nuʻuolemanusa, our village, (a.k.a, Nuʻusa, to visitors, strangers and palagi or Guʻusa to its descendants and those familiar with it) from three households where a blue light shone out of on Thursday nights, sharply at 9 p.m. *Or unsharply* if it were the case, whenever the TV experienced technical difficulties which meant the scheduled programs were indefinitely suspended and the screen remained that of a picture of waves breaking onto black lava rocks with the caption in large capital letters:

KVZK TV, PAGO PAGO, AMERICAN SAMOA.

The *Star Trek* introductory speech was a voiceover of our hero, none other than *the* Captain James T. Kirk of the USS Starship Enterprise. Captain Kirk's words not only infiltrated my medulla oblongata (telepathically via osmosis? *Star Trek* episode, "Is There No Truth in Beauty?"), and made me salivate for more and more knowledge of space and time travel like a Pavlovian dog, on Thursday nights at 9 p.m. but more specifically, they fired my imagination to the limitless possibilities among Samoan *girls* and *women* as captains navigating beyond the Milky Way galaxy as they might have done on canoes in ancient and future times, since no women were present on the very male-dominate *Star Trek*, that had its women merely as communication officers and nurses, or mysteriously exotic love interests and none in any significant decision making positions of power that I thought worthy of emulation.

I mean, sure they had Lt. Nyoto Uhura abroad the Enterprise who I admired. How could I not? She was a black woman from the United States of Africa, whose name in Swahili meant 'freedom' which already made me scream and fist pump, *Girl Power!* Lt. Uhura attended and graduated from the Starfleet Academy and then ended up being a cadet trainer herself at that fine institution that taught discipline of mind and body for Science! She was supposedly a Commander but did they once give her actual command of the USS Enterprise? In an emergency even? I really don't think they would have. And if they did, then God cut my tongue out, because I surely did not see *that* particular episode.

Still, *Star Trek* was the most exciting show on TV and won my heart almost immediately as a devoted student of Mathematics and Science.

TV was already common in other villages around Western Samoa, especially those close to Apia who already had access to the wonders of a new technology called video, where you could watch movies in the comfort of your own home. Something we loved at first but then realized quickly afterwards that it severely limited our contact with the outside world, especially special trips to the dark rows of the Savalalo Grand or the Tivoli where we watched and fell in love with John Travolta as Danny in *Grease* or Bruce Lee in *Return of the Dragon*. Not to mention sitting in the dark among boys and men, something that was highly frowned upon and considered inappropriate behavior for girls our age who were already menstruating and no longer reminded to shower twice daily; once upon rising and once after the evening meals when dishes were washed.

Gu'usa only had three TVs and they belonged to Tama Esimoto our pastor and spiritual father, Q's family and Nanamuolela's, our village sa'o or high chief.

Because it was the pastor's house, it was already a given that no one went there to watch TV, except the good girls of which I was. But it's rather awkward to watch people show intimate affection on Fantasy Island or Love Boat or Dallas while Tama Esimoto prepared his sermon and Tina Lakena was crocheting, looking up now and then and frowning instead at the Ford commercial that showed too much skin on the model in a swimsuit, excitedly jumping up and down once she exited the car. Then asking us whether we had driven Fords lately. And then immediately after that commercial break, and the show in progress would return, one had to excuse one's self and go home, too shameful to be seen curious about something which others might consider just a kiss, because kisses were believed to not exist in God-fearing Christian Gu'usa. At least the French kind that Hope and Bo were engaged in frequently on Days of Our Lives, or some of the guest visitors to Fantasy Island and passengers aboard the Love Boat.

The second TV was at Queeniveere's family and thank goodness Q and I were already friends before their TV arrived from her relatives in Kukuila who had sent it on the Queen Salamasina ferry and we were all there the day it arrived and saw them set up the antenna and within minutes, the entire village had gathered outside the louvers watching Pi'iga, Big Time Wresting.

Nanamuolela's, our village sa'o and head chief's was the third house with a TV but because he was the sa'o, no one went to their house on a Thursday night or on any night, except to drop off food and pick up plates where food was previously given as a sign of respect for the high chief and leader of our village. And even though his wife, Koligi would insist whenever she met our mothers in church or at the Women's Committee bingo to have the children come over and watch, our mothers knew better. They too were raised with the belief that the sa'o's house was taboo. It was a place whose dignity was maintained by the silence that surrounded it, which meant children and dogs were discouraged from going near its grounds so as not to disturb.

I guess you could say technically then, that there was only one TV in Gu'usa. That of Q's family. The one where everyone and their dog and cat and lizard would be crowded in to see and taste the new blue light while adults stood outside savoring its waves and radiance through the glass louvers.

Of course this meant that all the girls wanted to be Q's friend. Q the tomboy who never wore a dress. I was hers before the TV arrived, when we were 12, a lifetime ago, which made me the first to step into the USS Starship Enterprise and into the world of Science Officer Mr. Spock and Captain Kirk and Lt. Hikaru Sulu and Chief Medical Examiner Dr. Leonard McCoy, Lt. Commander Montgomery "Scotty" Scott, Nurse Christine Chapel, Communication Officer Lt. Nyota Uhura and the magic of the Transporter Room that could beam you just about anywhere you wanted to go.

What was exciting about *Star Trek* and made it different from say the Love Boat, or Fantasy Island or even Days of Our Lives, (despite its glaring gender imbalance), is that *Star Trek* gave you a glimpse of what human beings were capable of in the future and just how far one would travel to find and unravel the mysteries of the universe. Ideally, for the benefit of mankind.

I didn't realize that Saturday morning that I was going to embark on a similar voyage of my own. A life-changing journey that began when my mother asked me to drop everything and go to Apia on an errand. An errand that would take me into a strange new world where the rules of civilization as we knew it were instinctively abandoned and forgotten until the full weight of its reality glared and glared and glared into my eyes, almost blinding me.

I'm talking about the forbidden world of incest.

The final frontier.

Only my journey was not to benefit mankind or anyone else, other than the discovery and exploration and ultimate fulfillment of my own 17½ year old curiosities and desires and those of the one I came to call Night, who was my brother *and* my lover.

On one of the worst weekends to go shopping in Apia, the Saturday before White Sunday, my mother decides to ask me to leave the decoration of the church to Q and Cha and other girls in the choir and that I needed to catch the bus to town to buy her three giant white threads as she was running out of the last one with two more boy shirts and a puletasi that still needed to be cut and sewn, to be collected later that evening by a woman who would be traveling from Malaefou, a town village on the other side of the island.

I knew this would happen.

I knew she would run out of white thread, which is why I had suggested to her to buy three more when we were at CC's Stitches & Things two Saturdays ago.

But my mother being my mother, never listens to me.

I have just about given up on talking to her altogether as my voice seems to be nothing more than a noisy breeze to her, one that seems to either pollute the space where she breathes or doesn't exist at all.

I've come to the conclusion that my mother will only listen to me when one thing is certain, when I am dead.

✧✦✧

I quickly jumped into the shower and before I even turned the tap on, I could hear my mother yelling, Don't spend all day in there, girl! We haven't yet paid the water bill and Koma's bus just passed. He'll be back in fifteen minutes. Hurry!

I barely had time to wash my hair, so I decided not to. Instead, I cleaned myself as best as I could, fa'apako or duck-style and rushed out of the shower, quickly calculating what I would wear and whether my cousin Losaliga returned the skinny jeans she borrowed last week when their school had worn Mufty.

These impromptu visits to Apia are not as easy to execute as one might think. Especially when one shares one's best clothes with one's cousins, a fact of life that's best left unspoken. Just thinking about it makes you wish you were an only child, raised by extra-terrestrials in some far off planet, void of mothers, brothers and annoying younger sisters.

I looked through the shelf where we kept our daily clothes and noticed nothing, nothing a 17½ year old girl like me would want to be seen with on a bus headed for Apia.

I decided to look in the box where our family kept our good clothes and found my sister Litia's *Madonna The Virgin Tour 1985* t-shirt she won at the Women's Committee Bingo, and that was before I stumbled upon my miracle. Thank you Jesus! My skinny jeans were in there! Ironed and perfectly folded as only nerdy Losaliga would have done. I mean, who irons jeans?

I quickly took the clothes out of the box, dried myself before I threw them on, rolling the long legs to knee high and wrapped a lavalava around my hips before anyone could see.

Uncle Fa'avevesi, my mother's brother had banned us from wearing jeans. According to him, only girls and Women of the Night wore them. Which was perfectly ok with me. After all, it was 10 a.m. on a bright and sunny Saturday morning.

Still, the lavalava was extra insurance that he might not be at the plantation where he goes on Saturday mornings with his sons Chris and Emau and my twin brothers Aukilani and Ueligitone, affectionately called Au and Ue by everyone, except Tama Esimoto our spiritual father and pastor who never abbreviates anyone's name and would remind us that he did not baptize anyone with abbreviated names and that God will only recognize those who were baptized by their full names when they entered the pearly gates. Hmmm.

This would sometimes make me question God. I mean, if He were the Almighty, All Knowing God, Tama Esimoto told us he was, you would think he would have a good memory of all his creations, particularly those from our village who worshiped him with undying devotion. You'd think?

But who am I but a 17½ year old *Star Trek* fanatic from Nu'uolemanusa, Western Samoa who remembered every single episode of Season One, beginning with *The Man Trap* when the USS Enterprise visited planet M-113 to check on the man-wife team stationed there from Planet Earth only to find that the woman or the wife had been replaced by a strange and deadly shape-shifting creature.

How do you know all that Sia? I can't even remember last week's episode! said Cha. That's because you're not following the plot like Sia does Missy, Q jumped in. Admit it! You only watch *Star Trek* because you think Mr. Spock is sexy and could perform despicable alien acts on your fa'afafige body.

Ahhhhhhhue'e! Ua make'ia laka kupua, se! Ahhhhhhh! My riddle has been guessed! Cha cracked up laughing until soon we were all rolling on the floor, near the church steps.

✧✦✧

Before I left the house my mother had given me $25 tala. $15 tala for the threads and $10 tala for my bus fare and a snack.

Vave mai i le fale, my mother said.

Hurry home, she said vehemently, as she took a drag from a cigarette and walked towards the sewing machine. Her workplace and altar of worship.

Before she sat down, she picked up a pair of scissors and pointed them towards me.

Ma fa'apaku i luga le ga ulu. Kao ia, fa'akogu so'o.

And how many times do I need to tell you to wrap your hair up in a bun before you leave this house? I could just bake you in an oven!

I was standing at the bus-stop when Mr. Viliamu's ancient red Toyota pick-up truck passed before me. Instinctively, I waved at him, as his pick-up continued down the road before I bent to my feet and slapped about a dozen mosquitoes that had been circling there since I arrived at the bus-stop before I leaned against a post that said Nu'uolemanusa Tai, Home of the Owl.

Minutes earlier, I had neatly folded the lavalava I had thrown around me as a cover-up to my jeans before I left the house and was brimming with pride at just how resourceful I had become in avoiding the thousand-and-one rules that governed my life, every time I left the house.

Just as I was about to let my hair loose from the sloppy bun it was in, Mr. Viliamu's red pick-up truck reversed towards the bus-stop and he called out nonchalantly, in a voice I'd never heard before, nor recognized as belonging to him.

Girl, Can I give you a lift? he said, smiling at me as if he were meeting me for the very first time.

No, thanks Mr. Viliamu, I said politely, pressing my bag closer to my lap and then eventually holding it up to cover my chest.

I'll wait for the bus.

Have a good day, Sir, I said, waving at him politely, looking down at my feet that were already spotted with mosquito bites, allowing Mr. Viliamu time to bid me farewell before he sped off to wherever it was he was heading.

But from the sound of the motor, his pick-up was still stationed right there before me.

What does he want now? I asked myself.

And before I finished my thought he had already called out, How far are you going, Si'aula?

Apia, I replied, almost immediately.

I'm going to Apia, Mr. Viliamu. Then I need to make a stop at Gu'usa Uka on my return, I said, with a sudden urge to pinch myself for divulging more information than he needed to know.

He had only asked me where I was headed.

He didn't need to know that I had to stop at Gu'usa Uka on my return. Just as well I didn't reveal that part of it. The part about meeting up with Q and Cha at the Gu'usa Uka volleyball that evening whereby they were going to point out a particular someone that had been asking them about me and that I shouldn't worry because he wasn't from Gu'usa so it won't be like he was a maka'ifale or something but was friends with one of our village boys. And while Cha went on and on about how cute he looked and what a nice body he had, especially when he jumped up to spike the ball, my only prayer was that he liked *Star Trek* and whether he was sitting the Australian Mathematics Competition next month, which Mr. Viliamu had already registered us for and whether he was interested in meeting up at the Public Library one Saturday and studying together or something.

You are the most boring 17½ year old girl in the entire district Inosia Alofafua Afatasi! If I had the kind of sinful body you have girl, they would have to chain me down to a rock and hide the key! Cos, I would be traveling the world and going places no other girl has ever gone before! (Except Evelyn and her baby...oops...Did I say that out loud or is that only appearing as a Stan Lee bubble coming out of my head?).

How's that for being a true Trekkie! said Cha, as she sniggered with her hands to her hips as if she were a woman, scolding a child but with the most wicked smile across her face.

And Queenieveere, loyal and faithful Q, always to my rescue countered, Sia is a good girl, Cha. It's girls like her that give this village a good name and reputation. Who else wins the Inter-Island High School Mathematics and Science Competition twice in a row against the Apia schools? Huh?

I'm not talking about brains Q. We all know Sia carries a big bag of marbles. I'm saying, she needs to pay attention to her body and develop *it* as well. It's not all about brains you know.

Hey, why are you talking about me like I'm not even here? Don't treat me like a nobody. I'm right here! Talk to me Cha! If you have something to say, say it to me. Not to some abstract form of me. Ua iloa? You hear?

See, there she goes again. Using that vocabulary on us!

Well, isn't that what Mrs. Amosaosavavau told us to do? To make English alive by using the vocabulary we're learning in school? I fired back at Cha who was obviously unrelenting in her opinion.

Why do you have to be so square and do everything our teachers say? Huh? You're pathetic, Sia. I'm sorry to say that, but you really are pathetic, says Cha. I don't even know why I waste my time being friends with you. You're too clean. Too virginal. Too eh! Blah! That's what you are! She excused herself and walked away but called out before she completely disappeared, In case you're interested Miss Sia, his name is Nelson Solofa. He's the most beautiful Form 7th boy-man student on the planet. And I've had a secret crush on him since the 3rd Form. And it breaks my heart because he looks at me with lust but he wants you, boring, boring you with your head in Mr. Spock's brain and Captain Kirk's crotch! There! Fa la'ia! Goodbye now!

As Cha walked away from us, I found it difficult to understand why she was being so overdramatic! We'd known each other since we were children. She knew everything about me and Q and we knew the same of her. How she detested for instance being told by outsiders that her mother dressed her as a girl when she was a child because there were no girls in her household to do family chores which is why she was what she was, a fa'afafige. And I could still remember her indignant voice of protest as it rang and rang and rang in my ear and each time it did, I knew some cultural anthropologist had gotten to her! How dare they say that about the origins of my sexuality! As if I were some 2nd class citizen in a *Star Trek* episode whose sexuality was determined by the woman who gave birth to me and her choice of clothing for me which weren't the best at times, I would have chosen less bright colors myself but what does that have to do with poverty and not being able to afford the clothes I wanted? The audacity of such a thought! How preposterous! How utterly offensive to assume that I am what I am because of the chores I do and the clothes I was dressed in!

Not only is this offensive to me personally but to our entire culture as Samoans, Sia! I mean, think about it Sia! Think about it! You as a woman of Science and Mathematics know just as well as I do, that my sexuality had nothing to do with how my mother supposedly dressed me as a boy and the kinds of chores I did to help our family. I was born this way, dahling! With both man and woman in me! I am two-spirited! Why do people have such a hard time understanding that? I *am* the blessed child! I don't want to be a man or a woman! Why should I have to choose when I am both! And why should I be made to feel like I am a leper? That I am diseased? When everyone knows perfectly well that I am the end-possibility of the universe? God's most precious creation. The true expression of Her or His genius?

Cha's spirit and fierce intelligence was something that I secretly envied. I envied it because she didn't have to work as hard at it as I did. Mr. Viliamu would give us a quiz on Photosynthesis or Reproduction or Symbiosis and she would get every single answer correct. Without even studying for it! The way I had to. Granted I loved studying and lived for those moments of solitude where I found myself being astounded by an original thought that someone else had thought in history many centuries earlier, Hypocrates, Pythagoras, Isaac Newton, Marie Currie, the list goes on. But secretly, Cha is my real life heroine! Her ability to express herself openly and with wild abandon; ways of being that I was only able to dream about since all eyes were always on me and how I behaved and how my behavior represented not just me but my mother, my grandmother, my Aunty Aima'a, my Uncle Fa'avevesi, my spiritual parents Tama Esimoto and Tina Lakena and everyone else that I was related to by blood or through marriage!

As Cha walked away, I couldn't help but think of that episode called "Charlie X" that centered around a very dangerous young man, Charlie Evans, a passenger, traveling aboard the USS Enterprise, terrorizing the crew with his mental powers, the way she appeared to terrorize me but with the difference that I always knew Cha would come back and ask to be forgiven or I would do the same to her as we wouldn't be able to endure entire days without saying something to each other, as the silences that were born out of such rash moments were almost always so deafeningly unbearable.

I knew Cha would find being compared to Charles Evans offensive since there was an unspoken code to never refer to him as a male, (at least at this point in my life, she would say) that she was one of the girls. And that's exactly how we treated her. And everyone else around her. Except our spiritual father and pastor Tama Esimoto who always called her Charlie because that's the name she was baptized with and the name God would recognize her with when s(he) entered the pearly gates, preferably in a black suit and iefaikaga and not the dress Cha had been designing since we were in Form 3, which I reckon the angels would also envy since it radiated with a sequence of real diamonds and rubies that would blind even the Sun.

My thoughts returned to the red pick-up truck before me and to Mr. Viliamu's question of where I was headed.

Why did I have to tell him all that for? Idiot! I told myself, as I smiled right back at Mr. Viliamu, hoping he didn't sense the awkwardness with which I was calculating my next move.

Then you're in luck, girl! he said, with a wider smile on his face this time.

I'm headed to the Public Library in town. I can also give you a ride back if you want to meet up later after you've done your shopping, if you want.

As Mr. Viliamu was talking, I was already beginning to calculate yet again whether I should stay and wait for the bus or take his offer and go with him.

What harm would a ride from a teacher do?

It's not like he's some strange man that I didn't know who was trying to pick me up and drive me off to some unknown destination where he'd attack me and beat me and leave me for dead. Besides, not only would I be saving a good $6 tala in bus-fare, I get to ride with my favorite teacher, alone, in the back of a red pick-up truck and away from the noise of pigs and chicken and diesel fumes of an overcrowded bus that would take forever to get to town.

And with that line of reasoning, I decided to go with Mr. Viliamu.

But before I could hop onto the red pick-up truck, Mr. Viliamu called out to me.

Hey, what are you doing?

I'm getting into the truck! I excitedly responded.

I'm sorry but it's going to take me a minute, I added. Wishing I had worn something less tight as it was hard to lift my skinny jeaned legs over the tailgate.

Shh! Don't be silly! Come to the front! The sun will eat you alive back there, girl!

To tell the truth, I preferred sitting in the back of a truck and did so at any opportunity I got. Everyone I knew felt the same. Not only do you get to watch people walk by, you got to have the breeze against your skin and in your hair, which I had already decided to let loose once I got situated. But since this was someone else's generosity that is saving me money, I decided to be polite instead. Besides, I didn't want Mr. Viliamu to think I was ungrateful.

Mr. Viliamu had already opened the door before I came around to the passenger side of the pick-up which surprised me.

Thanks! I said, as I smiled at him with appreciation. After all, it's not everyday that a teacher opened a door for a student, I thought, as I hopped onto the seat, closing the door behind me.

You look nice, said Mr. Viliamu, who was wearing khaki shorts and a t-shirt that said

E=MC S.P.I.S.A.
South Pacific Islanders Science Association
University of Papua New Guinea
Port Moresby
1981

This time, I didn't say anything. Firstly, I noticed almost immediately that the square was missing from Einstein's theory of relativity, which I had remembered from watching NOVA the other day after school, when we were at Q's house and she told me to go turn the TV on and that I could watch if I wanted (which was a luxury of course) since we did not own a TV of our own and were in no financial position to get one any time soon. For one, my mother was technically the head of our household since it was her sewing machine that brought in the money and we relied on for a living. However, my mother always deferred to our Uncle Fa'avevesi who was older than her but hadn't worked since he lost his left hand in an accident two years ago while working on live electric wires. But that's a story to continue at another time.

Mr. Viliamu's missing square on his t-shirt made me wonder whether the South Pacific Islanders Science Association even noticed it themselves or whether it was some deliberate twist that only they knew and laughed at in their own time. And perhaps that's how things are at university. People are so smart there that they may not notice small things anymore. The small things that matter so much in relation to the big things. Small things make big things whole and complete. And I'm sure Einstein would have thought the same. But who am I but a Form 6 moepi/bedwetter trying to gather as much vocabulary as possible so that I could do what Mr. Viliamu told us to do on that first day of class when he told us to astound ourselves so that we might astound those around us.

But that's not really why I didn't say anything to Mr. Viliamu. Why did he think I looked nice? I mean, what was so nice about the way I was dressed in? I asked myself. Was it my hair? Which was in a sloppy fa'apaku/bun? Or was it my tight jeans? Instinctively, I touched my zippers to see if they were done properly. Just in case that's what he was referring to. You know how men are, Aunty Pisa, my mother's sister's voice flashed through my mind. They want only one thing and they will say and do anything to get it. Was that perhaps what he was responding to? Or was it the picture of Madonna on Litia's *The Virgin Tour* t-shirt that I was wearing? After all, I didn't wear make-up or fancy jewelry or anything that would deliberately draw attention to me. I had been told too many horror stories by girls who had been molested or raped or beaten or abused by strangers and worst by their own family members to ever galavant around drawing attention to myself. I was *terrified* of boys and men! *Terrified!*

And since I had this fear of boys and men, I was always on my guard. I read every action and reaction with great care. I didn't laugh too loudly or too cheery. And when I did, I never showed my gums which is the sign of a Woman of the Night and a slut and a whore said the womanly whispers at my house which meant that I smiled only when it was culturally and socially required and kept my mind firmly on our aiga, family, our lotu, church and on le aʻoga, school. Which is why I thought it odd that Mr. Viliamu would comment on my appearance like that, something he never did at school.

I also found it odd that he kept repeating 'if you want' as if I would have any objections to a ride from a teacher who happens to be Nuʻuolemanusa's oldest pastor's son, and oddest of all is when he kept referring to me as keige, girl, and not by my name which made me question whether he even remembered me.

How can he not? I asked myself, indignantly.

After all, didn't he know or have a clue that he was my favorite teacher?

I respected Mr. Viliamu and looked forward to his Science class more than any other class in school.

His class was the reason I woke up daily, to see what fabulous new adventures he was going to introduce us to that day.

I smiled lightly and brushed this oversight aside and looked out the window instead, watching seagulls glide above the waves.

You know what that means, don't you? said Mr. Viliamu.

Excuse me, Mr. Viliamu? I asked. Not knowing what he was referring to.

You're looking at the birds, aren't you?

Yes, I am, Mr. Viliamu. I'm looking at the birds.

And what is your Samoan scientific instinct telling you about those birds?

That they're hungry? I said, impulsively laughing out loud, which I regretted almost as soon as I had heard the sound as it escaped my tongue.

Is that a good guess, Mr. Viliamu? I asked, wiping the smile off of my face.

That's a brilliant guess! Yes, they are hungry. It appears they are hungry indeed. The birds are looking for fish. Look! Do you see those other ones to the east?

I quickly scanned the ocean. Embarrassed that I did not know which direction east was, until suddenly I spied on a school of seagulls hovering over a particular spot that I supposed Mr. Viliamu referred to as east.

Yes, I see them, I said. Now *they* must be really hungry, a 'ea?

That's how fishermen know where to direct their canoes, said Mr. Viliamu, with the same authority he used at school, only he was unusually over smiling, as if he was hiding something that had happened to him or something that was about to happen.

I guess that makes sense, I said, excited to learn something new on my way to town.

Yeah, it does make sense, aye? said Mr. Viliamu.

Our people were not only very scientific and mathematical, they had a spiritual connection to their surroundings and read nature's signs with striking precision. Like those birds out there, for instance. When you look closer at our Samoan language, you will find that it is intricately connected to nature. Do you know where the word manuia comes from?

I shook my head, acknowledging my ignorance. Preferring him to be the one telling me instead.

Of course you do!

We've just been talking about it, girl!

We have? I asked.

Ua kai fa'apea Mr. Viliamu po'o fea le lalolagi o feoa'i ai kaliga o lea. Mr Viliamu's probably thinking where my ears are galavanting about.

Manu and I'a of course mean bird and fish. The two words when combined forms the word manuia and means good fortune, which is why we say it whenever we wish someone well or after matai drink ava in a circle.

I listened intently to Mr. Viliamu as the breeze caressed both our faces.

He was a walking encyclopedia who knew just about everything there was to know and yet, he always made whatever knowledge he was passing on seem like it was a gift from God and that he was merely the medium with which such a gift was exchanged with those of us who needed to receive it.

Momentarily, I felt lucky and special that he stopped to pick me up. To share this knowledge with my ever curious and hungry mind that seemed to absorb everything he said.

A penny for your thoughts, girl, said Mr. Viliamu, drawing me back into the conversation.

I didn't know what he meant.

English I'm afraid to say, was not my best subject in school, which meant I paid more attention to it than any of the other classes I loved, like Science, Mathematics, Samoan, Social Studies and Health. I kept vocabulary notebooks and studied them and studied them and studied them until I knew meanings of words but found that there were not too many people in Gu'usa who spoke it. Perhaps I secretly loved English. Perhaps I didn't. Perhaps I did and I didn't. That's how I felt about English. It was a moody language. At times void of meaning. Empty. Perhaps this feeling of the emptiness of English comes from the blatant fact that I really had no relation to it just as much as it had no relation to me. It wasn't like my geneaology could be traced through it. Or that the veins in my blood were to be found in its alphabet, the way it is found on my mother's tattooed thighs. Besides, I did not want to appear fiapoko, like I knew everything, especially before my classmates who struggled with it as it was a language I too found hard to swallow and got stuck always in the middle of my throat, especially when I pronounced words like beach, peach, pig, big, and porridge.

And before I could respond, Mr. Viliamu asked me again.

Why are you so quiet? What are you thinking about? I'd like to know.

Does he really want to know what I'm thinking about or is he just being polite? Besides, why would the thoughts of a 17½ year old girl be of interest to an old man? He's at least 10, 12 years older than me! Not to mention the fact that he's a walking encyclopedia who just happens to be our pastor's oldest son which technically makes him my brother!

Nothing, Mr. Viliamu, I said, not wanting to disappoint him with my lack of enthusiasm.

I'm not thinking about anything. Besides, it's what you're thinking of that I'd like to know. Boldly smiling at him, supposing I had said something that he might find intelligent and would be proud of because it originated from him.

But instead he responded quite differently, as if he hadn't heard what I had said which disappointed me and I showed my disappointment by avoiding eye contact with him and stared instead into the ocean, watching her give birth to waves, listening to them splash onto the lava rocks below the cliffs of Si'unu'u which meant we were halfway to Apia.

Mr. Viliamu's voice echoed suddenly from a far away place, only he was no less than six inches away from me.

You might be embarrassed if I tell you what I'm thinking, he said, rubbing his stomach with one hand as if he hadn't eaten breakfast as he steered the pick-up truck with his other hand.

What is he saying?
Embarrassed?
Why would I be embarrassed?
Is he going to correct my English?
Should I have said a cluster or a crowd instead of a
school of birds?
They're birds all the same, aren't they?
But then Mr. Viliamu said something else. Something
he spoke through the language of his body movements.
He started scratching his knee and my eyes followed his
hand as it moved from his knee to his inner thigh so that
his shorts shrunk upwards and I caught a glimpse of his
pubic hair.

Immediately, my eyes darted out the window.

Not only was I embarrassed, frankly, I became offended
not to mention deeply ashamed.

A nervousness entered my body and I thought for
a moment that I was going to cry. After all, I had never
seen that part of a grown man's anatomy, and I suddenly
found myself thinking about all the males in my family,
my Uncle Afatasi Fa'avevesi, who is my mother's brother
and our aiga's main matai, lives with his wife Stella
behind the fale where my mother Alofafua and her sister
Aima'a, Gu'usa's traditional healer, and my grandmother
Taeao (short for Taeao'oleaigalulusa) and Ala (short
for Alailepuleoletautua), my grand-aunt who was deaf,
lived with all the girls of our family and boys under 13,
which included my 12 year old brothers Aukilani (Au)
and Ueligitone (Ue), identical twins who loved to play
identity tricks on people. The older boys, which included
our Uncle Fa'avevesi's sons Chris and Emau, as well as
our adopted brothers and other taule'ale'a or untitled
male relatives from either Savai'i, Manono or Apolima,
who are all technically considered my brothers, lived in a

house behind Uncle Fa'avevesi's house, closer to where the umukuka or kitchen was located.

With all these males around, you'd think I would have seen a full grown man's penis by now. And yet, the taboos that governed the movements of our brothers in relation to us, their sisters known as the feagaiga or the brother/sister covenant were so strictly observed and highly scrutinized that it meant I'd only witnessed a penis once.

Well, twice actually. But they belonged to my twin brothers Ue and Au who had been circumcised along with their friends and were waddling out of the ocean after one of them was stung by a jellyfish.

It was the funniest sight.

Q and Cha and I teased them so badly that their only form of retaliation were in empty threats that further paralyzed them by the state of affairs they were caught in.

Imagine the fastest boys of Gu'usa reduced to waddling turtles, calling out that they're going to 'get us' once their penises were healed. Because that's going to ever happen, ha! It was utterly hilarious and became a family and village joke recounted over and over by the women at suipi whenever they needed light entertainment to break the monotony of someone's winning streak.

I clung to the image of my brothers and their friends for safety as I was beginning to feel uneasy with Mr. Viliamu.

I didn't know how I was to ever look into his eyes again with the same confidence he had originally instilled in me at school, now that I had seen something so intimate as his pubic hair.

Perhaps it was an accident, I told myself.

He didn't mean to expose himself to me deliberately.

But then again, wasn't he the very same person who told our class that there were no accidents or coincidences?

That every action we make creates a ripple in the universe which means that all actions are interconnected?

How then could I possibly unsee what I had just seen?

Instantaneously, I told myself that this was a bad idea.

I never should have accepted Mr. Viliamu's offer in the first place.

I would have wholeheartedly given up the six tala my mother had given me for bus-fare to sit next to an old man who hadn't showered in a week in a crowded bus with babies crying and old women smoking Samoan tobacco, and Cyndi Lauper's Time after Time played over and over and over, not to see what I had just seen.

But it was too late I suppose.

As my Aunty Aima'a always says, *Once a cup of water is spilled, it can never be retrieved.*

Suddenly Mr. Viliamu said, You're quiet again. I can tell you're thinking about something because your forehead looks wrinkled.

Ha, I laughed, nervously, touching my forehead.

Really? You can do that? Know from my forehead what I'm thinking about? I asked rhetorically this time, not really expecting him to answer.

I looked out the window so that I could catch a glimpse of my forehead on the mirror so as to see what Mr. Viliamu meant. But Mr. Viliamu told me that there was a mirror right above me and reached across me to fold it down.

As Mr. Viliamu reached across me to fold the mirror down, his arm brushed lightly against my left breast and a tingling sensation surged through my body, from my head to my toes, which had never happened to me before.

Oopsy, said Mr. Viliamu, as he looked at me and smiled.

I'm sorry love, as he returned his arm to his stomach, caressing it, moving it towards his inner thigh, circling his pubic hair, this time, looking directly into my eyes.

Perplexed, I tried to avert his gaze and the piercing effect it had not only on my own eyes but on my entire body.

What is happening? I asked myself, as I closed my eyes and felt the sensation of Mr. Viliamu's arm against my breast, not to mention his penis which had increased immensely in size, bulging under his shorts which I was trying desperately to avoid seeing.

Is this osmosis?

Is this symbiosis?

Is this reproduction?

Is this metamorphosis?

What is this?

I could not find a single process in Science to name what was happening to my body and how it was responding to Mr. Viliamu's.

Nor could I comprehend how Mr. Viliamu's body was reacting to my own body.

What process was this? Really?

Could I call it a chain reaction?

Was it a voluntary or an involuntary muscular response?

But to what exactly?

I did not know.

Suddenly everything became a great big blur and for a moment I was swimming in a gray ocean, an ocean where there were no waves. No birds. And no blue skies above it.

Despite the haziness I found myself in, one thing remained certain. That the language Mr. Viliamu was speaking with his eyes and his hands was an ancient sacred language. A language that had undoubtedly been spoken by our ancestors before us and was older perhaps than the waves and the birds themselves, older even than the big blue sky.

It was a language Mr. Viliamu appeared to know intimately and spoke with the utmost fluency. A language I had never spoken before, and yet, I found myself drawn to it mysteriously if not instinctively as if I had a natural propensity towards understanding its nuances and hidden meanings.

I want you to do something for me, said Mr. Viliamu.

Startled that he finally spoke, I eagerly responded.

What is it Mr.?

Mr. Viliamu looked at me again. This time, his gaze pierced something in me that was similar to the brush of his arm against my breast. Only this time, I found myself looking boldly back at him as he tried to steer the red pick-up truck while holding my gaze simultaneously.

I want you to stop calling me Mr. Viliamu.

Why would you want me to do that for? I asked myself.

But instead, I remained quiet.

Then he spoke again.

This time, his voice caused the same sensation his arm had caused earlier when it brushed against my breast and his piercing eyes when they looked directly into mine. Only this time, his voice was like a fisaga, a gentle wind that caressed me and caused me to shiver.

I want you to call me by my name, Sia, he said.

But I *am* calling you by your name Mr. Viliamu, I found myself whispering back at him.

No, Sia, he said, looking out the window as we sighted the town clock, the Burns Phillip supermarket and the Nelson Public Library.

I want you to call me Ioage, he said.

Those were the last words he spoke before we went our separate ways, while the sun's rays danced on the glass of the NPF building windows, its reflection blinding me as I stepped into the street and made my way through the busy crowd, anxiously looking for a store that sold giant white threads while thinking about seagulls and waves and other unspeakable things that made me grin, inwardly.

Giant white threads are difficult to locate in Apia, especially during White Sunday weekend when shops are overcrowded with anxious customers pushing and pulling their way towards last minute buys and last minute sales. White Sunday was the one day of the year in Gu'usa and throughout Western Samoa where children were acknowledged as God's special gifts not only to their parents but to their families and villages and country itself. There was no other feeling like White Sunday to a child and to the adults that doted on them. The feeling that one was loved, loved entirely for all that was good and all that was bad and all that was best about one, was a feeling that everyone of us felt on that day. It never ceased to amaze me with each passing year. With all the hardships we had to struggle through and endure, White Sunday was the one day where it was all counted and we felt like we had been given a communal massage, which meant that one felt a certain rush through one's body as an entire congregation looked on as one recited one's tauloto or verse from the bible that one had spent the last four weeks putting to memory under the strict supervision of Tama Esimoto, our spiritual father, and Tina Lakena, our spiritual mother.

I spend the entire morning wandering aimlessly from one store to another, describing the giant white threads to storekeepers who kept directing me to other stores as if they themselves had never sold or heard of such a product.

How else are their store seamstresses sewing all these White Sunday dresses and shirts and puletasi and iefaikaga pinned to the wall? With Rumpelstiltskin-like thread?

The hunt for giant white threads took me all over Apia until finally, I arrived at the steps of CC's Stitches & Things, the busiest and most popular shop for women's fashion, accessories and threads in town.

I should have come to CC's directly. In fact, it should have been my very first stop the minute I was dropped off at the Public Library but since CC's is not known for its affordable prices, I, along with any other smart shoppers, thought I would look around at other stores and street vendors. After all, a tala is a tala. And if you're like me and live on the other side of the island, known to most Apians as the wop-wops or kuaback-lands and have to trek miles and miles to get to the capital, a tala does not go as far as one might think. And I was determined to stretch my tala or at least hold onto as many of them as possible.

Ceci, the owner of CC's Stitches & Things, was dressed in a very modern combination of a short red skirt and a transparent black top that was almost taped to her skin and showed off her hourglass figure. Her hair was sprayed and raised high so that she looked like Madonna, even though she was a Samoan of German and Chinese descent. I noticed this resemblance almost immediately, not only because we listened and lived and breathed Madonna as the most exciting singer of our generation, but she was worshiped by my sister Litia as her favorite singer since she won that t-shirt at the Women's Committee Bingo which I am prepared to go to war for upon my return home, on account of the fact that she's been saving it to wear on White Sunday tomorrow.

Ceci also wore large thick gold earrings and a small gold necklace with a pendant of a cross that had Our Lord Jesus Christ, hanging from it.

Ceci's face was fully covered in make-up that made her look like a sophisticated model out of a fashion magazine and she was wearing the highest red heels I had ever seen on a town woman showing off her long firm legs which complimented the lipstick she wore.

I stand six feet tall without shoes, according to our school nurse when she last measured our class at N.H.S. a few weeks ago, but Ceci loomed over me like a glamour woman from an outer planet, exuding a confidence in her walk and in her talk that I had not seen before among our women at home who had their own unique way of asserting themselves which had less to do with clothing, make-up and accessories but more to do with what they wore and carried inside of them: a sense of pride in where they came from and the genealogical lines they were connected to, which extended itself all the way back in history, to the original union between our ancestor Alofafua and the Sun which made women like my grandmother, Talune, my grand aunty Ala, Aunty Aima'a, my mother Alofafua and to some extend, all village girls and women and our entire aualuma, look like they were the tallest women on the planet, who exuded an almost celestial aura about them which made them appear just as powerful, if not, more.

Ceci greeted me with an over friendly smile and a confused gaze, as if we had known each other our whole lives.

Weren't you here last Saturday? she asked, her voice followed by her hands which seemed to move like those of a choir conductor's or ta'ita'i pese.

Yes, I said, looking at the mosquito bites on my feet.

It was a few Saturdays ago. I was here with my mother.

I remember now, she said. With a brighter smile on her face as she opened her red lipsticked mouth to speak.

I remember you telling your mother to buy three threads but I guess she didn't listen. Didn't she know it's White Sunday? Every other seamstress in town has already stocked up on white threads weeks, if not, months ago.

Tell me something I don't know, I told myself.

I tried to crack a smile at Ceci, but it got stuck in my throat as I listened to her recounting our visit to her shop weeks before, the sound of which opened a door to the great ongoing struggle I had with my mother, a struggle that will always be there as the great divide until I'm old enough to get a government scholarship and move out of the house and out of the country altogether, hopefully in a year's time, is my plan.

I suppose even then, my mother's arm will stretch and reach across the ocean and point at me in that insolent and overbearing manner of hers that always makes me feel unworthy and defeated. But we'll just have to cross that bridge when we get there.

Today must be your lucky day girl! Ceci said, extending her hands up in the air as if she were leading the choir in reaching a high note.

An order was canceled only minutes before you entered the store and if you still want them, I've got two giant white threads up for sale at $10 tala a piece and I'm more than willing to sell them to you, if you are interested.

$10 tala a piece? But that's double the cost of one thread! I exclaimed. Shocked at the sound of protest in my voice.

Like I said sweetie, it's White Sunday weekend. I can't imagine you finding giant white threads anywhere else. But since you look like you've just lost your marbles, I'll give them to you at $8 tala a piece and that's my final offer.

After a brief calculation, I realized that $8 tala a piece leaves me only $9 tala. Had I taken the bus, it would have meant I'd only have $3 tala to my disposal!

Suddenly, I became grateful for the financial advantage of having chosen to ride to town with Mr. Viliamu, (although I haven't quite processed the other thing that happened, the thing that has been under my skin since we went our separate ways almost an hour ago), otherwise, I wouldn't have been able to afford even a drink let alone a snack in this heat. Although, since our ride to town, food has become the furthest thing from my mind but I did crave an ice-cold drink and planned on buying one as soon as I could spot a vendor that sold some.

I nodded at Ceci and thanked her for the threads. She appeared to be a practical business woman who had a heart for us kuaback folks and I handed her the $20 tala bill which she took from me with a bigger smile, telling me to give her regards to my mother, and that to let her know that if she were ever interested, that she was looking for a seamstress in the Faleolela District as she is expanding her business.

And don't forget to smile girl, she called out. You'll never get anywhere with an attitude alone. But an attitude with a smile will always get you anywhere and everywhere.

✧✦✧

I don't know how I survived that first day. The day I discovered another layer to my self. A layer that was spoken of only as innuendos by the women of our house whose language of riddles whenever we girls were present and the matter of sex came up, was followed almost immediately either by suppressed laughter or strange silences that permeated the space where the cards of suipi were played along with their womanly night stories.

I had found the giant white threads sooner than expected, considering the overwhelming White Sunday shopping crowds. But instead of going directly to the bus-stop and catching the next bus home to avoid any unnecessary (but inevitable) suspicions, I bought myself a bottle of Coca Cola and sat under a pulu tree, sipping it, savoring the feeling of cold fuzzy liquid traveling down my throat.

The coolness of the Coca Cola was refreshing but I soon found myself thirsty again as if I were parched and almost immediately, regretted having bought it against my original instinct for a young coconut.

Serves me well I guess.

I'm a sucker for advertisement.

I'll buy anything sold during the Pat Mamaia Children's Hour on Saturdays. Especially when Mr. Mamaia himself was the one singing the praises of a product. It never fails and I guess that's why we earn our name as kuabacks. Oh well. What can I say? The one thing about sitting on the roots of a pulu tree in Apia that I *can* say, is that you get to watch and feel the pulse of a town.

And Apia is a busy, busy, town. One that exhausts and drains me, each time I visit it.

Suddenly I found myself drifting. Drifting in several directions all at once. Firstly, to the day I was told to take the laundry down to the river and wash the clothes because the government tap was not working.

It was a Friday afternoon, right after school.

I had been dismissed earlier for some peculiar reason, something about earning all the points I needed to earn for the mid-term and that my reward was early dismissal.

I remembered pleading with Mr. Viliamu that I didn't need to be dismissed early. That being dismissed early was actually not a reward as far as I was concerned. That being in school was my reward! But he kept insisting. A deal is a deal, Sia. That's what the class agreed to and you've not only won the deal, you've earned it. Now go. Bond with nature or something.

So I went home, determined to do just that. Bond with nature. If not, then at least try to bond with my mother. Good luck to me! So I went home.

When I got there the women of the house were playing cards and smoking and I was asked to serve them coffee and tea and Fijian tea biscuits with NZ Anchor butter and strawberry jam. Then I was told to take the Sunday laundry down to the river and to make sure to soak the whites in bleach for a good three hours before I handwash them and put them out to dry. So much for mother-daughter bonding.

✧✦✧

No one was at the river. I hadn't swam in the river since I started preparing for the Australian Maths Competition as I literally had no time whatsoever for any extracurricular activity other than studying, which occupied everything.

But that day, I remembered thinking about what Cha had said to me about being boring and how wasteful it was to have a body of sin and not using it as she would. What exactly was she talking about?

I had never seen my body naked before. I only saw shadows of my naked body at nights, caught unaware at times by the rays of the Moon. But to see my body. To actually see it as if reflected in a mirror was something that had never before happened nor occurred to me to do.

I decided to be bold that day and to look at myself. To see what Cha saw.

I stood on the bank of the deep end of the river that was calm and tranquil.

I could clearly see myself reflected in its depths.

I removed my clothes one by one and looked and looked and looked.

My breasts looked like giant ripe mangoes with large nipples that wrinkled up like prunes the minute I touched them. My touch alone caused me to shiver as if I were cold even though I was standing in the stomach of a hot day.

Then I looked at my own 17½ year old stomach and saw that it was as flat as a pancake with a small layer of fat under my belly-button. I felt my stomach. Stroked it, the way Aunty Aima'a did whenever I had a tummy ache. But I stroked it softer. Barely touching the skin. Then I spread my legs apart and was shocked at what I saw next, what was behind all my pubic hair. It was as if a nocturnal bud, not yet ready to bloom into a flower was there. Much like a sleeping baby butterfly with a small beating heart that pulsated the moment my eyes came in contact with it. It gave me chills and made me think of what Cha had said to me earlier when she accused me of having a body of sin. Is that what sin looked like? Giant mangoes, a sleeping butterfly and a bud, not yet ready to bloom into a flower?

I quickly put on my clothes and returned to the laundry and found that the twins's white Sunday shirts were caught in the current and were flowing downriver.

I ran after them as if I were running the 100 meters at school and caught them just in time but emerged all wet in the act as I had to dive in to rescue them, realizing immediately that I was not wearing a bra which made my nipples stand erect under the cotton shirt I was wearing that suddenly made me feel ashamed all at once while the trees and weeds and birds and ants looked at me and looked at me and looked at me but didn't scrutinize or snigger at me the way one of our house women easily would have.

Then I found myself drifting towards the red pick-up truck and what had taken place in it. How the memory of it had caused me to be unexpectedly sentimental and nostalgic. How was that possible? To feel nostalgia towards an event that took place no less than two hours before? An event that happened (in retrospect) without any memory of the radio ever being on. Was the radio on at all? I asked myself.

At my age, Samoan newspapers and the 2AP radio were our highest forms of entertainment. The continuing saga of Taki ma Lisa, a love-story about star crossed lovers engaged our lives with such fervor that it became my first thought of the day. Would Lisa escape the burning building she was trapped in and would Taki ever recover from amnesia? These were burning questions that engaged me as a 17½ year old student of N.H.S who was also obsessed with *Star Trek* and Mr. Viliamu's Science class and NOVA on PBS, who wondered along with other scientists as to whether or not we were alone in the universe and how would the universe all end? In the same Big Bang it was created? Without music perhaps? I asked myself with sarcasm in my own voice as I just now remembered that during the entire ride to Apia from Gu'usa, I didn't remember any songs being played on the radio or the voice of an announcer.

Was that what happened when one was struck by a meteor? You forget everything else around you? Is that what had just happened to me? And is Mr. Viliamu experiencing the same?

As my mind wandered (lonely as a cloud, that floats on high o'er vales and hills) I thought about Mr. Viliamu's request. The request about not addressing him by his surname but by his first name, something that would be utterly difficult for me to do.

After all, *he* is *Mr. Viliamu.* The most magical thing to ever happen to me since I started high school. Someone who had sparked in me an interest in my surrounding, my environment and my ecosystem. Someone who had impressed on me the tremendous importance of respecting our lands, our seas, and our skies. Who reminded us daily that we, as Samoans and as human beings have a responsibility to nature. To respect it. To honor it and to take care of it. After all, he said, Nature sustains us.

Our Oceanic people have known this truth since Fatu ma le Eleele, the original man and woman who were made by Taga'aloalagi. And how they practiced and witnessed scientific concepts and processes but had their own way of calling them. Which is why he insisted on teaching us in both English and Samoan. So that the concepts and processes our ancestors practiced, that we now teach in a classroom as Science, are never to be forgotten.

This alone is mind-blowing to a 17½ year old girl like me. Someone who's always been told that what is written in the books is palagi knowledge. Outside knowledge. Foreign knowledge. Which implies somehow that it is superior to our own ways of understanding this precious planet.

And then all at once, I was hit by an epiphany.

An epiphany so strong as if it had traveled the speed of light to make its way to my medulla oblongata, shining a bright light on Mr. Viliamu's request and gave me another way of looking at things.

Most importantly, how to decipher the hieroglyphics of his body language and what meaning they might hold in relation to my own body.

And in that instant, my heart swelled up.

As if the very depths of the ocean had poured itself into it and I found myself gasping for air until finally I drowned. Yet paradoxically, my heart started beating faster in ways that it had never done so before. Faster and faster as if it were a lali, a drum that was about to burst out of my chest and run towards the Nelson Public Library where my other body was waiting. Waiting for my heart to claim it. And somehow my feet felt the same way. Because with no command from me whatsoever, that was the exact direction they too were moving.

✧✦✧

At first, I didn't see Him and immediately my heart fell before a cliff of disappointment.

Miss? Would you like to sign up for a library card? It's free if you're a student, said an old woman librarian with glasses who directed me to the registration counter where a couple of Nu'usa High School students were standing, holding up library cards and looking on as another older woman librarian punched them in exchange for books.

I was startled by the old librarian's voice.

Startled too by the sight of the N.H.S students whom I knew individually by name.

Under normal circumstances, I would have run over to them and hugged them and asked them how long they had been at the library, which bus they had taken to get here and whether they were taking the same bus to return home.

I would have then sat with them and talked about whatever they were talking about and if they happened to be all girls, we would probably be warned several times by the librarian to keep it down or otherwise, leave because other students were there to study.

I found myself quickly thanking the old woman and walked instead in the opposite direction, towards the toilets where I could conceal myself until the N.H.S. students had left.

The first thing I did in the toilet was to turn the sink on and splash water on my face and my neck which was pulsating as if it were an open wound.

I looked at myself in the mirror and for the first time in my life I just stood still, scrutinizing my eyes as they watched me back and for a split second it appeared as if the image in the mirror was a whole other person, separate from me, even though she had all my exact features.

What if we had doubles? I asked myself.

Identical doubles that walked around like my brothers Aukilani and Ueligitone. Twins that were so identical that people couldn't tell them apart. Only we would not be of one gender but of opposites; man and woman.

Wouldn't that be something?

Could you imagine such a thing? A man who looked exactly like a woman and vice versa?

Perhaps I'd been watching too much *Star Trek*. Or it's all Mr. Viliamu's fault for telling us to astound ourselves, daily, with the endless wonders and possibilities of Science.

Suddenly, someone knocked at the door. A girl.

Are you finished? I have to go. Fast! Please?

I pulled out the lavalava from my bag and wiped my face. Feeling the texture of the cotton material as it pressed against my skin. Then I took a long lasting look at my face again in the mirror and saw that it had changed since I first woke up this morning and hopped into Mr. Viliamu's red pick-up truck who drove me to Apia. To the crowds and dust of a town bursting with a life of its own that was the complete opposite of village life with its own energy that was just as vibrant yet not as blatantly visible.

I couldn't quite put my finger on what the exact term to describe the change on my face. But it was a dramatic change nevertheless. Similar to watching cumulus clouds take shape and walk across the sky like the War Goddess Nafanua, bare-breasted and ready to take on an army of men and fight in the middle of a long day. Only I wasn't fighting an army of men but my feelings for one man. One man that I know will change my fate and the direction of my life the minute I decide not to decide.

Alas, there I was. Staring at myself in a public mirror that hundreds if not thousands of people have stood before, looking into it and seeing themselves perhaps too like me, for the very first time.

And I wondered, how many of them had looked into the mirror and saw themselves and asked similar life-changing questions such as the one I was about to ask my own reflection, staring me without a single wrinkle on its forehead, which was, What would happen if I were to ride back home with Ioage?

A pounding on the door broke my chain of thoughts and the girl's voice, whom I had forgotten altogether, hollered behind it.

What are you doing in there? I've got to go. Please open the door!

I quickly stuffed the lavalava back into my bag and opened the door to find the girl holding onto her dress with blood running down her leg.

I pretended not to see the blood and avoided eye contact with her and as I was about to walk out of the toilet stall towards the registration desk, I heard her say, Bloody kuabacks. You never seen a mirror before or what?

The girl's aggression took me by surprise. How did she know I was from kua? Was there a sign on my forehead that said, Hey, look, I'm from kua and I've never seen a mirror before?

Suddenly, I thought of my younger sister Litia who was the same age as the girl and wondered what she was doing. Whether she was helping Q and Cha with the church decoration or whether she was out at sea, fishing with Feutia her best friend or whether she too was somewhere waiting in line on someone using the toilet and that she was scared because she was unprepared for the Moon's visit.

I opened my bag and got out the one Kotex pad which I always kept there just in case and handed it to the girl under the stall. The girl took the pad but held onto my hand, gripping it tightly until suddenly I heard her crying. I wanted to ask her if she was ok. Whether this was her first time.

But then she squeezed my hand before she released it and said, Sorry sis. I'm sorry.

As soon as I emerged from the public toilet, Ioage saw me and smiled, a half moon smile that only I saw.

But instead of walking towards him, I walked the opposite direction, towards the Exit, determined to leave before anyone else that I knew saw me.

As I rushed out the door, His hand grabbed mine from behind, turning me towards him, pressing his mouth to my ear and whispered, You can't leave without me, you know.

The touch of his fingers against mine was explosive, like the supernova explosion on *Star Trek's* "All our Yesterdays" episode, that took place on the class M planet Sarpeidon. While the drama of rescuing an entire planet and all the obstacles and challenges faced by the USS Enterprise crew as it struggled to save everyone on Sarpeidon was engaging, I was the only one that marveled at the beauty of that supernova explosion towards the end, which made Q and Cha look at me strangely afterwards. Even Q, who was always on my side, barked at me, Sia, that supernova was going to annihilate all of Sarpeidon! What's so beautiful about that? Huh? Girl, you need to check your moral compass. I mean, I thought I knew you, Sia.

I thought I knew me too Q! Until my new obsession with Science and its wonders colonized my medulla oblongata! I mean, how can you let something like an evacuation that was going to happen anyway, deter you from marveling at the beauty of such a celestial phenomenon, special effects and all? I wanted to say. But our friendship was sacred. And I didn't want to add anything that would come between us, not even a stellar explosion, into that sacred space, which was our 'va' as friends. Although silently, and in retrospect, I wouldn't change my mind about the beauty of that supernova explosion and the radiance of its light which vibrated in my fingers the minute they collided with Ioage's.

But for reasons only I knew, reasons I decided after looking into the toilet mirror, I did not allow Ioage to see the stellar explosive impact of his touch on my fingers.

Nor did I allow anyone else to see it.

But I suspect Ioage knew.

Because he hurried towards the desk where he sat earlier and collected his books and backpack while I walked as fast as I could away from him.

I know what this is, Sia, he called out behind me.

This is what the old Samoans would have called speaking in opposites. Saying one thing but meaning something else. That's what you're doing, isn't it?

You're walking away from me when in actual fact, you want to walk towards me. Am I making any sense? Please, tell me.

I wanted so desperately to look at him then. To see the heated expression on his face as he pleaded for my opinion, but I couldn't. The thought of being spotted by someone, *anyone,* terrified me so much more that I couldn't for the life of me turn to see him.

Walking away from me is not going to solve anything, he said, as he caught up to me and stood directly in my path. It was then that I realized something that I had never noticed before.

That I was actually a whole head taller than him.

A fact, that was irrelevant in the past but gave me a new perspective as to how I saw him, in lieu of my recent private engagement with him where I saw another side of him that I would have never seen had I not decided to ride with him to town.

I suppose when someone you respected were to stand before you day after day, you lose sight of their actual physical size and they take on God-like attributes, like Gege or Moso or Vaea, or Superman, or Mr. Spock, a giant before a blackboard in a classroom full of students who have nothing but admiration for their very presence.

I know a smile is trying to escape your lips, Sia.

Come on, girl! Stop fighting it and give us a smile, he said, showing me his white teeth that glistened under the hot sun.

What is he trying to do, get us both killed?

As I thought these thoughts, an Owl appeared mysteriously out of nowhere. It hovered momentarily above us before it flew away. Disappearing as quickly as it had appeared. And in the shadow of its path I heard a whisper,

There's nothing to be afraid of, Girl.

He won't hurt you.

He can't.

But tread carefully.

Or someone is going to get hurt.

We avoided speaking or looking at each other when we first got into the red pick-up truck whose seats were so hot they burned my bum as soon as I sat down. I didn't want to see the impact it had on Ioage's behind especially with the shorts he was wearing but I found myself blushing all the

same at the image of him stoically collapsing onto the hot seat without a single word.

I don't know what he was trying to prove or why he didn't say anything but decided to just let it go. Whatever he had to say to me, he had another five hours to say it before I was to be expected back home. To home sweet home.

As the red pick-up truck drove through Beach Road, the emphatic sounds of Apia became more magnified along with the people and animals and buildings and other cars who had all suddenly taken on much larger forms than their actual size and I quietly closed my eyes, exhausted I was from the almost draining sight of it all.

When I opened my eyes again, I noticed that the people and animals and buildings and the other cars of Apia had returned to their normal size as the red pick-up truck sped far away from it, towards the first villages on its outskirts and it was clear that we were heading back towards Gu'usa Kai, to the point where our relationship had begun.

Is that what this is now? I asked myself.

Can what two people who just met for the first time and shared what Ioage and I have just shared constitute a relationship?

I thought about the word *relationship* and the day Miss Alabama, our peace-corps teacher who had been working with us on vocabulary and in particular, synonyms and wondered. Of the many synonyms *relationship* had, *affair* is the one that stood out most vividly in my mind.

Is that what this is? An event or sequence of events of a specified kind or that has previously been referred to?

Or was it going to be another definition?

An affair?

A love affair?

E.g. 'Her husband is having an affair'.

But Ioage was not married. He did not have a wife.

He was our pastor's oldest son which technically made him my brother and makes what is happening between us forbidden and taboo.

I knew I respected Ioage as Mr. Viliamu, my A Number One teacher.

But as the day progressed, that respect was slowly turning into something else.

Something I don't yet know. But I'd say that I was scared by it a bit and excited a bit by it, all the same.

Ioage hadn't said a word since we left the Nelson Public Library. What was he thinking, I wondered?

I remembered the first day he stood barefooted before our Science Class in his iefaikaga and his perfectly ironed shirt and long, long hair braided and wrapped around his head in a bun and introduced himself.

Talofa! Greetings!

O a'u o le tatou faia'oga, o Ioane Viliamu. I am Mr. Ioane Viliamu.

Ua fa'ato'a ou i'u mai i le Iunivesite a Papua Niu Kini. I am a recent graduate of the University of Papua New Guinea.

(The class laughed at the mention of Papua New Guinea as some of us still had fresh memories of Papua New Guinean women naked from the waist up as well as men wearing penis sheaths as photographed in The Samoa Times, during the 4th Pacific Festival of Arts, held in Papeete, Tahiti earlier in June). The class calmed down as Mr. Viliamu gave us a look that our own mothers would have given us at such a time, and then there was instant silence, before he proceeded with his introduction.

O a'u ua ta'ua o se Saienisi ma se Faia'oga o le Numera. I am a Scientist and a Mathematician.

O le matati'a muamua lava o lo'o o'u mafaufauina mo tatou uma i le tatou vasega, o le tatou naunau lea i lo tatou tiute i aso ta'itasi, ina ia tatou iloa Le Natura. The first thing I want to challenge you with is a daily commitment from each and everyone of you in this class, to know nature.

I le tulaga na iloa ai Le Natura e o tatou tua'a. The way our ancestors did.

Oute mana'o ina ia tou va'ai toto'a i lau, le vao, ma le ele'ele.

I want you to look closely at leaves, grass, dirt.

Aua ne'i tatou manatu fa'atauva'a iai. Don't just pass them by.

Oute mana'o ina ia tou u'uina le lau ma va'ava'ai lelei i ona ua.

I want you to pick a leaf up and look carefully at its veins.

Su'esu'e auili'ili ma va'ai toto'a iai aua o ua o le lau o lo'o taofimauina ai le fatu o le ola.

Examine it carefully and you will see that it contains the essence of life.

E le na'o le fafagaina o le tino le galuega a lau, ae o le toe fa'afo'isiaina o le malosi pe'a tatou mama'i.

Not only do leaves nourish your body, they will help heal it if we're ever sick.

O le malamalamaga lea a o tatou tua'a i lau, e le gata i le itu fa'asaienisi, a'o le itu fa'aleagaga. That's how our ancestors understood leaves, not only in a scientific manner but in a spiritual one.

O lo'u tiute, o le mafai lea ona tou malamalama i le tofa a o tatou tua'a ma lo latou tomai fa'asaienisi ma ala na latou fa'atino fa'atauanaina ai lea mataupu i aso ua tuana'i e ui e latou te le'i ta'ua lo latou tomai o le fa'asaienisi e pei ona tatou iloa ai le mataupu i le taimi nei. It is my mission to make you understand that Samoans understood science long ago and practiced it with great precision, even though it wasn't called Science back then but they knew and were very much aware of it.

E tai tutusa lava le tomai na io tatou tua'a ma le tomai lea na maua i le tofa a ni isi tagata anamua o le lalolagi lea tou te a'oa'oina i le Vasega o le Tala Fa'asolopito, le au Maia, le au Aikupito, Aferika, Saina, Monikoliana, Roma, Eleni, Initia ma o tatou uso ma tuafafine i le Vasa Pasefika. Just like other ancient civilizations you're learning about in History: the Mayans, the Egyptians, the Africans, the Chinese, the Mongolians, the Romans, The Greeks, the Indians and our brothers and sisters throughout the Pacific Ocean.

Ma e tatau fo'i ia te'i tatou ona tatou fa'atauaina tutusa. And it's equally important for us to do the same.

Ina ia tatou malamalama o le Fa'asaienisi ma le Numera o lo'o si'omiaina i tatou. To understand that Science and Mathematics are all around us.

E pei lava ole agaga a o tatou tua'a na latou fa'agalueina ma malamalama iai. Just like the spirit of our ancestors who practiced and understood them.

O lo'o iai i so'o se mea.It is everywhere.

O lo'o maua lea i le tino sasa'o o se fale, po'o se va'atele ma isi va'a po'o laina o le malu ma le pe'a, lea e taofimauina ai oloa loloto o o tatou mafaufauga ma o tatou manatunatuga. They're found in the perfect shape of a fale or a va'atele and other types of canoes or in the straight lines of the malu or the pe'a that hold our collective memory.

O lo'o maua fo'i i ona po nei, i se ipu ti vevela. Po'o se fasi aisa. Po'o se pepe o lo'o fa'apepepepe i le matagi. It is also found nowadays in a cup of hot tea. An ice cube. Or a butterfly fluttering in the wind.

E tele o'u fa'amoemoega mo outou. I have a lot of expectations of you.

O lo'u fa'amoemoega muamua lava i le tamaititi po'o le teineititi, o le mata'ala lea i le taimi o le tatou vasega. My first expectation of you in this class is that you pay attention.

Fa'alogo. Listen.

Ma fa'a'aloalo i so'o se tasi. Respect one another at all times.

A fia fai se fesili, tu'u i luga le lima. Raise your hand if you wish to ask a question.

Ma aua ne'i galo le fa'amolemole ma le fa'afetai i le o lo'o lua tuaoi. Remember to say please and thank you to one another.

E sa le fia fasi tamaititi seisi i totonu o le tatou vasega, toe sa le sana tato vale. I do not tolerate bullying of any sort in this class and that goes the same for disruptive behavior.

Oute talitonu ua uma ona a'oa'o lelei a outou amio ma le tufanua e tou matua. I am going to assume that your parents have done their job of discipling you and teaching you manners.

O la'u galuega o le a'oa'oina lea o outou. My job is to educate you.

Ina ia mafai ona tatala o outou mafaufau i ni manatu e sili atu i lo'o manatu o lo'o iai i le taimi nei. To open your minds beyond their current confines.

Ina ia fa'atumulia o outou manatu ma mafaufauga i vavega. To fill your thoughts and imagination with wonder.

Ma fa'amaofa outou ina ia mafai ona tou fa'amaofaina outou lava. To astound you so that you may astound yourselves.

E le ua na'o se potu a'oga le vasega lenei. This room is not merely a classroom.

O le *tatou* potu a'oga ma le *tatou* vasega. It is *our* room and it is *our* classroom.

A'e savali mai i totonu o le tatou vasega, ia taunuana ma oe, o lo'o e sau e te aoga. So when you enter it, never lose sight of the fact that you are here to learn!

We were all pleasantly surprised to hear someone from N.H.S talk like this. Especially a male teacher whose modus operandus won our hearts that very same day and we voted him a week later as the bestest teacher in the entire school. Unlike Mrs. Amosaosavavau, the known tyrant next door who taught English Literature and bossed poor Miss Alabama our vocabulary teacher and her students, as we could hear her through the thin walls tell Miss Alabama to please wear a bra next time she came to school as we didn't want to incite unnecessary problems with the students and that we needed instead to be examples to them (which upset the male population of our class and we could hear them say, Fai fua si keige o Eveliga ma le leai o soga papa, misi fo'i le kifaga o le aoauli se, something only boys would say in objection, that they would now miss out on their daily matinee), as well as warn her class that whatever they might think they knew about English, she knew more.

A warning for all the fiapokos who might entertain the idea of knowing it all, which made her the ultimate fiapoko in my book.

How do you expect us to be excited about flowers that grew in a landscape none of us have ever been to?

And why would such flowers be exalted?

Glorified?

And the authors of such poems glorified along with them?

As if our own local flowers and storytellers were unworthy of the same praise and attention.

Thank God Mr. was not like that!

His radical approach to teaching excited us about condensation and precipitation. Metamorphosis and symbiosis, in ways that made us not only understand such processes or relationships or chain reactions, but to know that our own people understood the same, in their own language, which made Science and Mathematics so much more personal and intimate not to mention alive.

Never would we look at clouds again without knowing which ones they were, whether they were low clouds, mid clouds or high clouds and what time of the day they appeared and disappeared.

Mr. Viliamu had taught us that all knowledge was inter-connected. That Science is connected to Mathematics and English which had its roots in Latin.

He said for instance the prefix alto meant high (which also means a voice range when singing, and is how Uncle Fa'avevesi, our Ta'ita'ipese and Choir master had classified my voice in our aufaipese or choir, as he warned me and Q to lower our voices and to sing gently, and that we didn't need to scream like a bunch of wild girls. *God is not deaf!* He yelled at us, as if *he* were deaf).

Alto is also given to mid-altitude clouds whereas stratus, is from the Latin prefix strato, meaning layer, which could also be used to describe the depths that each man, woman or child has within them and how we have the choice to show a layer of ourselves to whoever we choose, depending on the context of our relationship with that person.

In all, there were 10 different types of clouds, cumulus, stratos, cumulonimbus, stratocumulus, nimbostratus, altocumulus, altostratus, cirrocumulus, cirrostratus, or cirrus, each with their own personality; fluffy, detached, transparent, thin, continuous, gray, heavy, dense, semi-transparent, and layered which I use to describe my own moods and feelings and emotions at any given time.

Knowing these clouds and the way Mr. Viliamu drew our attention to their individual distinguishing features, made me utterly ashamed of my premature and juvenile judgement of Mrs Amosaosavavau and her exaltation of the English poet William Wordsworth who must have had a deep love and respect for nature, the way our own ancestors did.

Brothers and sisters are something else. This is what I've been thinking about a lot since my twin brothers Aukilani and Ueligitone brought the Aute Samoa and the Vaisina that cured my sila'ilagi/boil. I thought about them wandering the forest for an entire day without food or water, waiting for the forest to tell them what to do. Aunty Aima'a is wise that way. She is the wisest person I know. Giving Au and Ue the chance to feel the forest on their own without adult supervision. To have their own instincts guide them so that they could be in tune with their senses and how those senses are governed by a primal loyalty to our aiga our nu'u our district and our beloved country of Western Samoa, which was founded on God.

My twin brothers told me later that they would have died together in the forest if it meant giving me life. It moved me to tears. And I remember weeping for days, weeks, months even afterwards. The sacrifices my brothers were prepared to make for me makes me look at my own mother's relationship with her brother and our Uncle Fa'avevesi, who is known throughout Gu'usa Kai and Gu'usa Uka as the most generous man. Who will give away the shirt on his back to even strangers if they were to ask for it. He is our matai. And even though he has not been able to work for the last two years of his life due to the fact that he had gotten electrocuted when he was working on live wires and lost his left hand, his voice speaks loud and clear in our household, above that of my mother's who is the breadwinner of our household. Village people say that he could have easily become the saddest man on the planet because of the fact that he doesn't have a hand. But everyone thanks God and then my mother for being the rock that she is, that allows his voice to soar with her's as the wind beneath his wings. That is the feagaiga. The covenant between brother and sister that gives the fa'asamoa its strength and its beauty, said Tina Lakena, my spiritual mother and pastor's wife and Ioage's mother and our mother together when she was addressing the girls of the choir one evening.

And as Tina Lakena was talking, I found myself drifting on the soundwaves of her voice. Drifting and drifting in and out of the story of my own mother Alofafua and my father, Matua Solomua. How they met. How they came together. And how death intervened in their lives and transformed my mother into the woman that she is today with a perpetual melancholic look on her face, masking the true mysteries of her life which come alive whenever she lashes out at me.

Before my mother even knew what a relationship was between a man and a woman, Matua Solomua, who she had never met before, presented himself to our grandmother Alofafua with a proposition for marriage. Matua came from a respected family. He worked at the Post Office in Apia. His wife had died the year before during the Hurricane of 1966. Swept out to sea and her pregnant body was never found. When Matua, my father, came to my grandmother, his head was drooped and sad. So sad one could drown in the sadness that lived in the pupils of his eyes.

He was older than my mother by a good 7 years which meant he was 25 to her 18 on the night the tulafale, the talking chief, punctured my mother's hymen in our faletele, while our village people held their breath outside its blinds. When the tulafale walked outside with the ie sina, the white tapa cloth that my mother had sat on during the fa'amasei'au /deflowering ceremony, showing it off to the Night air, the people of Gu'usa proudly cheered. As if electricity had bolted through the crowd. Grabbing hold of every man, woman and child. Inciting in them a powerful urge to scream. To cry. To laugh. To cheer and cheer and cheer! Fa'auta i le taupou! / Hooray, she's a Virgin!

Exactly nine months later I was born.

I know he was my father, but I often ask myself, why would they agree to have their daughter marry a complete stranger who was more interested in death than in living? And sometimes too I often wondered whether my father drowned at sea or whether he was sired into the sea by the voices of his dead wife and unborn child. All I know, is that the love I see in movies, like the love between Danny and Sandy in *Grease* or between Superman and Lois is not the same love as what my parents had experienced which is why perhaps my father's death is more devastating to my mother. According to Aunty Aima'a, my parents grew into love. And if I should ever have any questions about it, all I needed to do was look at my reflection in the mirror. And those of my sister and my twin brothers. Therein lives the deep love my mother had for my father and vice versa.

Still, I don't think about marriage as much as the other girls. But sometimes, I do find myself wondering if I would ever get married like other girls in our village who grew up with both parents. I don't think about marriage as much as the other girls. It is something I don't wish to be engaged in. The loss of my father and his perpetual appearances in the sadness on my mother's face, is reason enough for me not to ever wish for the same loss on my own face. Our father drowned the night the twins were born and ever since then, I have had nightmares about the same happening to me which is why I don't go swimming. And I don't even go next to the water. Not if my own life depends on it.

✧✦✧

Ioage's silence was acute and I could see it from his firm grip on the steering wheel which made him appear as if he were in deep contemplation regarding what was unveiling right before the va between us, which had undergone an almost 180 degrees divergence.

A penny for your thoughts, I said, breaking the silence in that va which had reached almost deafening proportions.

I turned to look at him and saw the perpetual half moon grin on his face which restored my faith as I didn't know how to read his silence.

He bit his lower lip and put his left hand on my thigh as he continued to drive with his other hand. An electrical shock bolted through my body at the touch of his hand. A shock that was soon replaced by an ease and a comfort as if my lap was the most natural place in the world for his hand to be placed, to rest even. I looked at his hand and saw that he had a tattoo of a single line between his thumb and his pointer finger.

I wanted to ask him about the line.

Did it have a meaning? And if so, what was it?

But I decided not to, preferring to speak in the language of touch and movement which I was already beginning to understand as having the ability to convey so much more.

I took his hand in mine and caressed his fingers and was surprised at how that act stirred me, stirred me once more from my head to my toes.

While my fingers were slightly longer than his, His were definitely stronger.

And as I looked at the lines in his palms and pressed them against the lines in my own palms, I realized that they are the same lines that connected us both to people who once walked and fished and wove and sang and laughed and fought and cried and navigated this great big ocean, Mr. Viliamu referred to as *Lo Tatou Tina* or *Our Mother,* and all those who had gone before us but are no longer with us and that we were the ones to continue singing the line songs.

All at once, I raised his hand and held it with both my hands before I pressed it to my nose, breathing Him in.

And before I knew it, I slipped one of his fingers into my mouth and began to taste his strength which pulsated under his skin.

I didn't know what I was doing or whether I was doing it right or wrong but Ioage's facial expression convinced me that I was giving Him pleasure and I found that my heart was beating, even faster than when I had rushed from the pulu tree where I had been sitting, drinking a Coca Cola while musing about the day's events.

I had chosen to enter another world. A world with a mysterious language that grabbed me and shook me to my very core, with its powerful rhythms and exquisite sounds which I had discovered and enveloped me entirely, and for the first time in my life, I felt like I could breathe and exhale and breathe and exhale and breathe and exhale without having to think or watch or calculate my next move.

When I looked over at Ioage, I saw that his chest was heaving and that his penis had swollen again as it did before, only this time, I did not look away from it but rather, I reached over to Him and pulled his shorts upwards as he had done earlier, exposing his pubic hair which I circled and circled with my fingers.

Ioage looked at me and softly whispered my name as if it were a secret code needed to unlock a cave filled with hidden treasures.

Sia.

Sia!

Sia!!

Sole! Pupula ou maka i le auala! Keep your eyes on the road, man! I said, as he was about to hit a pig crossing with piglets.

I can't, with you doing that!

You mean this? I said, as I became a little bolder and released his penis from the confines of his underwear where it had been trapped. It was quite a shocking sight. A sight that was to become imprinted in my memory for the rest of my life, like watching Captain Kirk and Lt. Uhura kiss in that most unforgettable episode, "Plato's Stepchildren." Where for the first time a white man kissed a black woman on prime time TV. Those same chills were with me when I gazed at Ioage's penis as it continued to grow like a galactic flower, strange and beautiful.

Se auuuuua se, Sia. Please don't, Sia, said Ioage, as a moan escaped his lips.

I didn't know if he really wanted me to stop or whether it was code to continue. I decided to take the road less traveled like Mr. Frost did and continued.

Or this? I said, circling its tip which had started to turn purple reddish.

Ahhhhh, Ioage moaned.

Is that so? I responded. Then do you think we should stop? I mean, pull over? As I gently pulled on it.

Do you think we shoulddddd?

Should or shoulddddd? Ha!

Se soia, li'i. Stop killin' me! he said.

It's a question of safety, Ioage. Besides, imagine us on the 5 o'clock news: *Nu'uolemanusa High School Teacher Caught with Student in a Crash off the Si'unu'u Falls.* They won't care that we were in a crash or that we might be hurt or had hurt someone else. All they'll care about is that you, a pastor's son and a teacher was caught with me, a student and member of the Gu'usa aualuma. I'd say we pull over. Don't you think?

Why do I feel like I just got scolded?

Because the same woman raised us. That's why. Besides, it's because of what you're experiencing right now. See, your blood has rushed to your penis, causing what's clinically called a penile erection or penile tumescence, which means you've got a depletion of blood to your brain, but hey, you're the Scientist, I'm just your humble Student.

Ha! Ha! Ha! I have created a monster!

It's called Astound Your Teacher Day, mister. You didn't know?

Ioage's grin, which rolled into a small laugh and eventually into a roar, found us both laughing hysterically until suddenly we heard a loud sudden booming sound coming from the back of the pick-up.

I quickly removed my hand from Ioage's thigh and looked out the window to see what the problem was as the sound was most prominent on my side of the truck.

Ioage started to slow the pick-up down.

We were in an isolated uninhabited part of the island, high above sea level where there were no visible signs of a village, only lots of ancient trees and land and open sky.

Ioage got out of the pick-up and went immediately to investigate what had caused the booming sound. By the time I got out, he was already standing before the back tire which showed visible signs that it was no longer going to be able to be of any immediate use to the mobility of the truck.

Just then, an older man appeared out of nowhere carrying a bunch of bananas on his shoulders. It was

obvious from his dark, bearded, and stout appearance that
he was of Solomon Islander descent.

Ua a? he asked, as he removed the banana bunch from
his shoulders.

Car problems?

We both nodded.

Then he saw the tire. Do you have a spare?

I looked at Ioage and prayed to God he was going to
say yes but instead, he shook his head as if he'd been
defeated and said, Leai. No, E leai se sipea, we don't have
a spare.

The next village is a good 25 miles away, the man said.

I don't have a car myself but you can walk it in 4, 5
hours and if you're lucky, you might be able to stop a car or
the bus which runs by the hour but I haven't seen it since
this morning when it left for Apia. Well, let me know what
you decide. We live just a few steps away, below that Aoa
tree there. If for some reason you can't find transportation,
you and your wife may spend the night. I'm sorry we don't
have much, but that's all I can offer.

Before he left, Ioage asked the man, Ae se'i ta'u mai lou
suafa Tama, fa'amolemole. Could you please tell us your
name, Father?

O a'u o Lamaga. I am Lamaga.

Ia o Inosia lea a'o a'u o Ioane. This is Inosia and I am
Ioane.

Ia lelei. Good.

Fa ia oulua Igosia ma Ioage. Goodbye Inosia and Ioane.

Ia manuia ni isi fuafuaga o totoe o le aso Lamaga. May
the rest of what you have planned for the day be blessed,
Lamaga.

Lamaga waved at us and before he started walking away,
he called out, Ia fua le giu. May the coconut tree bloom.

✧◆✧

After some searching, Ioage was finally able to find the jack under his seat and was already starting to remove the flat tire from the wheel when a silver pick-up truck passed by and honked at us.

Seconds later, we heard it reversing towards us and an overly cheerful afakasi man with tanned skin, light brown hair and the bluest eyes, who immediately introduced himself while still seated in the silver pick-up by saying, Malo li'i bro! O a'u o Piliki! Hey bro! I am Piliki! as if he were expecting drums to roll at his own announcement of his presence, before he jumped out and asked almost the exact same questions Lamaga had asked us earlier, only he added bro to almost everything he said as if he were running for public office or was a member of a secret organization of the brotherhood and bro was their codename.

Ua a, bro? Car problems? Do you have a spare, li'i bro?

Ioage shook his hand and told him no. We don't have a spare. But that he'd appreciate it if he could give us a lift to some place where we could have it fixed.

I could give you my spare, bro. It's a bit dodgy but it'll take you to where you need to go, bro.

Piliki called out to one of the boys in the back to bring the spare down and to help Ioage install it. But Ioage thanked him for his generosity and insisted that he would install the tire himself.

The boys are fast, you know, bro? But if you insist, I'll leave you to it, bro. Good luck then, bro. And have a Happy White Sunday! Say hello to the wife, bro! And then he winked at Ioage who smiled back at him like they were members of the aforementioned organization.

Before Ioage could ask Piliki where he should deliver the spare tire, he had already hopped in his pick-up and was waving goodbye.

Magaia lau keige li'i Kams! Nice looking girl you've got there, bro! One of the boys called out before their pick-up made its way back on the road.

But before they sped off, Ioage smiled at him and said, Ha'e, se soia se, Stop it, man, and then winked at me before he called out, Fa ia oukou! Goodbye then!

While the silver pick-up truck sped off into the distance, the last thing I saw on the tailgate was a sign that said "Piliki's Bricks. Best Bricks in Town, Bro!"

As soon as Ioage installed the tire he walked over to me and said, Do you want to go swimming? I know a place not far from here. It's a lake. And with White Sunday shoppers in Apia all day, I'm sure it's going to be empty. Wanna go?

As enticing as that might have sounded to someone whose skin had been eaten alive by the Sun as Ioage had warned me earlier when I was about to jump into the back of the red pick-up truck, because I had been sitting on a rock next to the barren government road for what appeared to have been hours only it was probably no more than twenty minutes, waiting for the tire to be attached finally to the wheel, my mind was clogged with thoughts of the men that just left and how they acted towards us, particularly towards me.

First of all, let's look at how Lamaga acted. Lamaga with barely enough threads holding his lavalava together.

Lamaga was old enough to be both our grandfathers.

He walked barefoot, like Ioage did so at church and at school and everywhere he went which endeared him to the older generation of our grandmothers and grandfathers but made others who were less generous with their critique of cultural décor and aesthetics, snigger and whisper, Se makua makaga le fealuai e leai gi se'evae pei se kama fa'akau ula a'o le akali'i o le faifeau ma le faia'oga. Shameful that he should walk around barefooted like some man selling flower necklaces when he is the pastor's son and a teacher, a fact that earned him the nickname Mister Without Slippers.

And yet, Lamaga showed us both enough respect to last us a lifetime.

And he blessed us!

Now, let's turn to Piliki.

Piliki with the shirt that was unbuttoned and showed his very hairy chest and tight abdominal muscles, clad with heavy gold chains who wore sports shoes that appeared to be brand new and sports shorts, that revealed his pe'a, which I thought was about the only natural thing about him, his generosity, I filed away as nothing more but advertisement for a future business transaction.

I am not criticizing nor am I judging Mr. Piliki's appearance.

I'm sure there are many girls and women who find his particular manner of assembling his outward appearance alluring and attractive and I don't wish to be a rotten egg about it because, hey, I'm the one that shares clothing with sisters and cousins! I don't have the right to be critical of anyone who has brand new shoes and gold chains that they earned with the sweat of their own brow, but what I will be critical of is a personality that if not genuine, must be just simply exhausting.

It's apparent to me that Piliki was either a self-made man or a descendant of self-made men who've had to work for everything they've ever gotten and I have much respect and admiration for such men.

However, what remains a thorn under my tongue, is the way Piliki acted like I didn't even exist.

It was all bro this and bro that as if Ioage was the only human being worthy of his attention.

He didn't even look at me! The way Lamaga did. *Or* acknowledge that I was even at the scene. That I was present which I found highly offensive.

That Ioage participated in this act of my non-existence, was beyond comprehension, especially since he was supposedly the more educated one of the lot which made me not only angry at the men but even angrier at him, so that when he pressed his mouth to the nape of my neck and pulled me to him, I pushed him away almost immediately and started walking towards the government road.

Suga, o le a fo'i? What is it now? he asked.

But I continued walking as if I hadn't heard him.

Come on, Sia. They were just acting like men. If they were the chauvinist pigs you think they were, then they wouldn't have stopped now, would they? Besides, I didn't even know them!

I stopped walking.

I felt my anger rise as Ioage's words fell out of his mouth and into the air polluting the ancient trees and land and sky and my ears.

I turned around and walked straight towards him so that I was standing directly in front of him before I looked down at him and said, You didn't know them you say? But they were talking to you now, weren't they? Do you know what it feels like to be invisible? To be treated like you don't mean anything? Like you're just a brick or a piece of toilet paper flying in the wind? And you were so caught up in your own ego that you did nothing! You just joined them! One of the boys! Hoorah for you Ioage! I may be only 17½ but I have seen enough to know that common respect is something you don't abandon at someone else's convenience. You ought to know that Mr. Viliamu! Because you bloody well taught it to us!

Tears were in my eyes as I stormed away from him. But after a few steps I realized that I had forgotten my mother's giant white threads, the main reason why I had come with him in the first place.

I turned around and walked back towards the red pick-up truck, passing Ioage who just stood there, stunned it seemed from the impact of my words, words he hadn't expected to hear after he had spoken to me in that language he knew all so well, thinking that because I had a propensity for learning how to speak it too that it would mean we would forever be cocooned in its embrace, without a care about the realities of living in the real world, made up of pain and fear and shame and guilt and hurt; the almost inevitable elements of any young Samoan girl's life. But then again, how could he have possibly known that?

A giant gray Owl stared at me when I opened the car door. Its claws had opened the shopping bag and it appeared like it was shitting on the giant white threads.

I picked up one of the threads and realized that I would ruin them both if I were to ever attempt to wipe the shit off of it.

The knowledge of this caused me to break down.

Meanwhile, the Owl looked at me, and blinked its eyes before it flew off again, as if saying to me, What are you going to do now, girl? Huh?

Ioage started walking towards the car once he saw me sitting in it. I quickly rolled the windows up and locked the doors, my anger and frustration had now risen exponentially to a whole other level and I found myself sulking in despair.

What would my mother think when she sees the threads now?

What would my mother think when she sees the threads now?

What would my mother think when she sees the threads now?

Try as I might, there was no way I could explain to her what had happened. Not without digging my own grave.

Ioage knocked at the window and motioned to me to roll the window down.

He kneeled down on the government road and pressed his palms together as if in prayer and motioned to me again to roll the windows down as he silently said, Alofa ia Sia, fa'amagalo so'u sese. Please Sia, forgive me if I've made a mistake.

As frustrated as I was, I didn't have the heart to remain angry at him for long and started rolling the window down and opened the car door. But before I could let him in, I had to ask him something else, something Piliki said that took me by surprise.

What did Piliki mean when he said Say hello to the wife? Do you have a wife? Do you have someone out there who thinks you're her husband? Is there another? Huh? I want to know, Ioage. I want to know right now!

Ioage dusted his knees as he stood up from the government road and walked towards me. Sharp gravel was still stuck to parts of his legs, and when he reached me, he kneeled down a second time and collapsed his head onto my lap. Then he looked up at me and said, Look at me, Sia. You should know me by now. The only mistress in my life is Science. And Mathematics. And now, you. Which makes me a polygamist.

What's that?

Look it up in the dictionary when you get home.

Is it a word I'm going to want to keep in my vocabulary notebook?

Just don't tell them the context where you got it from, ok?

Ioage grinned when he said that, which made me very curious about the word. Note to self: look up polygamist as soon as you get home.

All jokes aside, Sia, do you really think I would be here with you if I were with someone else? A suga Sia?

I shook my head and watched him become more serious, more determined in his gaze as he took my hand and pressed it to his mouth before he continued again.

Why are you taking to heart something a complete stranger said to you? He was just, I don't know, I think he was jealous. Jealous because you're young and beautiful and you were with me. Men talk like that all the time. It's called shooting the breeze. They say things without thinking that someone might find hurtful. I'm sorry that you thought I was contributing to it. I'm guilty of it, I know. But you know what? You've taught me something today, Sia. A lesson that I'll never forget. And I'm truly deeply sorry for making you feel the way you felt. I must admit you're right. It went a bit to my head. I mean, I won't lie to you and say that when that guy said, magaia lau keige, I didn't feel flattered. I did. I mean, what man wouldn't? Look at you! You don't even know it, do you? The power you have over men like me. Men who have gone out and gotten educated and ended up having relationships with non-Samoan women, because there weren't that many Samoan girls at the university I went to and the few that I met I called my sisters and they called me brother and we immediately became the Samoan family because Samoa was so far away and we missed home.

Were you with a palagi when you were at university?

Yes. Not just one but with two.

And was it like this? Like how we are?

I'm not going to lie to you, Sia. I don't ever want to have to lie to you. But yes. One was like this.

And how come you're not married? I mean, you should be by now, right?

Because I was with someone my parents didn't approve of.

Was she a palagi?

She was an exchange student from China.

Was she beautiful? Like the women in Bruce Lee's movies?

Beauty is in the eye of the beholder, Sia. We grew into each other, not quite how this day has unfolded. It took me three months before I could even kiss her on the cheek. She was raised very traditional and conservative which at first appealed to me. But I had already been with a woman, two women, and she wanted me to still be a virgin and even science couldn't fix that. I told her that unless she was working on building a time machine, I wasn't the man for her, that is, I would never be able to fulfill her fantasy.

Wow! That's heavy. I mean, I'm exhausted just thinking about it and I wasn't even there! Was she also a Scientist and a Mathematician?

Yes. That was our connection. You too would have loved her mind Sia. She was brilliant, like you. And I mean, I could barely understand her in English but I knew her mind. And she did things with numbers that stunned and astounded me.

That's very beautiful Ioage. I love how you just said, stunned and astounded. It's very lyrical. It makes me feel like she's someone I would have liked to have met.

And she, you, Sia.

Can you give me an example of something stunning and astounding that she did with numbers?

Hmmm . . . now that you've asked, I can't think of a single one! Sole! There's so many! Ok, wait. I've got it. This is my personal favorite. She introduced me to Euler's Identity, known otherwise as Euler's Equation. And she showed me how to solve it, which is like traveling through a mathematical jungle. It's one of the most spectacular theorem in Maths. I know it doesn't sound like it, and I wish we had access to a blackboard so that I could demonstrate the fairly complex mathematics used to solve it but as my Uncle Vai used to say, Se fa'apu'upu'u Sole lau kala ua koeikiki ka le kaimi o pi'iga, Make your story short because it's nearly time for Big Time Wrestling.

Ha! Ha! Ha! We both busted out in a cacophony of laughter!

Then Ioage continued, Long story short, she showed me how we arrive back where we start, at the obviously simple numbers of 0 and 1. And you can just imagine my very Samoan mind, nurtured by the complexities of riddles, found this all so very inspiring. As sometimes, in the labyrinth of complexity, the answer is right there under our noses.

$$e^{i\pi} + 1 = 0$$

Euler's Identity a.k.a. Euler's Equation as Explained by Ioage Viliamu, Nu'uolemanusa, Western Samoa. Saturday, 12 October, 1985.

You just gave me chills Ioage. Wow! And I don't even know how you arrived at 0 let alone 1. But I can just imagine how beautiful it must have been to watch her make all those complex links to find yourselves where you started! Euler just blew my mind, Ioage!

I know, aye? I knew you'd see the beauty of it, Sia. It's nothing short of brilliance, isn't it? When I find myself alone, it's the one equation that lifts my spirits and makes me appreciate our interconnectedness in numbers, and as people both living and dead.

She sounds fascinating and intriguing, Ioage. Like an enigma.

You understand her as only one brilliant mind would understand another, he said. After all, brilliance attracts brilliance. And brilliant minds know not of the pettiness of mediocrity or jealousy.

If I'm to believe what you're saying, then what about two integers that have the same distance away from zero but on opposite sides of the number one?

Hmmm. Good question. Are you asking me mathematically or with relationships?

Both.

Auola! Se'i va'aia i le vave o legei both. Very impressive. I wonder who your teacher might be.

He's a very short and old man. He likes to squeeze 17 year old girl's nipples. Do you want his number? Maybe he could squeeze yours too!

Look who's catching up to the hoaxing game?

Ha! Are you saying that's another point for Team Blue? It's all right. You can have it. That was an easy one.

Oh thank you darling! I said, fluttering my eyes like Alexis Carrington would whenever she closed a business deal and was either celebrating with champagne in a bubble bath or just standing outside Colby Enterprises looking confident and wickedly beautiful.

Listen, said Ioage, as he interrupted my daydream of being Alexis Carrington, the most powerful and beautiful woman on prime time T.V., Back to our original hypothesis. Do opposites attract you say? It's complicated when applied to people because there's so many variables that you have to factor in, most notably, religion and economics. But personally? You're asking me whether I believe in the attraction of opposites? Nah. Not really. I know it sounds arrogant and goes against everything Jesus said and what was taught to us by our parents. But quite honestly, I don't think it's possible. Unless they were struck by some divine third force, that sealed them, miraculously, like having a child together or something. But even that, especially if they end up living separate lives after the child is born, then the force or power of the magnetism that drew them together in the first place, will eventually dwindle until it finally diminishes and dies. And even if you do end up together, you will always find something lacking in the other person. Unless you're the Night and Day, and believe in our ancestor's concept of celestial movement and how the Night recedes to make room for the Day and vice versa.

Did you know you just contradicted yourself li'i Ioage?

It did sound like it, didn't it?

Yep. It kind of did. Va'ai oe o lea e le'i momoe le pasese. Hey, be mindful of the passengers. We're still wide awake you know.

Ia sorry for my wrong, Si'aula.

Aua le koe faia. Just don't do it again, ua 'e iloa? You need to put the brakes on your brain and speed it down, Ioage. You're going too fast.

He pecked me on the forehead and said. It's what happens when I get too excited, which has only happened since you decided to hitch a ride with me this morning. Then he added, What did I just say again, Sia? Before you rudely interrupted me? he asked, with a grin on his face.

Rudely? Really Ioage? You sound like an old, old ancient old man.

No, really, I forgot.

Firstly, you said that opposites didn't attract. And then you proceeded to say that they did, from a Samoan cultural perspective. So you basically contradicted yourself.

Hmm. Let me think.

Think man, think!

Aua e ke saga ava'avau mai o lea ouke i'i, ouke le faipe, ua iloa oe lea? Koeikiki e foa i le ali. Don't yell at me, I'm right here and I'm not deaf, ok? Or I'll crack your head with this bamboo pillow.

Ha Ha Ha! That. Is. Classic!

Jokes aside, I'm missing something. I can't quite put my finger on it now but it's something that makes it work. Because it does eventually work, you know. I mean when you think about social and intimate relations, there was no such concept as romantic love in old Samoa. Romantic love is a purely American Hollywood illusion. Our people believed in something more long lasting. Something that wasn't just instant gratification.

Like us? I said, just to annoy him.

Oh shut up and listen, girl!

Ha! You become very manly when you're passionate and angry.

Stop it, you're making me lose my train of thought.

Lale e alu aku i le pasi a Koma lau train of thought! Your train of thought is riding on Koma's bus!

Stop it and listen to me! I'm your elder!

Hello? O Mapuifagalele lea? Se fa'amolemole lava pe maua aku si makou koeaiga lea e fiu e su'e . . . Is this the Old Folks Home at Mapuifagalele? Can you please tell me if you have our old man there, we've been looking all over for him.

Ia ua lava loa, e le malie, ua iloa? That's enough. That's not funny, ok?

Is this funny? I said, pulling his left toe.

Aua le faia le vaemakua. Leai se mea a le vaemakua o faia ia oe. Don't disturb the Big Toe, you hear? The Big Toe is not doing anything to you.

Doesn't the Big Toe *want* to do something to me? Huh? I fired back, taking pleasure in my growing confidence.

Hmmm that's a very complex question. In lieu of the fact that Big Thumbs are holding your nipples.

Ouch! Hey, stop that! I said, hitting him on the chest while pinching his inner thigh.

I'm not a bloody cow, you know, I said, pulling his other big toe.

I'm sorry, Sia. I couldn't resist. I remember watching this once in a movie, how they milked cows using these massive machines which they hooked up to the cow's teats, because we don't do that here. I just wanted to see if it was the same with humans.

Listen, I said, turning towards him and placing both my fingers onto *his* nipples, which I could feel under his t-shirt. Is that what you meant? I said, squeezing them tightly, the way he had just done to mine.

Ia aikae la'ia e kiga le mea. Now go eat shit, that hurts.

I'm sorry. I didn't mean to, he said, apologetically.

A minute went by before I said, I know you didn't mean to, Ioage. Just don't do it again because it really does hurt, ua iloa?

He said he was sorry again and then he gave me a wicked look before he did something strange that shocked me out of my skin. He slid his head under my Madonna t-shirt and lifted my bra upwards without undoing the hooks, and I could tell that his mouth was covering each nipple even if I didn't see what he was doing.

Aue'e! Sole! What if someone should see us?

But he didn't answer. And I suddenly felt myself

floating on a cloud, like a wingless bird, gliding, suspended in mid-air.

Is that better, Sia?

Hmm....no.

Is that better?

No.

And *that*...?

Ahhh....oh yes. *That... Hmm... That!*

I just wanted to finish my train of thought before you rudely interrupted me again, said Ioage, whose animated face was something extraordinary to watch, as it was different from how he conducted himself in school. In school, he would have said the exact same thing but differently. Not nearly as spirited as how he appeared before my eyes at that very moment which made me wonder whether that's how he usually behaved when he was away from his classroom and students or whether I was the one causing him to radiate as if he were a constellation at midnight.

I abandoned the question and answered him teasingly, preferring to be engaged with him and his energy directly, rather than being a mere observant or worst, a cerebral voyeur.

Which train of thought is that? The one that left an hour ago on Koma's bus? I asked, teasingly, smiling at how quickly he responded with such ease and conviction so that I could see directly into his spirit, which made me feel uplifted and safe all the same.

Be serious. Listen. I was talking about looks and appearances and how it's irrelevant to Samoans when it comes to the choosing of partners. And yet how it's the end all to Americans and their plastic cinematography.

Wait a minute. Why do you have such disdain for Americans and their cinematography?

I'm just going to pretend you didn't say that. Besides, I don't have disdain for all Americans. Just specific ones who control movie and media images which I'm sure ordinary Americans would also find just as disdainful if not more.

I don't get it, Ioage. I love movies like the next Samoan. Cowboys movies, karate movies, comedies and romantic drama and escaping into a fantasy world that is unreal. It takes me away from my own reality. So, why would you want to knock that?

Fair enough. But what if that fantasy was projected as a supposed reality?

Aren't all fantasies supposed realities?

You don't get me.

Then explain yourself more specifically, man!

I'm trying! But each time, you knock me down.

Kalofa e, i si kama o Ioage! Kakou e, kakou e, ua kafe le isupe! Poor Ioage! With snot running down his nose!

Oh, shut up!

Ha. Ha. Ha. That's what happens when you wanna play marbles with girls!

As much as he wanted to suppress it, He busted out laughing. And I laughed along with him. And somewhere between the roots and the bark and the leaves and the top of the moso'oi where we sat, our laughter hugged each other and smiled at each other, and told each other that this day will never end. That it would go on, and on, and on, forever.

Hey, maybe the variable you've been looking for is Time. Have you ever thought of time in the movements, of Darkness and Lightness? And how it might act to sustain that kind of relationship? A li'i Ioage?

Eureka! Time! Yes! Of course it's time! Why didn't I think of that earlier, Mei-ling?

Was that her name?

What do you mean?

You just called me Mei-ling.

Se kala mo'i? I did?

You look sad when I just said her name. You must miss her.

I'm sorry, Sia. I just got caught up in the heat of the moment. Please forgive me.

What for? I would have done the same thing if I were trying to prove that the square root of 2 was irrational.

Shooo hooo! Koe kau leisi au suipi keige lea! And another point for the Manu Samoa!

Eh, let's stop this talk of contradictions already. I just want to know something Ioage, do you miss her? Do you miss Mei-ling?

Yes, Sia. I do. I mean, I did. But it's been a year and in the last letter I received from her which was five months ago, she told me that her parents had also arranged a marriage for her.

I'm so sorry Ioage. I really mean it. But I know how your parents think because they basically raised me. And maybe Tama ma Tina are also thinking about Mei-ling and how difficult it would have been for her to live in Samoa. To live in Gu'usa. The wife of a pastor's son filled with so many responsibilities. Have you ever thought of that?

You're too young to know these things.

I am my mother's daughter as well your mother's daughter too Ioage. They've taught me how to eat fish well. To be mindful of the bones.

You've really been trained well.

Your mother, our Tina, had a lot to do with it also. It's strange to talk to you about her because she's your mother and because she is also my mother. She's my tina fa'aleagaga, my spiritual mother. And yet, here we are, a li'i Ioage?

Do you know what your so called spiritual mother told me to do at the airport on the day I left?

No. But by the sound of your voice, it was something you were not happy about.

She said, whatever happens outside of Samoa cannot be brought home to Samoa. That she didn't want me bringing home anyone else but a Samoan girl. And that if I wanted to, she was going to start looking for someone. Someone from Papauta or someone who would be able to carry the mamalu or the honor of our family lineage. Marriage is arranged for us with women we don't even know, but we do it because it's our duty. And it goes the same for our educated women who struggle with roles as daughters to traditional parents. Come back in four year's time, Sia, and tell me that that's not true. But that's not the point. The point is, Sia, I want you to know and to believe me when I say that I never expected this to happen. I mean, I'm not some pervert who became a teacher to look at or fa'atilotilo towards young girls like you. This whole day took me by surprise too. I didn't expect to be here at all. I was just doing my usual routine of going to the library on a Saturday while other men go fishing or to plantations or to work. Being the pastor's son is a privilege that has meant we never had to do all those things. Because everything was always provided for us by the aulotu. Food. Clothing. Education. But one thing I knew for certain after my first year in Port Moresby was that I wanted to return home and give back to the community that had given so much to me. The way my parents did, after raising us in Papua New Guinea ten years earlier when they were stationed there as Samoan missionaries.

That's why I'm here.

I want to inspire our students.

To let them know that there are opportunities out there that can be accessed directly from here. But that they should hold on strongly to their roots and to their identity because it gets easily confusing out there. I know this is not easy for you. Sitting here listening to some 30 year old guy give you all these compliments. But I can't help it, Sia. Your mind excites me. Your fierce intelligence inspires me and gives me clarity as to the limitless possibilities of the universe. Which I see in you.

You're curious about the world and you want to share it with as many people as possible. Just don't be surprised or disappointed when you go out there and find that some people may not necessarily like that kind of boldness.

Mortals are not used to bright stars like you, Sia.

That's what I thought of you after I read your first assignment on the 10 types of clouds.

I became especially fascinated at how you connected the description of each cloud with a human emotion and then your musings about the ancestors and how they too saw such clouds while they looked up to the Nine Heavens, long, long ago.

And those are precisely the kinds of connections I'm talking about when I stand up there at the blackboard. But most importantly, I saw in that first essay what I see with every essay you submit. That your excitement for learning is not merely for your own personal gain but rather to illuminate the path for others who are less capable.

And that's how I knew that your light didn't just shine for you alone.

It shines for everyone. And *that* is what attracted me to you. And your smile and you have big nipples. Ha! Ha! I'm sorry, I know that came out sleazy. I didn't mean to. I just wanted to share with you that you engage me wholly.

Mind, body and soul. But just understand this, Sia. That your light just might be too bright for some and it will end up making some even blind; the ignorant and the mediocre and the petty ones and the jealous ones, who may very well be the closest people to you.

Remember what Julius Caesar said in your English Competition play right after he was stabbed in the back?

E tu, Brutus? I whispered, barely hearing my own voice as I had become completely enraptured by Ioage's.

That's right, he said, You, too, Brutus? And do you remember why he said it?

Because the dagger in his back belonged to Brutus who was his best friend.

Brutus was his best man. His main man which is why it was so shocking.

Caesar was someone like you, Sia. He had your trusting personality. He loved everyone. Because he wanted the same justice for all citizens of Rome. And there wasn't a shadow of a doubt in his mind that everyone felt the same love and loyalty towards him enough to protect him from a conspiracy that eventually took his life. That's why it was so shocking to him to find out that the Senate and people he trusted the most, would conspire to kill him. However, my Samoan mind tells me that it wasn't the dagger that killed Julius Caesar, but rather, it was the betrayal of his friends and those he trusted most. I don't want to sound melo-dramatic. Or cynical. I don't want to scare you off. But that's human nature. People make mistakes. People have weaknesses. Like Achilles' famous heel. But that's no reason for you to stop shining, Sia. I'm saying all this to you now because I know in less than two months you'll finish high school and go off to where I've just come from, which is what I want to see happen to you and I expect nothing less from you. But I'll stop now. I've said too much. I just want you to know that young people like you are the reason why I returned. And you are so gifted. So perceptive, Sia. You see things that other people don't see. Things that even I don't see because I'm so scientific in my thought and so mathematical in my calculations that I'm caught up in the empiricism of it all, that at times, I lose sight of what's right before my nose. I know you're destined to do great things Sia. Your gifts will take you to many places far far away from Gu'usa. Places few of your classmates will ever get to see or be able to even locate on a map of the world if given the chance. But I just want you to remember to come back to us. And to remember this day. Like I will. *Always.*

A deluge of tears fell down my cheeks at the sound of Ioage's voice and his words as they surrounded us and I felt cocooned by its resonances and wished to remain in it indefinitely.

The day was not yet over and yet, the melancholic sound of his voice made me miss him. As if he were already somewhere far far away from me.

I looked up at Ioage and our eyes met. He held my gaze for a good moment that I wished would be multitudinous, amaranthine and endless.

Once more, as I was trying to say before you rudely interrupted me, said Ioage with a wide smile on his face, Samoans arranged marriages to strengthen inter-village alliances and to increase mana. What does how you look have anything to do with that? he asked.

Are we still on the subject of looks?

Yes, we are!

Why?

Because I don't want people to have romantic notions of how life was before the missionaries arrived.

Ok. Then how do you explain unions of women who were expected to marry men they'd never seen before in an excruciatingly painful ceremonial marriage where their virginity was tested, performed before hundreds of eyes to see? Especially when the man, or the chief or the son of a chief is already married to say 12 other women. What happens then? I asked. Is that real enough for you?

You have to remember Sia, these sorts of marriages were performed only between virgins and said men. It wasn't for everyone. So a virgin knew what was expected of her. She'd been groomed for it since birth. And would most likely remain with the man she married until she died.

Sounds depressing if you ask me. I mean, I don't think I could ever survive sharing you with someone else. Let alone a dozen.

Well, you see, you're looking at it from 20th century eyes, Sia!

I don't care what century eyes I look at it from, Ioage. I'll never share you with anyone. *Ever! Period!*

That, you will never have to worry about, my dear. Science and Maths are my only other mistresses. And I don't think I'll find anyone any time soon with your prodigious mind. *Trust me.*

Then he sat up and repositioned us both so that he became a chair with which I leaned back onto while he coupled my breasts in his hands and started caressing them through the Madonna t-shirt.

Thank you Ioage, I said. Looking up at him.

That means a lot to me. Especially coming from you.

You're welcome Sia, he said. As he bent down and kissed my forehead.

And when he removed his lips, he said, I've never had this kind of conversation with anyone before. I mean, since I got back from university where they were commonplace.

You should perhaps widen your scope and radius, I said, cheekily. Get around more, li'i Kama. Astound yourself with the knowledge that there are far more girls and women like me on our beautiful island paradise than you've been led to believe. More than you can count stars, mister.

Ha! Widen my scope and radius. Kau lau suipi! And, another point for Team Blue! Good one! Ok, I stepped right into that one. Before you say another word, will you excuse me while I remove my own shoe from my mouth thank you very much. Well said. See that's what I'm talking about! How did a girl like you get to be so bloody smart?

Don't underestimate us kuaback girls. We have a secret tree of knowledge that grows wild at midnight in the Garden of Wisdom. Its fruits are nocturnal and can only be accessed if you're not wearing a panty.

Ha! Ha! Ha! Ioage busted out laughing so loud, I thought he was going to choke.

You're killing me, Sia. You really are killing me, you know that, don't you?

I don't understand you. What do you mean exactly?

You've never heard that expression before?

I shook my head. No, I haven't.

When someone is saying that, it means they're overcome by emotion or that they were overwhelmed by an idea or a thought or something so profound and yet so simple that they're blown away by it. By how easy the other person makes it sound so that they too were thinking the same thing but were only sorry they weren't the ones to say it first. That's all.

Did Mei-ling kill you, Ioage?

Oh yes. Mei-ling killed me, Sia.

And the palagi women you said you were with? Did they also kill you?

I was only with two others. The first woman I was ever with was a prostitute.

What's a prostitute?

Someone who receives money in exchange for sex services.

You paid for someone to have sex with you? Why would you ever do that for?

I did, Sia. It was my first time. I was nervous. I didn't know anything and I didn't want to be with someone who didn't know what they were doing either.

Is she the one that taught you the language of love?

Not all of it. But yes, she was very loving and gentle which surprised me.

How so?

Well, because when people think of prostitutes, they don't necessarily think of a person with feelings. They only think of the stereotype. A loose woman with loose morals and values. I was astounded to find otherwise, Sia. Felicity sensed that I was nervous and put me right at ease. It was the most remarkable day of my life. One that I will not easily forget.

Felicity. What a beautiful name, Ioage.

She was a beautiful woman, Sia. She had a volumptuous body that made me experience pleasure with another human being for the first time in my life and she did so in the most gentle and loving of ways. And her heart was made of gold too which was a bonus I didn't expect. So I guess you can say she killed me.

I'd say she did, Ioage.

What about the other girl? I mean, woman?

I don't know if I should tell you about her.

Why not?

I don't think I'm ready yet to talk about her.

Well, at least tell me her name. What was her name?

MD. That's all I know.

Did you know her long?

I'd rather not talk about her right now.

That's ok, Ioage. We don't have to.

Thank you. Now, where were we?

✧✦✧

Ioage always wore his hair long and in a bun like mine which lead to much silent criticism of the fa'afeagaiga and the faletua, How can they tell our boys to keep their hair clean cut when their own son runs around like an uncivilized barefooted savage?

He told me to remove the band that tied his hair up and I was startled at just how long it was, longer even than my own hair.

I had never touched a man's hair before as my grandmother had told us that it was taboo. Especially a man with hair as long as Ioage's which reminded me of Samson in the bible.

I ran my fingers through Ioage's hair, feeling its thick heavy texture which I lifted to my cheeks and wiped my tears with it.

He turned around and looked up at me and saw what I was doing and took both my hands in one of his strong palms, while he reached up with his other and wiped my tears.

Se makagaga kele oe se. E le kagi se koa. Don't cry. A warrior doesn't cry, he said.

I sighed a great sigh then, while another deluge of tears began to flow down my face as he extended his arms around me and hugged me to him.

We remained in that embrace until I finally broke the silence when I asked him, Sole, do you think we might still have time for that swim?

Fern and vines and banyan trees and rows and rows of coconuts and blue birds and red birds and giant green lizards were just a few of the fauna and flora that surrounded the road to the secret place Ioage knew to be heaven on earth, pungent with the fragrance of pua and moso'oi that intoxicated our senses, or at least they did mine.

I held Ioage's hand and followed behind him as he led us further and further away from the government road and into the stomach of the forest. He carried his backpack, filled with all sorts of emergency supplies and a blanket which was in the cargo of the pick-up for just such impromptu excursions.

And as he kept walking, I couldn't help but stare and marvel at his calves. They were the biggest calves I had ever seen on a man, thickly pulsating muscle with each step he took. They reminded me of cartoon pictures of the Hulk which my twin brothers Au and Ue called Maso-man a.k.a Muscle Man. Only Ioage was not as big or as tall. But he had the same perfect proportions to his body.

As he led us further and further away from the government road, I couldn't help also but be stunned by the abundance of medicinal plants and trees, sasalapa, o'a, fau, tuise, lau matolu, magamaga, fetau, lau mafatifati, tauanave and all sorts of other leaves I recognized from when Aunty Aima'a and I would make treks to the Gu'usa Uka forest to collect them for her fofo, something I first began to do when I was 8.

Seeing them in abundance made my heart expand and in that moment, I felt the healing sacredness of their presence and remembered almost immediately the first time I met Ioage and how Ioage told us that leaves contained veins and that the veins carried the very essence of life.

Momentarily I thought about Aunty Aima'a and how much she would have loved to be here. I was convinced that she would have found it to be Christmas as any other traditional healer would. And then another thought entered my mind. The thought of MD and why Ioage didn't want to talk about her. And my own curiosity about Ioage's past, started to stir.

I had never seen a lake before and found my breath leave my body the instant I laid eyes on it. Intuitively, I closed my eyes and listened to the sounds of birds and bees and other forest creatures that made up the band of the most exquisite music I had ever heard.

As I stood there, stunned by the majesty of the lake, I looked over at Ioage and saw that he had removed all his clothes, including his underwear and motioned to me to remove mine, the same way he asked me to roll the window down.

My heart stopped at the sight of him.

So that's what a grown man looked like naked, I asked myself. As if I had come in direct contact with a sacredness that left me breathless.

I would have never known the sensual nature of Ioage's body as he was always impeccably clothed in the clothes ascribed to a Samoan man of his profession (minus the shoeless feet which I would have to agree with village murmurs and whispers that it was improper attire for a teacher of influence, but only for safety reasons).

Seeing him now made me feel moist between the legs and I didn't know what that meant, because it's not like I was peeing and yet I was wet all the same.

I put my hands to my eyes and then made Spock's sign with one of them, allowing a hole between my fingers where I spied at him, maka aiku, ghost style. The sound of his laugh echoed and echoed around the forest, causing a school of bats to flee into the sky, all at once, and then disappeared back into the woods.

The bats made me feel a sudden apprehension at the thought that we might be disturbing spirits and inviting ghosts, so I carefully unbuttoned and unzipped my jeans, paying extra attention at minimizing the noise level it might cause while I struggled out of them, before I folded them neatly on a rock, along with Litia's *Madonna The Virgin Tour 1985* t-shirt and I stood before Ioage with only my panties and my bra, like some tourist girl on holiday.

I was about to walk into the water when he whistled at me and motioned that I remove the last articles of clothing that still covered me before I should come any closer.

I motioned to him to keep his voice down.

As if he were already intoxicated, He took his pointer finger and pressed it against his lips and as he did, I started removing the last articles, the bottom off first and then the top until I stood completely naked before Ioage who had begun to walk towards me.

Naturally, as if it were my normal practice, I removed my hair from my breasts so that they were more visible to him and bowed my head to my feet, surprised not only that there was not a single mosquito in sight but that I had no shame whatsoever of being naked before him, which I know would have stunned my mother and the aunties and the faletua Tina Lakena, Ioage's mother (and my other mother) into strokes.

But I wasn't thinking of them or about anyone else.

All I was thinking of was Ioage and how safe I felt in his presence and in his arms.

And as he moved closer and closer to me, I realized, that he was one of only three people to have ever seen me naked in my entire life.

My Aunty Aima'a was the first, whose healing hands I can still remember as they anxiously traveled all over my body, massaging it with nonu leaves the week I came down with fever caused by an infection from a sila'ilagi/boil that made me throw up day and night and I thought I was going to die because I was positive I was going to vomit out all my insides. Until she told the twins to go into the forest and to feel the forest. Feel it and whatever leaves they returned with, those would be the leaves of the fofo that would help me, their sister, recover. The twins had left at the break of dawn but did not return to the house until twilight. My mother asked her sister whether the boys knew which leaves to bring. Why she didn't specify a leaf so that the twins would know what they're looking for! But Aunty Aima'a told her that therein was the problem. That we needed to trust the intuition of children and seek the purity of their hearts in council. Which is exactly what she was doing. A child also possessed wisdom, she reminded my mother. And because a child's wisdom is uncontaminated by the prejudices and discriminatory nature of an adult's mind, it is therefore more transparent, more lucid and more natural and organic. A child will recognize the healing powers of plants, roots, barks by feeling his or her way through the forest. Which is why she sent the twins. They will know, she said. Calming my mother's already anxious gaze which dissolved only when she heard the twin's foodsteps outside the paepae at twilight.

To Aunty Aima'a's great surprise, the twins did not return with forest leaves, even though they had been gone to the forest the entire day. When Aunty Aima'a asked them for the leaves, they told her that after an entire day of wandering in the forest, the trees spoke to them and told them that leaves were not what was needed but rather, showed her the roots of the vaisina, which they had to go to the ocean side to retrieve since it grew wildly at the beach and a basket of bright red Aute Samoa, Samoan hibiscus. They walked over to me and saw the black spots of death in my eyes and they wept as they both proceeded to chew the Aute Samoa and the roots of the vaisina, and applied it on the purple and badly infected sila'ilagi on my buttocks. It took less than a day for the Aute Samoa and the vaisina to make their healing way into my body and blinded the eye of the sila'ilagi and eventually killed it. But I still to this day believe that it was not the Aute Samoa or the Vaisina that killed the sila'ilagi and healed me, but rather, it was the alofa or love of my brothers for me which had compelled them to wonder the forest for an entire day without food or water or rest until the forest spoke to them and they in turn, brought the forest's advice to me, chewing the Aute Samoa and the vaisina in their mouths and pressing it lovingly to my own skin, healing me and sealing them both to my heart, forever.

The only other people besides Ioage and Aunty Aima'a to see me naked were the girls whenever we showered at the public showers, before we had our own family shower installed in the house, but even then, they never saw me with my panties off. And now, Ioage, who was walking towards me. Each step made my heart skip a beat.

As soon as he reached me, Ioage took my hair in his hands and wrapped it up in a fa'apaku, a bun so that it was only him with his hair almost down past his buttocks. Ioage had to stand on his toes to reach the top of my head and I ended up bending down so that he didn't feel awkward, and yet, I couldn't help but remark at the vast difference in our height and burst out laughing as soon as he stood before me.

Koʻa ʻe puʻupuʻu kele, se, I said. Why are you so short?

Galo ga aumai laʻu apafaʻi se. I forgot to bring my ladder, he said, which I found equally amusing.

Ua ga lou soaʻai ga ua ʻe saga umi ai? You're too tall because you sneak into the kitchen at night, he said, as he scratched his head with comedic perplexity.

Salapu, ke le pule. Shut up, that's none of your business, I responded, as a large full moon smile spread across his face.

Koeikiki foʻi se keigekiki po ia pi. I laughed, as a memory of me peeing on the mat until I was 11 flew into my brain and colonized the moment, which still haunted me but dissolved into thin air, at Ioage's teasing laugh.

Hey, se faiaoga i keʻi ua le aoga i se keigeikiki aoga. Fai aku ai foʻi. He laughed out loud before I motioned to him to keep it down.

Kekele o gei makasusu, se. He moaned. I moaned.

Ia ʻa kekele, aua le aia. If they're too big, then don't eat them, I said, as he remarked at the size of my nipples.

Aʻo le a le mea ua susu ai le mea a kaʻua e ke leʻi oʻo i le vai? And why is our cunt so wet when you haven't even been in the water?

Sole....Sole.....Sole!....Ioage!!

Sao faʻalalelei! Thank you! How beautiful! Now you look like a real taupou, Sia. You're a true ceremonial virgin, said Ioage as he marked my cheeks with the blood on his fingers, followed immediately by, Sia, did I hurt you? he asked.

No, you didn't, Ioage, I said. The feel of his fingers still vibrated though the walls of my cunt.

Are you sure?

Yes.

Promise?

You didn't hurt me.

I'm sorry if I did.

I'm not.

You know you're not a virgin anymore.

So that's what that Madonna song meant. 'Touched for the very first time.'

Open your eyes and look at me, Sia. No, you can't do that, you have to open both eyes. Shh, look at me, Sia. Look at me. Please. There's nothing to be ashamed of, aye?

I nodded. Touched by his concern. Understanding why he said what he did. But it still didn't answer the burning question that I'd always asked whenever I heard women talk talk talk about girls who'd lost their virginities before they were married: what did the rupturing of a small part of a woman's anatomy have to do with her character? And in my case, it wasn't like I had hurt anyone. Or stolen from anyone. Or killed anyone. And neither did Ioage. But if someone were to spy on us that very minute, the stories that would circulate *out of context* would be done so with such vicious malice and such cruelty I had no doubt it would kill a cow or a horse or a young girl (like me) who decides to hang herself or to drown herself or to slit her own throat in the middle of a stormy night if pushed enough closer to the edge.

If anything, Ioage and I shared a private, intimate and sensual moment of mutual respect with an urgency of touch that I knew sealed him to me and me to him and connected us beyond infinity.

What did the conventions of society have to do with that?

Why did such beauty need to be squashed and altogether killed by people's rules as if they too weren't young once and experienced what we just had?

And before I could answer any of these questions, Ioage looked at me and said, I see that nasty wrinkle on your forehead again, Sia. You're so far away. Come back to me, he said. Sia, come back to me.

Before Ioage started singing, I had always wondered about the meaning of this particular song as I often asked myself, why Samoans compared their lovers to food, as Ioage's voice ascended into the trees and caressed its branches and leaves. The songwriter for instance, was comparing his beloved to all the foods that were delicacies to us Samoans and Pacific peoples; corned beef from New Zealand, biscuits from Fiji, chop suey with tomatoes and beans.

In the second verse, the lover tells the beloved that if she wants to, they could get married at the government courts, and not a traditional wedding. And then interestingly enough in that same verse, the devil is implied to roam only among the uneducated who are warned that doing so, will lead to a baby of the night.

And in the last verse, he sings about their going their separate ways, that he didn't live far away but that if she had the time, to write him a letter and have it dropped off by a motor car.

As much as I loved the sound of Ioage's contended voice, which echoed and echoed through the forest and made ripples on the placid lake, I felt a bit melancholic by it all the same. Wondering whether it was an omen or a premonition for our own time together.

Would our time at the lake result in me getting pregnant? And if so, wouldn't our baby be called a baby of the day? And even though it's not night, it's the middle of a beautiful sunny day, with the Sun shining as we stood here staring into each other's eyes in the middle of a forest, would that then truly make our baby a baby of the day? But we were in a forbidden and taboo situation, I reminded myself, which meant that no matter how much light there would have been wherever we made love, our child would always be considered by society, a child of the night.

I wanted to ask Ioage about that. How he would feel about our baby being classified by people as a baby of the night? And since we're already married the traditional way, with trees, leaves, and a placid lake as witnesses, would we need to be married again at the government court house and be issued a certificate that said we were officially married? That we were then Mr. and Mrs. Ioane Viliamu? Would this then make our baby a baby of the day? And why was it so important for me how people called or labeled our baby? Wasn't the mere fact that he or she was conceived from the seed of two people who came together as one under a canopy of ancient trees and sky and light matter more than society's labels? I definitely had to talk to Ioage about that, to see what his thoughts were on the subject. But I filed that thought for perhaps another time. As he was far too merry singing about food than to disturb him with the ugliness of society's labels.

Ioage's voice soared and soared and soared like an Owl into the sky, without any of the self-analysis that was stuck in my own throat that prevented me from singing.

Oka oka la'u honey
O la'u honey fa'asilisili oute fa'atusaina
I se apa Hellaby,
Po o se pisupo sili po o se masi keke mai Fiti
Po o sina sapasui,
O ni tomato ma ni pi

Afai lava ua tonu.
Ua tonu i lou finagalo
Ta fa'aipoipo
Avane i le malo
E leaga o le ta'atua e tele ai le tiapolo
Nei maua sau pepe
O le pepe o le po.
Dear dear tofa o le a ta tete'a
E leai se mamao
Tele i ga'uta
A avanoa sou taimi
Telefoni ane i se itula
Pe fai sau letter avane i se motor car

Some time passed after Ioage sang the last two words of the song, motor car, which in Samoan would be spelled moto ka. And I fast forwarded my mind to three months from now, when that day in January would finally come, bringing with it a moto ka that would eventually take me to the airport, where I would fly off to my sister Simeamativa who lived in Los Angeles and had written to my mother to have me sent over so that I could continue my education.

Sia is hard working and is smart, Mama. I had read in my sister's letter.

She deserves a chance that is also our chance as a family. Please, I beg you to give her that chance. Give us that chance and you will see her soar.

The taste of salt is how I remember reading my sister's words that day. I never knew the extend of her feelings towards me until that day and a deluge of love suddenly poured out of me for her, for my sister, who had married my brother in law Freddy/Feleki who was the only palagi I knew who was confidentally fluent in Samoan and spoke it like one of us. Feleki's research was on architecture and how the fale was an expression of our social and political systems as Samoans, a topic far too heavy for my 17½ year old mind and yet, it was just as intriguing since it was connected to the ancestors, a theme that had become the all end for me since I first met Ioage who insisted on us making the connections between science and our ancestors and how they too understood and practiced science, in their own unique way.

It's interesting how you discover people in their words. Not the words they say before you, but the words they say when you are not in their presence. Loving and gentle and encouraging words which are hidden and not as easily pronounced as the aggressive and violent words which are ever so loudly audible and are painful and hurtful and have the capacity to inflict wounds that turn into scars that never ever heal. The loving, kind and encouraging words my sister had written in her letter to my mother for instance, would never see the light of day between us. But I knew that. After all, that's just how it was between sisters. At least between Simeamakiva and me which is what led me to conclude that perhaps people don't want to give themselves away with affection. Affection implied the possibility of appearing vulnerable even if for a second. People prefer cold stoicism to loving vulnerability and it wasn't just in our household that such truths were held.

Outé alofa ia te oe/I love you, for instance, was something you rarely heard in a Samoan household. At least not in ours. And yet, I knew and we all knew that it was always there. Ever present. As if by vocalizing it, it might disappear? Love's presence in our family and village life was like an invisible blanket that made us feel safe and warm on a cold, cold night. One that didn't need to be unnecessarily spoken of because we always knew and felt and were aware of its omnipresence, which gave us an inspired sense of identity and of belonging.

I was feeling the same feelings towards Ioage. The feeling of being wrapped in the softest blanket. One that made you feel warm and fuzzy inside and made the world a gentle and wondrous place to be in. Even more so on a warm hot day like this on an island in the middle of the Pacific Ocean.

Talk about paradise's paradoxical irony.

As Ioage's voice swirled and swirled and swirled around me like a protective buffer that shielded us both from any aiku that might be lurking in the thick forest or in the lake, I caught it with my own voice. And together, we sang like two hungry people whose hunger was satiated by the mere thought of Hellaby corned beef, biscuits from Fiji, tomatoes and beans and the presence of the beloved as butterflies continued to dance and dance and dance above the mosooi blossoms.

I finally mustered the courage to open my eyes and was pleasantly surprised to look directly into Ioage's own eyes.

He saw my reaction and pointed at his feet and that's when I noticed that he was standing on a small rock that made him appear taller than me. A mischievous smile spread across his face.

Sneaky, yet genius, I said, as I saw his feet planted squarely on the rock which made me laugh out loud.

Well I had to do something so when you write about this moment in your book one day, you'll say something like, 'Then she opened her eyes and looked directly into his tall, strong and manly gaze, and instantly, her mouth ached to be conquered by his mouth, ached too, especially for his passionate and wanton tongue.' And not, Then she opened her eyes and couldn't see him, even though she knew he was around somewhere below her knees. Then she bent down at him because he couldn't reach her. Ha ha! Laki le iai o si ma'a lea i'i, pegei e le au le kama o le aka! Shoooo hooo! Just my luck this stone was here, otherwise, the movie's action hero wouldn't have been able to reach the leading lady's lips!

And that's when I started busting out laughing.

The one thing I've come to know and enjoy so much about Ioage is his ability to take me through the entire spectrum of human emotion. It's unlike anything I've ever experienced in my 17½ years. Like greedily biting into a mango or swallowing a double rainbow all at once. Without sounding like a broken record like some of my friends do when they're praising a boy or a famous singer, Ioage simply blows my mind! Wide open!

Then he suddenly turned from me and got something out of his backpack.

Chewing gum? Really, Ioage? I said, hoping he would give me the bigger half.

It's called a condom. I doubt you've seen one.

How do you know what I've seen and not seen? Huh?

I know, trust me. I know.

No you don't.

Yes I do.

That's mighty presumptuous of you, Mr. Viliamu.

Ehh . . . this is not the time for this, Sia. Just . . . se soia se!

Stop, what?

I'm trying to . . .

Ioage struggled to open the wrapper and took the condom out, but before he could finish his sentence, I grabbed it from his hands and upon closer inspection blew air into it until it was inflated like a balloon.

Are we going to have a party? Where are the guests?

Se aikae ia se, he said. Stop being sarcastic.

And I laughed out loud again.

Then he laughed too as he slid his fully erect penis into it and led me towards a clearing in the woods where he had spread the blanket earlier and we both laid down on it, looking up to the flowers of the moso'oi being lightly caressed by the blowing afternoon breeze.

I may have been taller than him but he was stronger. I felt his strength all through me as he guided himself into me and slowly began to thrust. The first of which made me wince as my fingernails dug into his back and drew blood, his name the first word that flew out of my mouth.

Ioage moaned and when I opened my eyes, he looked at me and whispered if I was ok.

He was surprised when he heard me say no and repeated it as if it were a question, that confused him all the same.

I think something's wrong, Ioage.

O le a? What is it? he said, between moans.

It hurts Ioage, I said.

It hurts.

He pulled himself out of me and I saw his penis with the condom still on it, glistening, all wet as if it had been in the rain.

Does it hurt a lot or a little? 10 being the worst pain, what number would you use to describe how you're feeling?

A 5? I said, hesitantly.

Are you sure it's not a 7 or an 8 or a 10 even?

Then in that case, it's an 11.

An 11? Are you sure, Sia? An 11 you say? But I don't understand it, he said with a look of utter perplexity.

But it hurts, Ioage. It hurts, I said, almost in tears this time.

Shhhh. Come here. Listen, I'm hearing you but I don't understand it, Sia. I mean, you're wet, he whispered.

You're dripping wet, Sia. Do you know what that means?

No, I said, shaking my head and shrugging my shoulders.

I don't know what it means, Ioage. Am I going to die? I asked, looking at a large black ant crawling in circles on my big toenail, like a dog biting its own tail.

Die? Sia, what are you talking about?

It was something I overheard Ioage. One of the aunties was talking about dying and going to Pulotu after she, I mean, after her first time doing it which was a long time ago I guess, because she's old and doesn't have teeth.

Listen Sia, said Ioage, as he lifted my face so that he was looking directly into my eyes and said, Forget about what your old toothless aunty told you. That's just women's talk, you hear? A girl like you wouldn't understand that kind of talk anyways. And you're not going to . . . well, we'll talk about dying later. Anyways, didn't your mother tell you what to expect? I mean, didn't she prepare you for this day? Well, perhaps not *this* day. But for when this day should come? She knew this day would come Sia. She knew it because it also came for her.

I shook my head. Suddenly ashamed at the very thought of my mother who would kill me for sure the minute I get home or at least the minute she learns about what I had done and would most probably crucify me to a tree if she were to ever find out *who* I had done it with.

Listen Sia, of course you wouldn't know what it means to be moist. To be wet as you are now. It just means that you're excited, Sia. That you're sexually aroused by the sight of me. Just like I am, with my penis that got erect by seeing you near me. The wetness you're feeling or experiencing means you want me to be with you, just as much as I want to be with you, which is a very positive and good sign. Millions of girls and women around the world suffer from dry vagina, meaning their vaginas don't get enough lubrication in order for sexual intercourse to take place which usually happens when a girl or a woman is forced into having sex with someone they don't want to have sex with or simply someone they're not attracted to, which is obviously not your problem as we can clearly see. Getting wet is nature's way of lubricating your vagina so that it can easily receive my penis, no matter what size it might be, without pain. I hope this is not sounding like a biology lesson because it's actually quite sexy what's happening here but I just want you to know that from a scientific point of view and from a man's, everything is going as it should, considering how we feel about each other and your body's physical response to those feelings we share. So I really don't understand why it's hurting as badly as it is, Sia, because it shouldn't and I'm sorry that it is.

Ok, Ioage. I nodded, agreeably to everything he said.

Then he pulled me to him and held me in his arms before he continued.

Listen to me, Sia. This was a bad idea from the start. I say we take a swim, come out and lie here fa'akulisi/like tourists and get dried by the sun and then pack our things and head back to Gu'usa. What do you think a suga, Sia? Huh? Tell me.

No, I protested stubbornly. I don't want us to head back to Gu'usa. Not yet. I want us to continue. I've dreamt about this moment happening for such a long time, Ioage.

And how does it happen in your dreams? Tell me, Sia.

I dream that it's going to hurt but I just want it over with so I don't have to think about doing it again just so I get to say I've already done it like some of the girls at school.

Why would you dream that Sia? That's not a dream. That's a bloody nightmare if you ask me!

A nightmare? Then let it be my nightmare Ioage. I want it to be my own private and personal nightmare. Something that belongs to me and me alone.

Then find some other accomplice, Sia. Find someone else to share your nightmare with because I refuse to be part of it. Frankly, I find it offensive to say the least.

What do you mean, Ioage? But I thought you only wanted one thing, like all men do. I mean, that's what some of the aunties keep saying. That men want only one thing and once they get it, they move onto the next flower, like philandering bees.

Do you really believe that, Sia?

Yes, I do, Ioage. It's what I've been conditioned with my whole life.

You sound like Pavlov's dog.

And you're the bell I'm hearing, Ioage! *And that's why I'm wet!* I'm salivating at the sound of you near me!

Be that as it may, do you still think I'm a, what did you call it, again? A philandering bee that goes around stinging every woman I lay eyes on? Is that how you see me, Sia? Really?

Let's see. Wasn't it you who said that all men are mortal? That Socrates is a man. Which makes Socrates mortal?

So you're saying I'm a fucking bee?

No, I said you were a philandering bee. You chose to add the word fucking to the bloody syllogism, not me!

How do you get to remember everything I say? Damn you Sia. It's not fair.

Then be damned yourself for being such a what did you say again? A fucking good bee of a teacher.

And how did you get to be so fucking smart? A li'i keige lea/Aye, girl?

I'm not going to answer that because it still hurts, Ioage, ok?

It still hurts? he whispered.

Yes, Ioage. It still *fucking* hurts.

But it shouldn't have, Sia. That's what I've read and it's what I've known as I already told you. I'm completely puzzled by what's happening. But like I said, maybe this is a sign that we shouldn't have gone as far as we already have.

Are you angry, Ioage? Huh?

No. Why should I be angry?

Cause I know a girl who kept saying it hurt but the guy kept going as if he didn't hear her. But Pela said he heard her. She was convinced of it.

Well I'm not that guy, Sia. Look at me! I'm not that guy. Ok?

I'm sorry, Ioage. I didn't mean to imply that you were.

I know what you meant, Sia. Listen, if you insist we continue, then I know another way.

There's . . . another way?

Remember in Science there's always another way. Well, in making love there's not only one way either, there are many, many ways. As many as you can imagine. There are even ancient cultures who devoted huge portions of their lives to nurturing the principles of pleasure and of how sexual gratification and most importantly, sexual satisfaction led ultimately to harmony in every other aspect of a person's life. Our people also believed in this same principle and did not view sex with disdain but rather with respect as a force of connecting and bringing families into alliances that would foster stronger bonds of peace and harmony so that those virtues are passed onto the next generation.

I was both startled and dumbfounded at Ioage's confident knowledge of history and his fluency in the language of love. When Ioage said this, my mind couldn't help but wonder. I mean, sure we've seen dogs and cats and cows and horses do it. And once when Q, Cha and I spied on some Swedish tourists down at the waterfall who were fondling and kissing each other as if they hadn't eaten in days. Other than that, I've never really seen any of my own family members or other relatives engaged in such an act. Perhaps because we were a largely female household, whose financial source was my mother's sewing talent. None of the women in my family were married except aunty Stella who was married to Uncle Fa'avevesi. But I could never imagine them engaged in anything other than hymn singing and prayers which they were genuinely devoted to.

And what way is this that we're going to try next? I wondered.

After all, I only knew for certain that there were only two ways to make love and we saw them weekly with Krystal Carrington and Alexis Carrington of *Dynasty* and Pamela Barnes Ewing of *Dallas*. Alexis who was passionate and wicked, got whisked off to bed and then a man would repeatedly thrust himself into her as if he were hurting her and she would have a big old sinister smile on her face as if she enjoyed the power she felt while she was being loved by some big oil tycoon. And if it were Pamela Barnes Ewing who was nice and good or angelic Krystal Carrington, she would just lie there and smile while Bobby Ewing or Blake Carrington lovingly caressed her and whispered to her to stop asking him how his day went with the big oil tycoons of Texas he had to meet that day and to just kiss him and make it all disappear so that it would just be the two of them left in the world. And then the show would cut to a commercial of Calgon soap and its wondrous properties that help its user get transported to another world altogether.

Yes, really, said Ioage. Zapping me out of my sudden T.V. flashbacks that did not include the strangely exotic and mysterious femme fatales of *Star Trek*, which were numerous.

And what way is this that we're going to try next? A li'i Ioage?/Aye Ioage? But before my thought could be formed and spoken, Ioage's voice interceded suddenly.

Shhh. Lie down again and let me have a look, ok, Sia? I promise you, that whatever pain you experienced earlier, this will make it disappear, once I'm done, Ua iloa?/Okay?

I shivered when Ioage said the words 'once I'm done'. He had a determined look on his face and I knew that whatever pain I had experienced earlier, I trusted that Ioage would not only identify its location, but it's source. And I found that I was excited by my own anticipation of this new position Ioage was proposing so that I nodded at him and laid down intently as he had told me, closing my eyes, but I could still feel the same wind that caressed the moso'oi blossoms above us. And yet, my mind was filled with a curiosity so foreign to me that when I opened my eyes again momentarily and looked up to the flowers on the moso'oi branches, they appeared further and further away until the moment Ioage parted my legs as he had done earlier and I felt something else being inserted in me that was not his penis but rather, his tongue? What? My head darted towards Ioage's and saw him wink at me as he inserted his tongue further into me. What is he doing that for? Is he going to use the same mouth to eat food with?

But before I could answer my own rhetoric, Ioage saw the baffled look on my face and said instead in the softest and most gentle of voices, I'm kissing you, Sia, to make it all better. Is that better? he asked.

Hmm....hmm...hmm...I found myself murmuring as if all concept of language as a communication tool, had left me and my eyes were tightly closed the further he inserted his tongue deeper into me.

How does that feel now, Sia? Huh?

I'm, I'm, I'm, I'm I'm . . . What's happening to me Ioage? Ahhhh . . . I shuddered and my body vibrated in a million different directions while I felt Ioage insert his three middle fingers into me in place of where his tongue had been.

Shhh . . . I think you just had an orgasm, Sia. Wow! Girl, you're burning like a black star on fire.

Indeed, I felt like I was burning as Ioage said I was. Like I had a fever and my heart was beating a million times faster as Ioage's tongue returned to where his fingers had been and continued to dance and dance and dance in the black hole between my legs that was exhibiting such strong gravitational force not even light could escape it, and yet, I felt an unbearable lightness of being at that very same moment as if I were being beamed-up somewhere outside the confines of my own body and that of the imaginary USS Enterprise that was an ever present resident of my medulla oblongata, out far and beyond the Milky Way galaxy as we know it and into the wider unknown so stunning it became utterly incomprehensible to me and yet, my skin reacted as if I were stung by a bee, that had been injected a mysteriously magical and other worldly potion into its epidermis, the millisecond my inner ear detected the vibrations of Ioage's voice and my eyes immediately became wide shut once he opened his own eyes and looked at me and said, You died so beautifully just then, Sia. How do you feel? You just died girl. And I'm the luckiest guest at your funeral.

Gosh Ioage, I feel light-headed but wow. I don't have the words to describe what just happened. What just happened to me, Ioage? Huh? A funeral, you said? What do you mean? Tell me.

Now you know what's it's like to die a small death and I was the only one that saw and witnessed it.

I don't understand, Ioage.

That's what your toothless aunty and the women of your house were talking about earlier.

It was like I was in Heaven, Ioage.

Or Pulotu, as your good old aunties would have it.

Ioage smiled at me and continued to eat me as if I were an octopus in coconut milk, Hellaby corned beef, tea biscuits from Fiji or some other Samoan delicacy and a moan escaped my lips again and I closed my eyes and saw shooting black stars exploding beneath the Milky Way that appeared as close to me as the very air I was breathing.

Open your eyes Sia, said Ioage. Look at me and watch me taste and eat you. Watch me, Sia. Watch me.

I opened my eyes and immediately came in contact with Ioage's stunning eyes whose gaze had pierced me and I shuddered once more. But then he closed his eyes, closed them as if in prayer again. This time, Ioage's tongue felt like a popsicle that had been placed on the parts where I felt the original pain. And within seconds the pain was gone. Just like that. As if it was never there in the first place.

As Ioage's tongue circled and circled me, I wondered to myself whether the pain I felt was real or whether I had imagined it. After all, we were told very early on, as soon as we were visited by the Moon that sex was something bad and dirty and nasty and that no good girl would want to be engaged in it until she was properly married in a ceremony that involved not only our immediate family that we live with but our extended families who lived in other villages and in other outer islands not to mention our own village and that only sluts and whores enjoyed it, not good girls. I considered myself a good girl as I did everything my mother told me to do in the quickest of times. And obeyed my brothers whenever they told me to go home in the evenings whenever they saw that too many boys had showed up to the volleyball net which happened in the evenings on the malae.

Suddenly, without any initiation of my own, another moan escaped my lips. A moan I knew now to be intrinsically connected to what Ioage was doing to me with his tongue which felt like licking an ice-cream cone while floating down the Gu'usa river on a hot, hot day such as this.

I wanted to reach down to Ioage's hair once more, like I had done earlier. To touch it or to at least hold onto it. But touching a man's hair especially without his permission is considered taboo according to my grandmother, and so I refrained from it.

I decided then to just lie back and close my eyes and to feel the wondrous sensations of Ioage's tongue as it circled and circled and circled me and as it did, I felt like I was a cumulus cloud swimming across the sky, listening to Madonna sing *Like a Virgin*, smiling at the new knowledge I had of Death when I would hear the lyrics again on the radio, Touched for the very first time.

My thoughts were broken suddenly when Ioage whispered to me, 'Sia, Do you want us to give it another go, now? A suga Sia?

Without thinking, I immediately said yes, almost too eagerly as the pain for all practical purposes was gone, as if it was never there in the first place.

Then, Ioage entered me again, and for some reason his penis felt larger than before. But I was no longer shocked by it's entrance as I had been earlier. This time, I looked straight into his eyes and he looked right into mine and I started moving my hips then according to the movements of his own hips. Until later it appeared like we were performing a dance. An old and ancient dance. A dance that ended with the universe vibrating at the explosion of stars and constellations all across the galaxies, one that made me feel like I had just dived into a black star in the middle of the day and died. And lived. And died. And lived. And died. A thousand small deaths.

I have a gift for you, said Ioage, when I opened my eyes.

What is it? I said, half expecting a gift wrapped package. But instead, Ioage showed me the three fingers he had used earlier to break my virginity and later to penetrate me towards my first orgasm and I saw that they were still stained with my own blood.

What do you want me to do with them, Ioage? I asked.

I want you to smell them, he said, as he pressed them to my nose.

Then he moved up towards me and we breathed my scent in together.

It's a strong and strange scent, I said.

That's because it's the scent of a woman, said Ioage. *My woman.*

Tears swelled in my eyes when Ioage said the words 'my woman.'

Are those happy or sad tears? He asked. A suga Sia?

They're both, Ioage. Both happy and sad.

Why do you say that? Tell me. I want to know.

I'm happy that I lost my virginity to you, Ioage. I wish all girls who've ever told me a sad story about their first experience would get to meet men like you, Ioage. Men who listen when we tell them something is wrong. When we say no, it hurts. And respect us enough to stop and to say, I'm sorry. How can we do it so that it doesn't hurt? The way you did just now, Ioage. There are so many girls that walk around thinking sex is a horrible, dirty and nasty act they have to endure just to have a boyfriend or a man or just to say they'd done it just to do it. To get it over with.

Catching that ride with you this morning has turned out to be the most special decision I've ever made in my entire life Ioage. Thank you for stopping and offering me a ride because it's lead me to this place. This wondrous and magical place. *With you.* Do you understand what I'm trying to say, Ioage?

Ioage nodded and said yes, Yes, Sia. I know what you mean. You have to understand that for some of us men, sex is a conquest. It makes us feel important and masculine to have conquered someone else. Especially if that someone else is a girl that everyone else wants and desires. A man wants to be able to say to his mates while shooting the breeze, Yeah, she walks around like an angel but with clipped wings. She's a fallen woman and I'm the one that made her fall. She fell because of me!

But that's just cruel, Ioage. It's ugly and cruel, not to mention savage and barbaric, I said, turning suddenly away from him which he noticed almost immediately and pulled me back to him.

I'm not the enemy, Sia. You just said so yourself. Just because some men act like dogs doesn't make all of us the same. That's actually an insult to dogs. But you know what I'm trying to say Sia. You're absolutely right. Such acts of cowardice are savage and barbaric and cruel and ugly, as you've said. But that's just how it is in this world we live in, Sia. Some people are so petty and small that the only way for them to feel any sense of self-worth and importance is if they attacked and conquered someone else. Usually someone weaker than them. This has been my experience at least. Of listening to these guys as they rave on about their conquests over a cold beer. Which never ceases to stun and sting me Sia. As if the girl in question was an object, not someone's daughter or cousin or sister. That's what our parents taught us Sia. To always think of the va. The space between people that one interacts with on a daily basis, even one's enemies. There's always a right way and a wrong way, my father would say. And that God gave us free agency to choose which way one's conscience can live with and whether your decision was one that enabled you to look into your family's eyes the next day and feel pride that you made the right choice. It's what makes us civilized, and human, Sia. That we were raised by people who understood the intrinsic value of each life and how our treatment of one another is an expression of how we too, would wish to be treated. As for offering you a ride? Well, you only have to look at my Buddha face to know that it was entirely my pleasure, my dear.

I was speechless and completely overwhelmed after Ioage spoke. His words wrapped themselves around me like the invisible blanket that wraps every Samoan who grew up not hearing their mother or father say the words 'Oute alofa ia te oe/I love you' in the open not because love was absent but because of its omnipresence which was strongest when left unspoken and made me understand what Aunty Aima'a had said once, 'Not everything is meant to be spoken Sia. But rather, to be felt. With the heart. That's the true essence of our Samoan way and to a larger extend, our Samoana way, which is the way of our Pacific people born and nurtured by our Oceanic Mother, Moana."

My eyes fell on Ioage after Aunty Aima'a's image faded and I heard myself saying to him, Thank you, Ioage. You have no idea what it meant for me to hear you say what you've just shared. Then I moved closer to him and felt his heart beat against mine.

In a way, I'm glad this happened to you, Sia. I mean to us. As it's given us a chance to discuss it and know how the other person is feeling. Real life hits us in the most mysterious of ways. Something negative turns suddenly into something positive.

Like the movements of Malamalama / Lightness into Pouliuli / Darkness and vice versa, I added.

Koe suipi oe keige lea / Another point for you! said Ioage. Go the Manu!

As I was chuckling at his excitement over scoring points with every hint of a profound thought, Ioage added one of his own, saying that the same principle of the interconnectedness of Malamalama and Pouliuli is very similar to the ancient Chinese philosophy of Yin and Yang and how such opposite forces are actually complementary rather than opposing. Their interaction, leads to a more stunning system where the whole is greater than the gathered parts. *That* is the beauty of nature that I was talking about that first day I stood before your class, Sia. Besides, I'm the fortunate one. The lucky one, Sia. I know any guy would take my place in a heartbeat but I'm going to just throw that thought towards an uninhabited island, along with all the other negative thoughts I've had in the past, where no one would see them.

And now tell me, what's the sad part, Sia? Huh? You said you were both happy and sad. Why are you sad Sia? Tell me.

I'm sad for all the reasons you've just outlined which I've heard from the other side with girls I know and in the anguish I heard in their stories which would make your heart bleed Ioage. But that's just a small part of why I was sad.

And what's the bigger part? A 'ea? Ka'u mai keige lea. Tell me, girl.

I'm ashamed to tell you.

You shouldn't be. Remember, this is me, Sia. Ioage. Your Ioage. Tell me. Please.

Ha! You know when you first told me to remove my bra and panties earlier, it was as if it was the most natural command I had ever heard someone say to me, Ioage.

Why do you think that was?

Because I knew that I was with someone who wasn't going to judge me, Ioage. Someone who was excited about me as much as I was excited about him.

I'm sorry if I hurt you earlier, Sia. I had no idea that you would feel that way because your body, I mean the biological mechanics of your body and how it was responding were all signs that you were excited and that you wanted me, the way I wanted you and still want you.

There's nothing to be sorry about, Ioage. I think it was all in my head, you know? A phantom pain that had grown and festered in my head after listening to all those tragic stories.

That's most likely what happened, Sia. But I don't want it to be the entire blame. I want to take responsibility for my part in it too, you know.

That means a lot to me, Ioage. Thank you.

I hugged him to me and he hugged me back with a renewed intensity that wasn't there before. Shhh....I don't ever want to hurt you. Do you hear me, Sia?

Yes, Ioage. I know you won't.

And you'll always be honest with me and tell me like you did just now if something was wrong or if something didn't feel right, you hear?

I hear you, Ioage.

Promise me you would never lie to me, Sia. That you wouldn't pretend on me. Do you know what I mean?

No, I don't.

I don't ever want you to feel that you need to endure pain just to make me happy. It wouldn't be right and it would be an insult that would offend me deeply. Promise me that, Sia. Promise me that.

I nodded and gave Ioage the biggest promise I'd ever given to anyone, to God even.

And then he kissed my eyelids and stroked the sides of my face and said, I know you won't ever lie to me, Sia. I know it.

Now I want you to do something else.

What is it Ioage? Anything. Tell me.

I want you to taste yourself, Sia, he said, as he motioned to me to open my mouth and he inserted two of his fingers into it. Then he moved away from me and returned to my cunt where his tongue made the most exquisite sounds.

Touch your breasts, Sia. I want you to touch your breasts, he said as his tongue continued to penetrate deeper and deeper into me.

Now, say my name as you touch yourself, he said.

Ioage.

Say it again, louder.

Ioage!

Then he showed me his penis and said, Look at him? He heard you, Sia. He wants to know what you want to do with him.

Put him in, Ioage, please, Ioage, please.

A smile as big as the two moons on Mars spread across Ioage's face when he heard my plea. He looked as if a cyborg from Planet X had kidnapped him and stretch his facial skin so far back that he appeared to be an ancient Chinese sage as he searched in his backpack for a condom.

This is the last one we have, he said, opening it and inserting himself into it.

I watched how quickly his fingers moved as he inserted himself into the condom. Then he looked at me and winked at me and said, Are you ready, keige lea?/aye girl?

Yes, I nodded, assuringly.

Then he thrust himself into me again and again and again, each thrust caused me to moan in a strange manner that I did not recognize, even if it were my own voice, until finally, Ioage collapsed on me, panting, like he had just run a long race, instinctively grabbing my hand, as if he too were afraid that it may have all been a dream.

And while he was panting next to me, I looked at his penis and it was still erect with the condom filled halfway with a white liquid.

So this is sperm? The picture in the biology textbook doesn't even come close, Can I remove it now? A li'i, Ioage?

Do you want to?

Is it going to hurt you?

He shook his head. No. And then added with a wider smile, Ia a koe hurt o lea fa'ako'a uma gei aku a ga hurt. Se kao ia oe se! What do you mean does it hurt? It just got hurt! Eh, bake you in an oven!

I simpered along with him as I held his penis in both hands, and gently removed the condom despite his sarcasm, masking his desire.

I couldn't help but noticed how beautiful he looked at that moment. I know we're only supposed to say women are beautiful and men are handsome but at that particular moment, Ioage's face and his armpits and his neck and his chest and his stomach and his thighs and his calves and his pubic hair and his penis and his mind and his spirit all put together made him the most stunning being I'd ever seen in my entire life.

And for a second, I wished that time would stand still, so that this moment would remain as it always is, dazzling and magnificent.

I see that nasty wrinkle returning to your forehead again, Sia. You're so far far far away this time. Come back to me, said Ioage.

I smiled at him and closed my eyes instead and felt the sun's rays on my breasts.

I had been thinking about the song Ioage had sung earlier. Thinking and thinking until his last thrust which caused all my thoughts to dissipate and disappear momentarily.

Would I have a baby and would it be called a baby of the night? And even though it's not night, it's the middle of a beautiful sunny day, with the Sun shining as we lie and make love in the middle of a forest, would that make our baby a baby of the day?

But we were in a forbidden and taboo situation, cloudy and murky. Would that make our baby a baby of the Day? Or would it still be considered a baby of the Night?

I wanted to ask Ioage about that. How he would feel about our baby being classified by people as a baby of the night? And since we're already married the traditional way, with trees, leaves, and a placid lake as witnesses, would we need to be married again at the government court house and be issued a certificate that says were officially married? Would this make our baby a baby of the day?

Ioage's voice had soared and soared and soared again like an Owl into the sky, as he began another new song, without any of the self-analysis that was stuck in my own throat that prevented me from singing.

He took my hand in his and pressed the song lines to his lips. Then he winked at me and encouraged me to sing and that perhaps he shouldn't have sung earlier about corned beef and biscuits and chop suey and fried tomatoes and beans because now he's starving and there's nothing else around to eat but to devour me once more to satisfy his hunger.

Chills went through my spine when he said that.

And I found myself being utterly fascinated by the language of love as it unfolded and revealed itself before my very own eyes. It was then that I climbed onto Ioage's chest and offered him my breasts to eat. To nourish him. To sustain his energy. As we still had another few hours before it was time to leave.

O OE O LA'U UO MONI
YOU ARE MY TRUE FRIEND

O oe o la'u uo moni, e le galo oe i le agaga
    You are my true friend, unforgettable to my heart
Ta fia fa'atasi pea ma oe i lenei olaga
    I wish to be with you always in this life
E manatua ai oe i ou foliga ata'ata
    I will always remember your buoyant face
Laumata fiafia. Amio tausa'afia
    Your gleeful eyes and exuberant ways
O la ta mafutaga
    So, about our relationship
Ua ou le iloaina lava
    I really don't know

Le mafuaga ua alai o lenei mala
    The reason for this curse
Se mea a faigata, o lo'u nei fiafia
    O what a wearisome thing, my happiness
Ae ui ina liua, pei o le vai o Sina
    That might be transformed like the pool of Sina
Fa'ali maia funa o sou manatu
    Show me what you're thinking
Pe e te alofa moni ia te a'u
    Whether you really and truly love me
E faigofie ona fa'apu'upu'u
    It's just as easily made short
Pe afai ua e musu
    If you no longer desire it
Fetu e, o le lagi, Figota o le sami
    O stars of the sky, creatures of the sea
Se'i ta'u maia e se tasi, po'o fea ea la'u honey
    Can someone tell me, where my honey is?
O oe o la'u pele ea
    You, my beloved you
O la'u manamea e toatasi
    My one soulmate
Lenei ua mou atu, e aunoa ma se tali
    You have disappeared without a say
Sau ia oe lau dear, o le sa ou filifilia
    Come now my dear, the one that I've chosen
E moni ai le upu tusia, pupula le gata ae fasia
    It is true that the snake is beaten before it's very eyes.
E ui ina ou lagona, lagonaina le mafatia
    Even though I am in despair
Ae tu'u pea ia, fuga e, i lou faitalia
    But it's up to you darling, whatever your decision
Tofa soifua la'u pele lo'u au
    Goodbye my love, my darling

Mo'omo'oga ua le taulau
  Desires unfulfilled
Ua motusia talu le tuinanau
  Broken because of lust
Fia fa'atasi e fa'avavau
  I want us to be together forever.

I could still hear Ioage's voice as it swirled and swirled and around me like a protective buffer that shielded us both from any aiku that might be lurking in the thick forest or in the lake. He reached out to me and said, Come here.

And as I moved towards him, I was already thinking, So *this* is what it's like to have real sex? Blows my mind, I thought. Ioage simply blows my mind.

A penny for your thoughts, Sia, he said.

How was it, the second time? Tell me.

It's not what I expected, Ioage.

No? A look of concern spread across his face when I said what I did.

No, I said, taking one of his hands and combing my fingers through his.

How so? Did I hurt you, again?

That's what puzzles me, Ioage, I said, perplexed.

I don't understand, Ioage replied, as if afflicted by my response.

No, it wasn't like that. It wasn't like that at all, with a full moon smile brimming on my face.

What are you saying? he said, with a smile on his own face.

It's beautiful, Ioage. Sex is beautiful. And you're beautiful.

He appeared more relaxed and was delighted (although he did a terrible job of pretending he wasn't, when I asked), Can we do it again?

E, kaula'ikiki! Hey, Cheeky! he said, with a wicked smirk on his face.

I was not joking Ioage, can we please do it again?

But we just did!

But can we do it without the condom? I just want to know what it's like to have you inside me without some obstruction.

We're fresh out of condoms. I didn't even think we were going to need the second one, being that it is your first time so I wasn't sure.

Did you know we were going to need a condom, Ioage?

Frankly? No. I never thought in my wildest dreams this was going to happen. Please believe me when I say that. I didn't pre plan this, Sia. This just happened. And I take full responsibility for it.

So if you didn't know this was going to happen, why did you then carry condoms in your backpack?

A man always has to carry condoms, Sia. Not just to prevent a woman from getting pregnant but to stop the spread of venereal diseases. We are human and we have human needs, Sia. Sex is the most primal need a man has. They say if a man were stranded on a deserted island without food or water and when at the time of his rescue, he were to be given the choice of food, water or sex, guess what he would choose?

A trip to Disneyland?

Se kao ia oe se! Bake you in an oven!

Hey, kama lea. There's something else on my mind that I've been meaning to ask you but wasn't sure when. I guess they'll never be a right time for this conversation. The conversation I know you've been avoiding since her name first came up.

But we just had such a beautiful moment, Sia. Why did you have to go and ruin it for?

Before you go ballistic on me, think about it Ioage. What better time to talk about this than now? Huh? Please? If you, I mean if we don't face whatever demon this is you think you're carrying, it will continue to weigh heavily on you as time passes. You know this.

Sia. Sia. Sia.

I'm here Ioage. I'm listening. Please, Ioage, please?

Apparently, I fathered a boy.

Apparently? What do you mean, apparently?

I didn't know her.

But you made love to her, didn't you? I mean, you made love to MD, didn't you, Ioage?

No Sia. I had sex with her.

With MD?

Yes, Sia. Christ! Yes! With MD.

Pardon my 17 ½ year old ignorance, but tell me, Ioage. What's the difference between making love and having sex?

See, this is why I didn't wanna talk about this.

We're not doing anything else until this is talked about, Ioage. It's the only way for us to move forward. You can't just pretend it didn't happen. You have to face it. Now, tell me. Why do you say 'apparently' when you know you 'had sex' with MD?

Do you really want to hear this? I mean, are you up to it?

I just don't want to see you sad anymore, Ioage. I've always detected a sadness about you since the first day I met you. It seemed to weight on your spirit and stifle you.

I could feel it then and I'm feeling it even more strongly now. I know that this has a lot to do with it, Ioage. Am I making sense?

Shit, Sia. Nothing gets past you, does it?

My mother says it's a curse. Aunty Aima'a says it's a gift. So there! I'm a walking contradiction.

But with a big bag of marbles.

Yeah, that's a real comfort, you know.

Don't play small Sia. An aoa tree was never meant to be a pot plant to be kept indoors. You shouldn't be ashamed of your gift. Because it is a gift.

I know what you're doing here, Ioage. You're using me as a diversion. Come on, Ioage! You've gotta be serious about this. We have to talk about this. This is about you and MD and your son.

I don't even know his name, Sia. And frankly, my dear, I have no interest in knowing and have deliberately distanced myself since I was first told.

Just tell me what happened, will you?

A month after I arrived in Auckland, I met my cousin Pulupulu for the first time. He was a big shot. The smartest one in our family, he was studying for his Master's in International Business at Auckland Uni. He knew all these kids from Parnell, Mission Bay, Herne Bay. Rich kids from extremely affluent families. Families whose names you saw on wine bottles and boutiques and billboards and salons and restaurants.

Pulupulu had been in New Zealand since he was 13, and went to school with a lot of these guys so he knew them.

What exactly did Pulupulu have that gave him such influence in these kids lives? Was he selling them drugs?

I reckon you've been watching too much Hawai'i Five-O, Sia. But the answer is no. There were no drugs.

Did he threaten to beat them up? Tell me.

No, he didn't, Sia. Pulupulu was barely 5'1. He couldn't and wouldn't hurt a fly. Unless he was pressed to.

You're getting me all curious about this Pulupulu. What did he do exactly, Ioage?

Pulupulu was a cerebral kinda guy. Small man, big brain. They paid him to do their homework.

But that's being dishonest!

But that's the way of the world, Sia. Pulupulu was an investor, who made big killings trading and buying stocks and bonds and that kind of action which you'll know more about once you get to America; all funded by his dealings with these guys whose parents ended up consulting him on interest rates and trust funds accounts and all sorts of other financial dealings which Pulupulu simply called the fruits of an open market capitalistic society. I mean he reveled in it. He owned those guys. And he became known in their social circles as the Sam Don of discretion. That's what he sold. He sold them his own version of intellectual property and discretion but at a very hefty price. One must give him credit for creativity. No doubt he had a Napoleonic complex but what a brain he had. It was quite astounding for someone who got beat up as a boy and teased for being a dwarf with a limp.

And what does MD have to do with all this?

Pulupulu was only seen with palagi women. White women. Blondes. And MD was the blondest of them all. She was a fashion model. Her legs alone were taller than Pulupulu. But that didn't stop him. She was his girlfriend. And she was rich.

The plot thickens. Where do you come in?

I'm the fob Coconut, that's NZ slang for those of us who had just arrived from Samoa only I was on a government scholarship. Went to church. Attended all my classes at

Auckland Uni. Had a part-time job stocking the aisles with Prakash & Sons, a dairy down from our house. One night I got a call. It was Pulupulu saying the action was hot at one of these super rich homes he happened to be in and whether I wanted to come down and join him. He needed a driver. He had been drinking and sniffing JJ which was code for cocaine. Anyway, I was in a whole other world from the one Pulupulu was describing. I mean, I was calling the bingo for the Youth that night, for crying out loud! After we broke down the tables and chairs and cleared the gym and submitted the money to Uncle Iakopo, my father's brother and pastor of his parish, I told him I needed the car to go pick a friend up who was stranded downtown. I didn't mention Pulupulu's name as I've come to understand it being the synonym of trouble.

Long story short, I got to the party a little after 1 a.m. Immediately, I knew it wasn't my scene. Firstly, the music was this techno punk new age stuff that I called senseless white noise. Then everyone looking like they were ghosts. Like they were surrounded by wealth and not a single person looked like they were genuinely enjoying themselves without the aid of some artificial substance which was either sniffed up their noses or injected into their veins or simply poured down their throats. And they looked like they were attending a funeral or the death of something as they were all dressed in black.

Where was MD at this point?

She was dancing behind me.

You didn't know?

No. I mean, I was not dancing. I was just standing there. She was dancing. Alone. Pulupulu was not with her. Then she started talking to me. Are you the gorilla he sent to fuck me? she asked.

I wasn't sure who she was talking to. I turned and when her eyes met mine, she repeated what she had said before, adding, contemptuously, Well, if you came to fuck me King Kong, then let's go in the room and get fucked or did you prefer to spread me open right here for everyone to see? I heard you fobs enjoy performing for an audience.

I'd heard that kinda talk before, Sia. The first time was not directed to me but to Mr. Prakash at the dairy where I worked. An older palagi man had come in to buy a bottle of milk. The bottle fell right before he got to the cash register where Mr. Prakash stood, smiling at him, happily waiting to cash him out.

Now look what you've made me do, you big dumb over-cheerful baboon! Do something to clean this bloody shit off of me!

Mr. Prakash came around and motioned to me to hold off.

Let's get him cleaned up, John. But don't touch him, the way your eyes are telling me you want to. Do you hear me, son? Just go in the back and get the mop and the bucket and leave it to me.

My feet found themselves moving to the back but my fists wanted to merge with that man's face. To hurt and damage him, the way he had obviously hurt Mr. Prakash. But by the time I returned with the mop and the bucket, the man had already left with what he had originally come to shop for, free of charge, including a box of Earl Grey and some strawberry shortcake.

Mr. Prakash later explained why he did what he did.

John, peace should be respected at all times in this dairy. Never forget this. It is easier to react with anger and violence but the highest form of action is to perpetually meditate on peace and on ways to manipulate opposing forces so that their dual nature facilitates an outcome that you are able to smile at, at the end of the day. It's that simple, John.

But he humiliated you, Mr. Prakash. He called you a baboon and treated you like you didn't matter! Like you were an untouchable. Like a doormat!

He will think about what he said as he drinks the tea I gave him and adds the sugar and the milk and eats the strawberry shortcake that I gave him. He will think about these things John, and it is my hope that the next time Mr. Goodman drops a bottle of milk, that he would be more conscientious of the way he treats those around him at the time he does. Do you see it now, John?

Yes, I do Mr. Prakash. My father would have done the same thing, sir.

Oh, I have no doubt he would have, John. Your father sounds like a wise man. He is in your eyes. And your face is his.

Sia, you may not want to hear this next part. The part where I turned into a monster, the complete opposite of my father or of Mr. Prakash.

Shh, don't, Ioage. Just tell me what happened. Please. Tell me!

I slammed MD against the wall and ripped her mini-skirt up, tore her panties off and fucked her and fucked her and fucked her and fucked her and fucked her the way she wanted me to fuck her. And each time I did, the imagine of that milk bottle dropping to the floor and smashing everywhere jabbed at me so that I saw Mr. Prakash nod at me to go to the back and fetch the mop and the bucket. Calling me son at such moments when he knew it best because he could taste the fury in my breath when the word baboon flew out of that man's mouth. Fetch the mop and the bucket, John, he had said and I did like an obedient son. Meanwhile, the crowd had gathered around us as if around a bonfire and they were clapping and cheering and

chanting Kong! Kong! Kong! while MD squealed like a pig
as I rammed myself into her and when I finally came, I was
covered in sweat and so much anger and contempt and
hate and right before I left, I spit on her. And the crowd
went wild, Sia. I had never seen a bunch of savages in all
my entire life. They repulsed me.

I went home and sat under the shower for hours,
Sia. Hours! Until Uncle Iakopo came in and got me out.
Dried me and clothed me. I simply became mute. I was
like a zombie. But Uncle didn't ask any questions. He just
went about the business of taking care of me as if I were
a helpless child all over again. Made me a cup of hot milo
with ginger biscuits, my favorite. Then tucked me to bed
and he prayed to God that whatever it was that ailed me,
that I found peace in God's loving embrace and grace. And
as he was speaking, I found myself thinking back to what
I had done and it was then that I realized I never even had
a clear idea of what her face must have looked like, Sia.
I don't even remember what she looked like except there
being a sinister smile on her face the minute I collapsed
into her after I came.

A year later, they were married. And Pulupulu and her
live in that very same house, with their only son. Apparently,
my son, since Pulupulu could not have children.

Ioage, he, I mean, it sounds to me like they used you!

It took me the last four years to figure it out, Sia.

I am so sorry, Ioage.

Come here. Please, come here.

Hush, it's over, I whispered. You're home, Ioage. That's
all that matters. You've made your way back home, to us
and to me.

I held Ioage close to me as he continued to sob and sob
and sob, the anguish in his voice pierced my own voice and
we found ourselves in a weeping embrace until we could
weep no more, and fell into the hollow tunnel of sleep,

while dry moso'oi blossoms fell and fell and fell, slowly, onto the merciful and forgiving earth.

You were snoring you know.

I was? he said, with his usual half moon smile on his face.

You frightened the coconut crabs and the wild boar.

And the wild boar? Thank God I was here to protect you from the wild boar.

Protect me? You mean, frightened the poor thing with your loud snore.

Hey, what can I say? I'm the master snorer!

You've got that right, mister.

What time is it, Sia?

We have another 3 hours.

I asked you what time it was, not how many more hours I had left as your love slave.

Now that you've mentioned it, can we please do it again? I want to feel you again inside me, Ioage. Please, Ioage, Please?

No, Sia. Listen, ideally, that's what I'd like more than anything, believe me. But I can't.

Why not?

I just can't, Sia.

I thought we'd already decided it was over. Now that I know what really happened with MD. You were set up, Ioage. Your cousin set you up in the most sinister of ways. But we've seen now how twisted it all was. It's over as far as I'm concerned. Out of sight, out of mind.

You don't know what you're asking, Sia. The reason why I'm wearing a condom is so that you won't get pregnant.

If it's not about MD and Pulupulu, why would you not want me to get pregnant? Isn't that why God made man and woman? So they can be fruitful and multiply?

Sia, believe me when I say it's not about MD and Pulupulu, ok? That's out of my system now and frankly, I really would appreciate it if you were to never mention them again.

Of course, Ioage. My lips and my heart is sealed.

Thank you. Now listen to me carefully. There's enough people on this island adding to the population and going nowhere. You've got somewhere to go, Sia. Places to go and people and ideas to meet. And I can't be in your way.

What do you mean?

I don't want to say something insensitive that might hurt you. But I'm not going to be the last man you're going to be with.

You're not? That's cruel, Ioage. Not to mention highly offensive. I *can't* believe you just said that to me.

I just . . . This is difficult to explain.

Please do. Explain! I want to know because what you said was like a dagger. And it's piercing through my flesh to my heart, like the one Brutus used to kill Caesar!

I was afraid you would say that.

Then why did you say it? Huh?

Because it needs to be said.

I don't understand, Ioage. There will *never* be another man. *Never.*

I know. That's what you're saying now and my heart and soul and body and mind will always love you, too, through time and space. But I also know, that it's selfish of me to want that.

Now you're confusing me. Don't you want me, Ioage?

I want you, Sia. More than you'd ever know. But I can't have you.

But I'm giving myself to you, Ioage! I'm asking you to make a baby with me because I want to! Otherwise, what's the point of being a woman if you can't make a baby?

Many women can't have babies Sia. But that doesn't make them any less of a woman. My point is, we are in a very fragile spot. And it's all my fault. I'm the adult. I should have been able to stop this before it's become what it is now.

A sadness spread across his face when he said that. But I wasn't listening to his words and responded eagerly instead, quite the opposite of what he had been trying to convince me of.

But it's already the second week of October. I finish high school in less than 6 weeks. That means if we make a baby now, I would not be in school anymore by the time it's born. Besides, our baby is going to be the first Samoan in Space. We'll be the Marie Curie and Pierre Curie of Samoa, the Pacific and the world!

Ha. Ha. But that's not what I want for you, Sia. Don't you understand? I don't want you to stay here and be like all the other girls who do that because they don't have options. Or at least they think they don't have options. But you do Sia. *You do!* What did Pistol say in Shakespeare's, *Merry Wives of Windsor?*

I wouldn't know. Mrs Amosaosavavau only read *As You Like It, Hamlet* and *Julius Caesar* with us. Oh, and *The Black Tulip* both in English and in Samoan, *Le Tulipe Uliuli.*

Pistol said, *Why then the world's mine oyster. Which I with sword will open.* What do you suppose he meant? Just by listening to the words.

Can you repeat it again? Please?

Why then the world's mine oyster, Ioage said, slowly this time, *Which I with sword will open.*

That there's a pearl of great value to be found in an oyster? Help me out here. I said.

And what happens once you open the oyster, Sia? What happens to the pearl?

It means that once you find the pearl, you can basically own the world and do anything you set your heart to?

That's precisely it Sia. You can do anything you set your heart to. *Anything.*

But you have my heart, Ioage. You have my heart!

And you have mine Sia. That's why we can't do this. Ok? It would haunt me.

But that's not your choice now, is it? A li'i Ioage?

Hey, look at me. We, Us. Do you know what this is, Sia? Do you know what we've just done? What I've just done to you? This is taboo and forbidden in the fa'asamoa for two reasons. Firstly, because you're a teine o le nu'u. You're a village maiden and I'm le atali'i o le fa'afeagaiga, the pastor's son. The sacred covenant between God and his people, which makes you my sister! Secondly, I'm a teacher and you're a student. It would be devastating for Gu'usa. Think about the implications. Think about your family. My family. Our village will be the laughing stock of other villages. Do you honestly think you want to be responsible for that now? And are you willing to put that kind of responsibility on yourself and another life and me? It will mark him or her for the rest of his or her life, Sia. Is that the legacy we want to leave? You're old enough to know this too, Sia. It's not like I'm telling you anything you don't know. This is serious. We can't make a baby for those reasons. Not now. *Not ever!*

Ioage's voice scared me. It made the reality of our situation grave. I turned away from him and looked at the lake, the very placid lake that will always be the only witness to what we've just shared.

Ioage turned me over towards him. I'm sorry if I sounded harsh.

No, you're being logical, I said, with a dash of melancholy in my voice as the pain of the truth hit me.

That's what you always told us? Isn't it? To be logical. Use reason. And that's what you're doing right now. You're reasoning it out. But you know what?

What? said Ioage, as he looked at me, sitting above him with an urgent conviction burning in my eyes.

What good is reason and truth and virtue if all we have is a memory? Huh? A memory of the most incredible day of our lives? And I can only speak for myself. I know your concerns. I hear you. But please don't treat me as a child. Or as your sister. Or as your prized student. I want you to treat me as a woman, Ioage. As the woman you've just made me be at this early stage of my life. And as a woman, I've also done my own process of elimination. And I know I'll be off to America at the beginning of January and I don't know what's going to happen after that. Whether I'll ever be able to come back to you. I'd rather go with a part of you than go empty-handed.

Why do you have to be so bloody clever and brilliant? Huh?

I do have my Ela moments.

That's not possible. Not you. *Never.*

I smiled at him as he sat up and placed my legs around his waist so that they were to the sides of his body as if they were hugging him and moved himself closer towards me.

And then he took my head in his massive hands and he kissed me for the first time.

It was shocking at first.

To feel someone else's tongue in your mouth. But then the kiss made me wet again and the deeper he kissed me, the more wet I became and I saw that Ioage's penis was also hard again.

He told me to turn around, to place my hands on the forest floor to support myself so that I appeared like a soft table of pulsating flesh, filled with alacrity and solicitude and vehemence as I felt him guide himself into me from the back (the way we've all seen dogs do it) and started to thrust again and again and again until I found myself exploding with uncontainable pleasure and momentarily, my brain became inert and not a single thought transpired through its walls and when I finally opened my eyes and came to my senses, I shivered at the shocking sounds that escaped my lips, until the final scream I heard when Ioage's sperm was finally released in me and appeared to frighten all the birds of the forest which made me smile a strange and peculiar smile yet I didn't want Ioage to ever stop. *Ever.*

After the fourth time, Ioage said he had to rest.

You take all my energy, girl. You realize we need to get going.

Can we just do it one last, last, final last time before we go? Please Ioage? Please, Ioage? Pleaaaase?

I'm not a machine, you know, he said. But I could see that he was secretly delighting in my pleas and was pretending to scoff me off. Or at least that's how I read him.

I hate false advertisement, you know, I said, with a wicked smirk which he responded by shaking his head and smiling and taking a big breath and then he pulled me up and buried his head in my bosom which made me want him again especially as he circled his tongue around and around my nipples.

And while he moaned I couldn't help but bite my tongue as quickly as the words flew out of my mouth as I knew I may have sounded more like a toddler who was throwing a tantrum because they hadn't gotten what they wanted. And yet, Ioage's moans told me otherwise.

Fiafia kele oe e mea, a ea? You love making love don't you? he said, as he paused from sucking on my left nipple.

I pressed my lips to the song lines in his palm and looked deeply into his eyes and whispered back.

Only because it's with you.

He smelled my hair. And then he closed his eyes and pressed his nose against mine and we breathed each other in. I don't know what Ioage thought I must have smelled like at that very moment as the scent of his sperm and our sweat was viscoused and sticky between my thighs. Additionally, we were lying directly under a big mosooi tree whose pungent fragrance was intoxicating and yet, I could smell Ioage. I could smell him. *All of him.* And he smelled of the trees. The fern. The vines. The leaves. The bark. The roots. And the land.

And I suddenly remembered old man Lamaga's last words before he left us.

Ia fua le giu. May the coconut bloom.

Suga, we'll only have time for a dip. We have to go soon. I don't want your house to be worried about you. Besides, if you want your spaceman, then I suggest you just go in quick and come right back out, ua iloa?

Can we just lie here? I just want us to lie here and not say or do anything.

You say that, but then you're the one that keeps wanting to do it again and again. Koeikiki fo'i e lavea i lo'u agavale. I might backhand you with my left hand.

And you don't, Ioage?

You know I do, Sia.

Ioage, I said, as I took his hair onto my lap, Would you be offended if I were to ask you something personal? Something I've always been curious about since I first saw you in church after you had returned from university?

O le a? What is it? You look serious and you're scaring me.

It's nothing to be scared about. Or at least I don't think it is.

Then go ahead, ask me. Ask me anything, he said.

Thank you, I said, as I started combing my hands through his hair.

I don't know if you've heard the rumors, not that you would care, but people talk about you and your hair. They say you're setting a bad example for the youth. Why do you grow your hair like that of a woman's? I mean, I would understand it if you grew it and then let it hang. But I've never seen you with your hair down until now. Is there a reason why? I mean, is this your way of rebelling against Tama ma Tina? Tell me. I want to know.

Remember how you raced out of the library and I told you that you were acting in opposites?

Yes. I remember.

And I told you that old Samoans spoke in opposites? Saying one thing and meaning the other?

Go on.

Well, come here, and lie next to me, because it's going to be a long fagogo/story, he said, as he made space for me on the blanket and tapped his shoulder where I could lie on while he began to tell the story of his hair.

When the LMS missionaries arrived in Sapapali'i in 1830 they were shocked by many things which will take up the whole afternoon and the night and tomorrow if I list them. But I'll tell you only about hair and religion as those are things that I think you, as a young and brilliant Samoan woman needs to know and understand before you leave us a few months from now.

Missionary men had their hair short as is the fashion now, while their women had long hair, also the current trend. One of the first things they did was to reverse what they had seen which was quite traumatic to our people and threw the spiritual world and living world totally out of sync. Spirit women were the only ones with long hair and they desired the long hair of beautiful young men. Besides, the new trend offended them as they wanted no other competition from humans. Our elders understood this so as a compromise, Hair, was always wrapped in a bun. It was grown, to match the wants and rules of the missionary man but then it was held up in a bun to show respect for the Maidens of the Spirit world, specifically Telesa and Sauma'eafe, whose names were not casually uttered for fear of igniting their wrath.

Before the missionaries arrived, Samoan men wore their hair long, which as you know is now the opposite to what we have. Ironically, long hair on women is what the world thinks of when they wish to picture or imagine a Samoan girl nowadays. But in the old days, it was a women's fashion or style to have *her* hair shaved with only a curl behind her left ear to signify her virginal taupou status.

While I was at PNG, I noticed how devoted the people there were to their culture and their traditions. They had an inherent pride in them, and a spiritual aura about them that connected them intrinsically to the land and the sea and the skies and their bodies and most importantly to each other and their ancestors.

I know we have that too in Samoa.

But I was and still am disturbed by our propensity at selective memory, which means that we tend to remember or want to remember some things, things that are flattering to our present identity as the most Christian people in the Pacific and on the planet, at the expense of other less flattering things, things closely linked to our sexuality and our conception of the next generation, which is a natural human impulse. For instance, did you know that men had multiple wives? That women were systematically deflowered by a talking chief in a ceremonial marriage called the fa'amasei'au that took place in the middle of the malae while the rest of the village; men, women and children, looked on? Did you also know what happened on poula nights? It's nothing like the saccharine, tamed ones we know now. Poula nights were the sacred clowning nights where all the rules were thrown out the fale and that common women, women without status which were different from the virginal taupou, would parade themselves before the men, showing off their genitalia to incite desire towards copulation which was seen as a way to increase one's mana and social station? And that grandmothers or grandaunts were responsible for the care of a girl of high status's vagina from birth until she was married? That they massaged the outside and combed the hair and even dyed it red to make it more beautiful? A woman's vagina was sacred, Sia, as was a man's penis. They were not dirty or nasty or attached to any of the negative connotations sex is known today among our people, because both were sacred. They ensured that the song lines would remain strong and be continued. That the lines that criss-cross on our palms, the lines of life and of the continuity of life, remain strong and life-giving.

There is so much more that I learned while I was away, Sia. I feel that I've learned more about Samoa from being away than when I was here. I also learned that our ancestors were highly conscientious of maintaining the balance and equilibrium of nature which was the foundation of their spirituality and spiritual beliefs. Samoans were polytheistic. Which means they did what? Come on, Sia! Hurry! Prefix, poly.

They prayed to many Gods? I said.

Yes, they did, Sia. They prayed to many Gods.

When the missionaries first arrived, they noticed that unlike the Hawaiians and the Tahitians which they had previously encountered, who erected sacred temples and sacred idols and statues as a respectful way of worshiping their Gods, the Samoans had none of it. It surprised them at first. And yet still they were shocked that such a people as the Samoans, with all their navigational and war feats, did not have idols or temples or other places of worship.

And for a few years afterwards, because of the continual absence of a more tangible and more physical manifestation of a place that showed the presence of worship or exaltation of a higher being, a creator for instance, that's what they then became known for; barbaric, savage, wild, inferior, and godless Samoans.

It wasn't until a few years after 1830, that the missionaries discovered Samoa's polytheistic ceremonies of worship and along with it, their own ethnocentric faux pas.

They came to know that each village had a God as each family had a God. Samoans worshiped the strength of Nature, in Trees, such as the Aoa and the Ifilele, and sea creatures, such as Malie, Sharks, Pusi, Eels, and Fe'e, Octopus, and land creatures such as the Atualoa, the Centipede, the Pili, Lizard and flying creatures like the Pe'a, Bat, Gogosina, Seagull and many, many, many more. Nu'uolemanusa, the name of our village for example, is originated in the worshiping of the Lulu or Owl.

Those early missionaries who brought the gospel to Samoa were determined that it was not only good for the gospel to be merely heard by the people, but that it be spread. There's an interesting reason for this. On the surface, (and as you've stated in your cloud essay, our ancestors were experts at the rhetoric of surfaces and layers), the missionaries appeared like they were truly interested in saving Samoan souls and dragging, I mean, bring them to know the one and true God, Jehovah and his son as we've come to know him, Jesus Christ. But what is not terribly known because it is unspoken in the matters of converting an entire people's souls, is that of its economic advantage. Saving the soul of the Barbaric and Wild and Heathen Samoans was big business. The more reports that were send to England showing through documentation any increase in the numbers of converts, meant that more funds and financial assistance were poured into the missionary stations. The most drastic conversions happened in the Hawaiian Islands. Where the fast spread of Christianity was like wildfire. And made riches and very wealthy some of the oldest missionary families in places like Laie and Hau'ula on the North Shore of the Island of Oahu. This is where Samoans' system of customary lands and land ownership comes into play. As you know, land in Samoa isn't owned by a single individual but by a aiga. A family with roots as far stretching as there are many stars in the night sky. It the pule or authority of the matai that guards and protects these lands and ensures that everyone with a right to any land is guaranteed that right through the strict observation of genealogy and respect for the song lines, which guarantees that no one in Samoa should ever complain of being homeless. Long, long story short, in order to prove that one had truly accepted Jesus Christ as his Lord and personal savior, one had to eat one's family God before the missionaries. It was a shocking and traumatic experience for our ancestors, whose stories of cannibalistic feasts were widely known to the missionaries. I will not sit here and say to you that our people were not cannibals, because they were. But like I had jokingly said to you earlier about the word polygamist, it's all about context and meaning and nuance of meaning. Human flesh was eaten by high chiefs only, who were considered to be Gods among a village. The eating of human flesh was done on what was called the Chief's Day. And it was widely known that the last Chief's Day came to an end when the son of one of the highest chiefs, Chief Malietoa, sacrificed his life for the life of his best friend who was delivered to be eaten for the Chief's Day. Chief Malietoa was so broken when he saw what his son had done, that he made a vow then and there that he will relinquish his rights to the practices of the Chief's Day and told his aiga and his nu'u that he was no longer going to accept their offerings, which was culturally seen as the highest form of respect. Other high chiefs heard of the very touching story and were moved by it as it went straight to their hearts. And since then, The Chief's Day was no longer practiced. To ensure this, coconut leaves were no longer used to wrap larger offerings such as pigs, an insurance that the unknown baking of a human body would never be seen or heard of again. So when our ancestors heard the condition set by the missionaries for conversion, it made them weep. The deliberate desecration of one's family or village God was such an inconceivable idea. It was the highest of offenses! A riddle they simply could not fathom. And momentarily they were broken by it and felt defeated by it all the same.

But as you know Sia, even the most difficult of riddles has an answer. It might not necessarily be the answer you hope or pray for. But it's an answer nevertheless.

And so they did what they did which is what they had done for hundreds if not thousands of years. They sought the counsel of their Taula'aitu, the high priests and priestesses of their village and family Gods.

All over Samoa, prayers were being offered in the lowest of voices.

Tu'u maia se Tali, Le Atua mamana e! Give us an answer, Oh powerful God!

Se tali e mafai ona matou talia pe'a matou va'aia le Laina o Pese e aunoa ma se ma'asisasi ina ia mafai ai ona fa'a'auau le matou malaga!

An answer that we could look into the song lines without shame or regret and be able to continue!

And so, after long nights in the forests, the Taula'aitu, the Anchor of the Spirits finally emerged with the answer they had been looking for.

Aua le fefefe. Don't be afraid, they said.

Fa'apotopoto uma mai tamaiti ma aiga. Gather our children and your families.

O le a tatou a'a'i ma tausamia o tatou Atua! We shall eat our Gods!

And when it came to Nu'uolemanusa, they gathered all the Owl eggs in the forest and brought them to the village. And when the Moon was high in the sky, the Tauala'aitu blessed the eggs for the last time and sang long lamenting songs that took on a new life at the break of dawn.

This puzzled the missionaries.

First, they cry during the Night. And now that it's Daylight, they're happy. What is it with these wild savages? These wild heathen savages!

Before the sun was up, they all gathered outside the church building, calling out to the missionaries.

Ua matou o mai e amata le tatou taeao! Le Taeao'oleaigalulusa!

We have come to begin our morning! To begin with the eating of the sacred Owl! And so they did! Eggs were passed from the oldest to the youngest. Without a single sign of lament. Or of regret which made the missionaries proud. Proud that they had done their job. That they had led these heathens away from the Darkness and into the Light.

But what the missionaries in their arrogance failed to understand, is that the Samoan mind has a different way of looking at the movements of Pouliuli, Darkness to Malamalama, Light. Light is not superior to the Dark. Neither is Dark superior to Light. Like symbiosis, they co-exist so that Dark is Light and Light is Dark. Light recedes to make room for the Dark in the similar way that Darkness will make room for Lightness. So that when our village people kneeled before the missionaries and drank their sacred Owl's eggs which was viewed by the missionaries as a monumental symbol of victory and triumph over the Death and final destruction of our God and our heathen ways, the Owl circled the village one last time and started to cry one last cry before S(He) entered the body of each man, woman and child, its now new home.

So as you can see, on the surface it appeared as if the Owl was killed that day! But below the surface, below the layer, the Owl had migrated from the forest and into the people of Nu'uolemanusa where it resides still to this day.

Why do you think my father wrapped me in cloth and took me to the Taulasea, your Aunty Aima'a, and Nu'uolemanu's traditional healer when I was 10 after a scarlet handprint was seen across my face as a result of whistling at twilight? Sure, my father's first impulse as pastor was to pray to God and to Jesus Christ his son to save me, his eldest son, from the wrath of Satan that had befallen our house.

But when the third day passed and the handprint become redder and redder, he sought the council of the

Taulasea who he knew, had a direct connection to the Owl.

Tell me, Aima'a, what should I do? He is my eldest son. He is my heart. Tell me, what this boy has done to offend the Great Owl? Whatever he has done, spare him and take me instead.

Susu mai lau susuga i le fa'afeagaiga, Esimoko, Welcome, your Lordship, Pastor Esimoko, thank you for your visit. We are very honored indeed to have you visit our humble house of healing and to know that you still honor the old ways. But it is not the Great Owl who finds Ioage's behavior offensive. But rather, it is the Maiden Herself, whose name I cannot utter because of its sacredness. She has advised that Ioage should respect the evening as Her time of rest. As you can see, the mark on his face has slowly disappeared since your arrival.

But Ioage is marked by the Maiden. And that mark he will always carry behind his knee. As a reminder and as a warning to him, to respect the va. The sacred space not only between the living but between the living and the dead.

And from that day onwards, I became solely responsible for ensuring that the va was never disrespected again. That the mirrors were always covered in the evenings, so as not to capture the image of the Maiden as she combed her hair. Or that the suitcases of visiting relatives were always closed and not left open like coffins. When I heard my father pleading like that for my life in exchange for his, my heart jumped out of my skin and hugged his heart. And since then our hearts have always understood each other, No matter what happens, I know that my father will lay down his life without question for any of us, including you Sia, his most prized student and spiritual daughter.

That's what makes what we're doing so wrong, Ioage. It is a complete opposite of everything he ever taught us. I feel closer to Tama now, more than ever because of what you've just shared, and yet, at the same time, I feel I'm light years away from him. Do you know what I mean?

Ioage nodded in melancholic agreement. And a sadness fell suddenly before us then and covered us both, like a wet blanket that had been left out in the rain, cold and heavy as we both shivered under it, in a soggy embrace.

Ioage continued the story of when he was a student at Port Moresby not only to teach me about the history of Samoa he had learned from books but to take us both away from the graveness of our reality as star crossed lovers caught in a black hole that seemed to be abandoned by the universe.

My contact with Papuans, inspired me towards wanting to get a pe'a, a tattoo, but when I expressed this desire to my father, he was vehemently against it. You may not know this, but the sons and daughters of pastors are banned from having tattoos because according to Christian beliefs, Christ had already made the ultimate sacrifice which means it would be offensive to further spill blood, willingly.

I wanted to get the pe'a. I wanted to be tattooed.

But I respected my father more than my own individual desires.

And so on the day I went to the tattooist and canceled the operation, I didn't know that my father had followed me. And when I saw him, he bowed his head to me. And for the very first time in my life, I saw my father weep and weep and weep.

Ioage held me in his arms and pressed my face to his chest and we laid there for what seemed a short eternity. And then I tasted salt all over again on my face. And I . . .

Shh, kagi so'o se, kai omai gi aiku fasi a'u. Shh, you cry too much, some aiku might hear you and come beat me up, which made me laugh again as he held my hand and led me to the lake.

So what else is in your backpack a li'i kama lea?

Oh, you know, the usual necessities. Batteries. Matches. Candles. Toilet paper. You never know when you'll have a day like this.

I feel safe and secure already, I said, nudging him to his side.

You should. I also have an AK 47 in there, just in case we get attacked by extra-terrestrial ninjas with colossal and gargantuan heads.

Ha! My, what a scintillating and colorful imagination you do possess, kama lea/aye man.

All the better to astound you with my dear.

Do you have any scissors in there?

Why do you ask?

I want you to cut my hair.

Cut your hair?

Yes, cut it off. Now that I know that it's not even mine. That it doesn't even belong to me. It's someone else's idea of how I should look. Cut it off Ioage. Please. Cut it off.

Hey, shhh. I didn't mean to upset you by telling you that.

You haven't upset me, Ioage. You've just woke me up. And now that I'm wide awake, I'm really really really angry!

Shhhh....Se soia. Onosa'i. Shhh....Stop it. Be patient.

I just want it off, Ioage! The same way you had that epiphany that lead you to grow yours long.

Hey come here. Put your head right here next to me. It's ok. Everything is going to work itself out. In its own

Time. But you do know why you can't cut your hair, Sia. Right?

Why not? It's going to grow back anyway. I just don't want it on me right now. Right this minute. Suddenly, it has no appeal to me anymore Ioage. It's become meaningless, because it's all been a lie. A great big fat lie. And it's bloody criminal if you ask me Ioage. Cut it off. Please. I'm begging you.

We can't cut your hair Sia.

Why not?

It will be like spitting into God's face and into Lamaga's blessing.

How so?

In old Samoa, pregnant women were the only ones that grew their hair. It is the symbol of life. And growth.

Ok then. But I'm cutting it the minute my womb is empty again.

That's *my* woman.

To my stupendous surprise, my mother did not notice the Owl shit at all and sighed in great relief when she saw me, thanking me for saving White Sunday in her own rare quiet way, by nodding at me and speaking the language of intimate silence between a mother and a daughter, a language I've had to maneuvre and navigate like eating a bony fish for the last 17½ years of my life, always with the fear of possibly swallowing a bone or two, the risk of which far out weighted the delectable taste of its flesh. Which is how I have come to understand my relationship with my mother, thanks to Ioage. An odd moment transpired then between my mother and me after I handed her the cotton threads. A moment unlike any that I had ever experienced with her in all my 17 ½ years. I felt like she was looking straight through me and saw me in all my transparency. And as she took the giant white thread from my hands, I noticed what appeared to be a smile on her face. It wasn't a big smile. Nor was it an obvious smile. But it was a smile nevertheless. What she was smiling at, I did not know. Perhaps it was the joy of seeing the giant white threads which she needed to complete the sewing of the day as the Malaefou woman was stopping by that evening to pick up the clothes she had sewn for her. Or perhaps she knew what had happened to me at the lake as only a mother would know. But instead of tearing her hair out and mine, my mother spoke to me in the language of silence, the way Ioage spoke to me in the language of love. And when our eyes met, I did not look away. But found myself gazing and gazing and gazing, drowning in her deep brown and knowing eyes.

When we reached the pick-up, after the lake, something I despaired to do because I knew I would have to face the foul scent of the Owl's faeces not to mention the utterly stained threads that had already ensured a beating or at the very least a scolding that would be heard all over Gu'usa and played over and over whenever anyone wanted to tease or mock me later on, something I was already prepared for. I showed Ioage the threads with a sudden melancholy and he immediately squeezed my hand and told me not to worry. That he apparently had the perfect solution for it, which calmed me down because beyond a shadow of a doubt, I believed him, and was prepared to be astounded.

And then like Mary Poppins, he took out of his backpack a bottle of vinegar. Which he said he carried for his health because it stabilized blood sugars, was good for the heart and was meant for just such emergencies.

According to Ioage, vinegar feeds and grows naturally occurring bacteria which dissolve the acid in the Owl faeces faster than water or any other chemical. And the moment of proof came when my mother, the most critical woman on the face of the planet did not even detect a problem or the original smell I had experienced when I first saw the Owl scrutinizing me as if saying, So you want to be a woman before your time? Eat my shit first and let's see what happens girl-woman.

Once the threads dried I thought of the Owl. I know she's trying to protect me. But like my mother, she too needs to learn to trust me. To let me make my own decisions. Fall flat on my face and scrape my knees with my own mistakes. After all, isn't that how one learns how to ride a community bike? Through overcoming personal failures and obstacles put there so that we can learn of our own strength? Our own resolve?

Ioage, tell me what's going to happen to us if they ever find out?

No one's going to find out. I mean you'll be in your first trimester by the time you leave and that's not really going to be as obvious. But your spaceman will be an American citizen. So instead of Owls you'll be flying like Eagles in the land of the free, which will become your new home. Just stay away from movies with grass huts and skirts and people named after certain days of the week. Ua iloa? And if you're serious about it, I have an old professor who specializes in Aeronautics and lives in Clearwater, Florida. He works for NASA and the Kennedy Space Center. He could hook my boy up.

Ha.Ha. Now he's your boy? It's going to be a she, mister. You mock me now but in 20 years time, ke'i a le kou aiga ua ku le Starship Enterprise i luma o le kou muafale ae la'a mai i fafo Spock ma vala'au mai, Ia beam aku si koeaiga ulu kula lea i luga, Scottie! You mock me now but in 20 years time, you'll have a sudden visit from the Starship Enterprise and Spock will walk out on our front yard and call out, Beam this old bald man up Scottie!

And we laughed again. So much I nearly peed.

Besides, people say that all the time, that no one will ever know. But the truth is, someone always does. Aua e magigo lava le maka o le vai, that's my Aunty Aima'a's favorite saying. That whatever lies in murky waters will always be revealed. *It never fails.*

That's just superstitions.

Is it? Listen Ioage, look at me.

O lea a? What is it?

I don't know how I'm going to be able to act towards you when we get back to Gu'usa. I mean, seeing you at church. In school. I'm afraid I might say the wrong thing, like accidentally look at you the wrong way, the way that might give us away. Most difficult is reverting back to Mr. Viliamu after having called you Ioage. I mean, what's going to happen to us? Huh? I just want to disappear!

Don't say that, Sia. Shhh.....Don't.

But it's the truth Ioage. That's what I feel like doing. I just wish Time would stop at the lake or that Time didn't touch the lake, so that we could just live there in that warp for the rest of our lives. Away from everyone and suddenly I'm reminded of that *Star Trek* episode called "The City on the Edge of Forever," which is my ultimate favorite.

It starts off with an explosion atop the USS Enterprise, caused while on investigation of temporal disturbances from another planet. Lt. Sulu is hurt. Badly. Dr. McCoy,

Chief Medical Officer, administers him a shot of cordrazine but the ship gets shaken and so Doc accidentally shoots himself and gives himself an overdose! He finds himself in a state of delusion and escapes from the Bridge to the Transporter Room where he beams himself to that planet of doom not far away. While the mood of the rest of the episode is melancholic and sad, especially the last part when Sister Edith Keeler, a woman interested in man's future and the stars, whom Captain Kirk falls in love with and sees killed before his very own eyes, a death he could have prevented as he knew beforehand that the only way for history to be realigned was for Edith Keeler to die, a fact Spock had shared and explained to him earlier, which horrified him, he stood there, and watched the woman he loved get run over by some truck. It must have been just horrible for Captain Kirk. Just horrible! What lover wouldn't be horrified? I asked myself. What human being wouldn't? But now that I know what it's like to feel and be the beloved of a lover, I find that whole concept of choosing one over many a beastly dilemma to have to be faced with. I know that I would have easily chosen Ioage over the demise of the entire human race, I would. That's how much Ioage has come to mean to me. Killing him would be like killing myself. I could never live with the thought that his heart was not beating close to mine! He has turned me into a shameless woman. A woman who would chose him over her aiga, her nu'u, her itumalo, her country and even the human race. Which of course would bring tons and tons of shame not only on my family, but on every earthling who knew me. What I'm interested in, and found most profound from that episode which would end up saving Earth and everyone else in the universe, is the idea that there is a Guardian of Forever on the planet, whose job is to be the doorway to any time and space. While the old Samoans did that in their dreams, where they would wander Pulotu and the galaxies, almost kinetically and in their dreams, I wished at that very moment that Ioage and I knew the Guardian of Forever and that he would grant us a portal where we would exist in perpetual bliss at the lake, without hurting a single soul but to love and to be loved. *Forever.*

But Sia, if we're caught in the time warp of forever, you won't be able to finish high school and go to university and become a brain surgeon or a heart specialist or a kick-ass academic or a writer and deliver your spaceman, said Ioage, bursting my bubble, just when I thought I had come up with something compelling. Remember always to astound yourself Sia. Rather than dreaming up ways of escaping reality, your perpetual duty is to face reality and all the challenges it throws your way. Don't wish for the easy. Go through the hard and tough. Because it is only there and then that you truly discover just how remarkable you are. And you should never forget it. Ua e iloa? What did I say that first day in class? Astound yourself so that you may astound those around you.

How can I astound myself when my heart hurts, a li'i Ioage? When I looked into the Owl earlier at the library, the Owl told me that you won't hurt me that you can't but that someone was going to get hurt. I didn't know what it meant. But now I do.

I know. I don't know what's going to happen, Sia. We're not Gods or God. We're human. With our moments of weaknesses. We make mistakes.

Are you saying this is a mistake?

No. It isn't. And you shouldn't either.

I can't breathe, Ioage. I think I'm drowning.

I can't breathe either, Sia. I'm drowning too.

That Night, the night after the White Sunday final practice I sat outside the church steps and looked up at the Stars and started crying. I was carrying Ioage's seed inside me, which means I'll never be alone. But what about him? What's going to happen to him? If his prediction is true, that he will not be the last man that I will ever be intimate with, then what would happen if this baby lives? Would the person I end up with, love Ioage and my baby the way he would love me? The thought alone made me burst into tears and I started sobbing and sobbing like an inconsolable baby.

✧◆✧

Whoever did this, we're going to tear them apart, said Q. Tough girl Q who wants to love me the way Ioage does. I've known that since we were 12 when we were showering at the paipa and she suddenly wanted to play a game of comparing who has the biggest breasts. The largest nipples. And when I showed her mine she said instantly, wow! And asked me if she could touch them.

I let her touch them.

And when she did her eyes were closed. And mine were too as I felt her fingers caress my nipples until suddenly she started squeezing them so hard it hurt. And it's the one memory I have of her that she keeps reminding me of, despite the fact that it happened almost 6 years ago, before I started wearing a bra.

I looked at her and I saw myself reflected in her eyes. Only I was worlds away.

What it is Sia? Tell us, said Cha. Is it that Solofa boy? Did you finally meet him? Has he said anything to you yet? Tell us, please. Enquiring minds want to know!

Oh, Cha, Cha, Cha. My spirited and bold Cha. My one and only fa'afafige friend, sharp as a razor who tells me the truth about everything, boys, clothes and how I needed a new wardrobe. She's the only one who can critique village people and get away with it unscathed because once the laughter dies down the truth she speaks of lingers. And I know that that gift of hers or that ability of hers to make our village people laugh while they contemplate (or not) what she has to say, comes from a spirited place inside her as she carries the spirits of both man and woman, which gives her that special spunk, that extra sparkle and twinkle in her eye.

Cha who kept reminding us that when she finishes high school she'll go to Hollywood via New Zealand and Australia and that she's going to be a star! The biggest star singing sensation Samoa had ever seen. She's going to hop on the Cha Cha Cha express. Get her breasts done. Take hormone pills like Aunty Von. And get a university degree like aunty Von too. A girl can't get ahead with looks alone, you know. Which never failed to put a smile on my face.

Now that you're smiling, tell us, who did this? Huh? Va'ai iai ouke sasaea le guku. Ka'u mai. Huh? I'm going to tear her mouth. Tell us.

But I couldn't. I didn't even have the heart to tell her that I had completely forgotten about the Solofa boy that she had tried to hook me up with. Or that my body had now known the language of love and is no longer the bore she used to think I was. Far from it. But even that I couldn't disclose to either of them.

I didn't mean to be condescending, I just didn't think they would have understood where I was coming from. After all, they're still living in the world where Ioage is Mr. Viliamu. Mr. Viliamu the A Number One Teacher. Selau pasege le kakou faiaoga. What an awesome teacher we have world. And for a minute I became nostalgic again and longed for that look that Q had on her face, the look of a girl. A girl who thought about bible studies, knew all the books of the New and Old Testament and could recite them backwards. Knew scripture better than God himself. Excited about Days of Our Lives and *Star Trek* and PBS Nova (well, not really Q, that would be Cha and me, as Q was more of a Big Time Wrestling kinda girl) and would hurry home after choir practice so as not to miss Marlena and Roman and Hope and Bo and other TV stars who had absolutely no idea about our reality and yet we wanted so desperately for our lives to unveil like theirs. Still, I wouldn't exchange any of that for what I had come to know in the last 24 hours of my life.

In the last 24 hours I'd learned a whole other language.

I've touched a grown man's hair. Felt his fingers through my fingers. Caressed his pubic hair, seen him naked before me, breathed him in, his scent caused my cunt to get wet while he deflowered me with his fingers, and thrust his seed into me, marking my cheeks with my own blood, which I understand now for the lipstick girls used to mark their faces during cultural performances.

I never understood that before. Lipstick. Hymen Blood. Lipstick. Hymen Blood. Lipstick. Hymen Blood.

Sa'asa'a mai loa! Se'ese'e malie! Se'ese'e malie! Lalo! Shoooo hooooo!

Now dance! Glide with grace! Glide with grace! Now bend Downwards! Shoooo hooooo!

A ifoga, said Ioage, is a traditional ceremony where the offender seeks the forgiveness of the offended party by appearing outside her or his house, with matai members of his or her family.

The offender would then kneel before the house, his or her body and those of his or her family's matai would be covered with a fine mat, if it were a serious crime such as rape, adultery or murder.

The offending party will wait outside the house until the offended party decides to accept their apology, which could take hours under the scorching hot sun or rain and thunder if it were the case. The offender and his party will endure whatever weather conditions that prevail until the offended party decides to forgive them.

In the old days, the offender did not merely kneel with other matai, covered in fine mats but appeared at the break of dawn with piles of stones, banana, ta'amu and mango leaves, a long stick and a knife or some other sharp object as if to say, Here I am. Take this stick and put it to my neck and strangle me with it. Then take the knife and gut me. Stuff me with stones and mango leaves. Then use the remaining stones and leaves for the umu where you shall bake my body like the pig that I am.

This was how utter humility was shown by someone who knew they had offended someone else. It is the ceremony the whole of Nu'uolemanusa Tai are prepared to witness in retribution for the crime of deflowering one of its virgins and member of the aualuma of the London Missionary Society congregation. And would be performed by me, the pastor's son. The son who will bring nothing but disgrace.

Why do you say that? You didn't rape me.

But I deflowered you.

And what's my part in this deflowering ceremony?

Ha'e, se aikae ia, koeikiki e lavea i le ali vae kasi. Eat shit, or I'll hit you with a one legged bamboo pillow.

Haahahahaha. Like I keep saying, you're very manly when you're angry. But please, don't flatter yourself, mister.

When is the moto ka coming to take you to the airport 'a suga, si'aula?

Ko'a sau gagei i le po. Later on tonight.

You know I can't be at the airport. I won't be able to survive it.

I know. And I don't expect you to be there either. I can't put you through that, Ioage. Especially since I heard Tama ma Tina / your Father and your Mother are going to be there with the Aukalavou / the Youth for Christ and the Au a Keige / the Girl Guides. That's why I am here, Ioage. To see you and to hold your hand and feel your warmth for the last time.

Sia.

Sia!

Sia!!

Ea kama lea? A? / What is it? Huh?

I just wanted to say your name one last time while you're still with me.

Oh Ioage.

Say it again.

Ioage.

Again.

Stop it. I can't.

Yes you can. Please. Say it.

Ioage.

Again and again!

Ioage.

I'm going to miss you too, Sia.

I'm missing you already, Ioage.

But at least you won't be alone once your spaceman starts kicking.

I think he just did! Give me your hands. Do you feel that?

That's impossible. It's too early. You're only in the first trimester and barely at that. They say the baby usually kicks at the 5th or 6th month, when body formation is complete. It must be a phantom kick. You think he's kicking, but he's not.

Since you've had chirren already, I'll take your word for it.

You know just how to get to me, don't you?

I'm going to miss this nose, Ioage. This big flat beautiful nose that has breathed in the scent of a girl and a woman simultaneously. And these ears. These soft and tender ears that listened and heard the exquisite sounds of you each time you entered and exploded into me, whether from the back or from the front or when you would make me sit on you and your mouth would greedlily cover my breasts while you helped me move up and down until I saw the Sea of Tranquility and afterwards, came face to face with the limitless and vast expanse of infinity! And this chest, this magnificent chest where I laid exhausted from the very thought of you near me. And these thighs that held the fragrance and scent and musk of you. And these calves with the strength to lift the globe and carry it across the Milky Way. And this scar behind your knee. Like a lonely nocturnal flower at dawn. And this straight line tattooed between your thumb and your pointer finger. I never asked you before, but what does it mean?

It was supposed to be an illustration of perpendicular lines but I passed out before the tattooist could even get to the second line. Imagine a full tattoo? A 'ea? I opted for the hair instead, and my father told me, when I finally had the guts to go up to him and told him what I had decided, Now, you're a man, Ioane. Whether you know it or not, God has just blessed you with a tattoo that will remain in your heart and be your compass wherever you go.

Ahhhh. What a beautiful story, Ioage. Talofa e, ia Tama. You really are the apple of his eye, Ioage. This, you and me. This, will devastate him, Ioage. And I'm not even going to think about what it will do to Tina Lakena. I shudder at the very thought of it. And I haven't even factored my own aiga and our nu'u, our village.

No it won't, Sia. My father, that is, our father is a tough man, Sia. This, *us*, as difficult as it is will humanize us before the aulotu. As sometimes, people feel that because we are the children of pastors that we are angels on earth without problems. But this, what's happened to us will teach them hopefully to not be as judgemental and more forgiving towards others and to be more kind and gentle. But I don't want to think about anyone else right now, Sia. All I want to hear is your voice. Talk to me, Sia. Tell me. What else are you going to miss about me? A li'i keige lea? Aye, girl?

I will miss these dark, black nipples, Ioage. And these provocative and cheeky fingers. These big titanic toes.

Yeah? You're going to miss the Big Toes?

Yes. I will desperately miss the Big Toes.

What else, Sia? Tell me.

These hardworking elbows. I will miss the hardest working elbows on this side of the Moon. Ova le ovakaimi a gai kulilima se, fai aku ai fo'i. These poor elbows have been working tirelessly over time. And these great and broad shoulders that have carried and carried and carried my legs until you made me scream and I frightened all the birds of the forest, causing ripples through the very placid lake. And these strong and muscular buttocks that thrust the life force into me so that the song lines see continuity. And how can I ever forget this back with its mountainous and monumental craters? I don't think there's another back this strong or as beautiful in the entire galaxy.

Go on.

And these lips. These thick and ravishing lips. And this tongue! This wicked, wicked, wondrous tongue. And what words can I use to describe this mouth? Oi aue! This poisonously delicious mouth! And this sensuous neck. And the nape of this neck that makes me wet and drip.

And? What else? Tell me, Sia. Tell me!

This scent, Ioage. This musky scent of the earth in your armpits. And this beautiful and gorgeous cock. This splendiferous, opulent, beaut of a cock. Too bad I never got a chance to taste it, a ea?

There's still time, you know.

But it's not enough, Ioage. I'll just have to save it for my dreams, aye?

Are you sure you can wait that long?

I want to leave some part of you for prosperity, you know.

You take care of yourself out there, you hear?

I will. I promise.

If it's a girl, name her Taeao'oleaigalulusa. Morning of the Eating of the Sacred Owl.

And if it's a boy?

Spock?

Hey! Don't joke about it, because you know I will! He'll be Spock V. Afatasi Ioane. Son of his father, Ioage.

Poor boy. He'll be the laughing stock of his class.

Or the King at those *Star Trek* conventions! I interjected. I had actually seen a PBS documentary on the cult of the trekkies. How some people might lead their entire adult lives as Spock, Hikaru Sulu, Dr Leonard McCoy, Lt. Hadley, Scottie, or Captain Kirk! Blows my mind!

Maybe it could be his nickname then. Sipoki.

Hahahahahahhahaha! Now *that* is hilarious!

Shit, I didn't realize what that would sound like when translated. Hahaha! Ok, hey, that *was* pretty funny!

Ga'o le akali'i lava o Ioage e fa'aigoa kogu a i le mea ga kupuga mai ai. Ia sao fa'alalelei! Only Ioage's son will be nicknamed by the true origin of his birth!

Ok, jokes aside Sia, if you really want to know what's in my heart, it will be that he continues the song lines of our ancestors. If you don't mind Sia, please name my son after his grandfather and my father, Esimoto. I know you're going to be a modern woman so he doesn't have to take Viliamu and it's ok with me.

As you wish, my Liege.

I wish we were strangers in the night Sia. Or that we met somewhere else, light years ago. Then I don't have to say goodbye and you don't have to leave.

Shhh.... You're going to ruin it, Ioage. Stop.

I don't know how I'm going to survive without you, you know?

Another Lolita will come. Trust me. And she's going to be more lustrous, refulgent and brilliant.

And what does The Raven have to say about that?

Never, nevermore . . .

You've gotta get going now, Suga. Say your farewells to your other friends and families.

Ok, I will. But before I go, I want you to say something to me, Ioage.

What do you want me to say? I'll say anything. Anything you want me to say, Sia. Tell me!

Say something deep and occult. Something so astounding that it will blow my mind into cosmic dust and carry me on my long, long journey.

Hmmm . . . something profound you say? Let me think...

Think man, think!

Hmmm . . . Ok, Come here. I think I've got it.

But first, kiss me while you say it, Ioage.

Like this?

Not so rough. Not as if you're intoxicated. But rather, kiss me deliberately and softly. Kiss me tenderly, Ioage. Run the tip of your tongue over my lips and rest for a while over each lip until your electric impulses bounce between your brain, your tongue and your skin. Like you're drowning but you don't want anyone to rescue you. The very act of drowning *is* your rescue!

Shit that's deep, Sia.

Tai le alofa, Ioage.

I got goosebumps just thinking about the science of that. I never thought there was a science to a kiss.

You should break out more li'i Kams, like I did. Expand that radius boy!

Se ga'o ia. You're too cool. Damn.

Remember that first day when you introduced yourself to our class and you said, O la'u galuega o le a'oa'oina lea o outou. My job is to educate you. Ina ia mafai ona tatala o outou mafaufau i ni manatu e sili atu i lo'o manatu o lo'o iai i le taimi nei. To open your minds beyond their current confines. Ina ia fa'atumulia o outou manatu ma mafaufauga i vavega. To fill your thoughts and imagination with wonder. Ma fa'amaofa outou ina ia mafai ona tou fa'amaofaina outou lava. To astound you so that you may astound yourselves.

Ioage clapped as I spoke. Then when I finished he said, You've remembered every word Sia! Bravo bella! Bravo!

That's because I come from ancestors who wrote their histories on their legs and their waists and their buttocks and their inner thighs and their bellybuttons, permanently. Who used to navigate the largest body of water on the planet by the stars and the directions of the winds and whose stories were whispered from one generation to another and I can still smell the fragrance in the ula they wore on the malae as they sang and danced with pride beaming on their faces after a virgin had been deflowered and I am ashamed that I wasn't able to wait until the same fate was mine, even though the missionaries had democratized that institution, I still believe and respect its origins, as it is also my duty and responsibility to our aiga's name and honor, But I couldn't possibly be with a man whose mind I didn't respect, Ioage. You know that, don't you? I just couldn't. Not after I've come to discover and explore and know yours. And what a mind it is, Ioage! It is an arresting mind! It is exquisite and magnificent! Ravishing and sharp like a fish bone and just as complicated. And I am humbled and feel honored to have had the chance to collide with it. Even if for a brief moment. But back to what I was saying about losing my virginity to you, I'm sorry to offend our cultural values by saying this, Ioage, because, like you, I too believe in the 'we' that defines us as men and women who are intricately part of the web of aiga, family, nu'u, village, itumalo, district, atunu'u, country so what I am about to say might make you ashamed of me and make you think twice about me, but I can't think otherwise because I am now a Night woman, who craves nothing but coconuts that fall in the middle of the night. But I hope you'll understand and forgive me, Ioage. That as important and as significant my aiga and family is, my heart belongs to you, Ioage! You and only you! There's no one else but you! Not even God can come between us! There! I've said it. May lightning strike me down now, any minute. But I tell you now, Ioage, as only a shameless woman will tell the man she wants more than life itself will tell you. That I will eat stones and drink fire if it means spending one more day with you. The way we did that Saturday before White

Sunday when I decided to take a ride in your red pick-up truck. And that's why I will willingly and wholeheartedly carry the guilt that has weighed heavily on me since we left the forest and the lake that day. And I'm going to have to carry it with me for the rest of my life until they return my body to the fatu ma le eleʻele, the earth where it came from. But before we cross that bridge, which I hope is a lifetime away, I just want to hear your voice, Ioage. Now say it, I'm ready to be astounded by you one last time. But this Time, kiss me violently. Devour me with wild abandon and desire as if you've been stranded on a deserted and uninhabited island and I'm the first wo(man) you've seen in weeks! Months! I'm here, Ioage. Now, kiss me!

Wheeeeew! That's a mighty tall order you've got there Sia. I hope I can live up to it. And I understand what you meant about being a Woman of the Night because guess what? I *am* the Night! And you *are* the Day. And no matter where you go, you will always be closer to me than you think. In the song of the early morning bird or in a double rainbow or crickets chirping at twilight. My heart belongs to you too, Sia. And I realize the incestuous nature of our taboo relationship, but like you, I would endure poisonous fins being stuck in my eyes and my body gutted like a pig and stuffed with stones and baked in an oven than to lose one hour of that precious day at the lake with you.

What am I going to do with you, Ioage? A ea, kama lea?

I want to be your man but I don't want to disappoint you, Sia.

You're doing fine, Ioage. As you always have thus far.

Give me a minute, ua iloa?

Are you nervous? You shouldn't be. Alo loa i ou faiva. O ou mama na.

Tai le alofa. Are you ready for me, Sia?

Yes, Ioage. I'm ready.
Are you positive?
I'm wide open, Ioage.
I'm coming, Sia.
I'm here, Ioage.

✧✦✧ ✧✦✧ ✧✦✧ ✧✦✧
✧✦✧ ✧✦✧ ✧✦✧ ✧✦✧
<<<<<<<>>>>>✧✦✧* Tatou <<<<<<>>>>>> ** **
.........* .... ;;;;;;;;;;;;; ** ^^^^ ....TATOU
✧✦✧*o ... * .,,,te manumalo....,,,^ ...;;;..... ....'" '' '''
......'" '''* * * * * .... * ^
;;;;;;
** * TE MANUMALO <<<<>>>>
* * * o* ...
.....pe'a tatou.... ;;;;;;;;;** ** * ^^^^ ^^ * * * **<<<<>>>>
PE'A TATOU ✧✦✧✧✦✧.......;;;............"'"""""""""" ✧✦✧ ....
fa'ato'ilaloina....** *
.....i tatou lava... ✧✦✧ ooo * ✧✦✧ ✧✦✧** oo * *^^^^
FA'ATO'ILALOINA ^^^^ * ^^ .... ;;;;;;;;;;;;;;;;;
I TATOU LAVA....... **..>,,>,,> ..*...ae le'o '"""""""""""""
.... * ✧✦✧✧✦✧* ** ✧✦✧ .... AE LE'O ;;;; ooo
....isi. ISI.
>>>>>>> * <<<<<<<<< ✧✦✧ >>>>>>>>

Ahhhhhhh!!!!! It's marvelous, Ioage! It's just as I expected! Dazzling and magnificent! I can see the Southern Cross and the Milky Way! You've just blown and stretched my mind so far it's going to take me a millennium to catch my breath. Say it again Ioage, Please, please, please, say it again. In English this time.

We triumph through conquering ourselves, not others.

It's perfect, Ioage. Perfect! Like a positive integer that is equal to the sum of its proper positive divisors.

Thank you, Sia. That means a lot to me, especially as it's coming from you.

You are welcome, Ioage. It's also very philosophical and subtle and yes, sagacious.

You're making my oceans flow and I'm tasting my own salt, Sia.

I will lick the salt off of your oceanic eyes, Ioage.

I didn't know it was going to be like this, Sia.

Did you honestly think it was going to be any different from what it is now, Ioage? Really, Ioage? *Really?*

I just thought . . . I thought we at least deserved a chance at happiness, considering.

Considering?

Considering, all the shit that I've been through. That *we've* been through together and *are* going through.

You mean with Pulupulu and MD and what happened to Mr. Prakash and your life in New Zealand? Or is it the incestuous and forbidden web of love and deceit that we are tangled in, a li'i Ioage? Which one did you you mean, exactly a li'i, Ioage? Huh? One or the other or both? Because whichever door you choose to walk through, I'll have to say, I'm truly sorry for you, Ioage. And if I have one gift to give you, it would be to erase that chip that's on your shoulder right now. Erase it so that you don't walk around this earth thinking anyone owes you anything for your pain and the pain of the lives of those around you. Wasn't it you who taught me not to escape into a supposed fantasy but to grab a hold of my life and live it? Huh? Or was I wrong in assuming that you were a strong and principled man whose main purpose in life was to perpetually astound himself so that he could do the same to those around him? Please don't tell me it's all been an act Ioage. Please convince me otherwise. Tell me, Ioage. Tell me!

Like I said, you don't miss shit, don't you?

That's because I had a kick-ass teacher who held me accountable, Sir.

Show me the bastard so I can give him a piece of my mind.

That's not so hard, darling. You only have to look in the mirror to find him.

I fucking miss you already, you know that. Don't you?

Ha'e, aua e ke makagaga. E le kagi se koa! Hey, don't cry. A warrior doesn't cry.

Are you sure you liked it? What I said earlier? Is it as profound as you had hoped and said that it was?

I would never lie to you, Ioage. You should know that by now.

I still want to know, Sia. Is it everything you had ever hoped for? Did I astound you?

Hey, come here.

Is this close enough?

Give me your ear.

Whisper it to me, slowly, Sia. Whisper it so that I melt into your voice.

Not only did you astound me, I am delighting in your radiance! It's like looking into Euler's Identity and it's just as spectacular, Ioage. And it's going to be the words that take me beyond the number 1 and the infinities of o and into the Vast Expanse beyond Heaven and Pulotu.

I am one lucky bastard, you know that?

How so? I'm leaving, Ioage. What's so lucky about that?

Because I have the shit, man. And because you are the shit.

I am?

You know you are, girl. I don't care how far you go away from me or which parallel universe the USS Enterprise ends up taking you, you are forever my woman, Inosia Alofafua Afatasi.

And you are my man, ad infintum, Mr. Ioane Viliamu.

Ga'o lo'u gofo aku lava i Samoa a'o lega o le 'a 'e fealua'i mai ma le ka faku, keige lea. I will remain in Samoa while you wander the world with our heart, girl.

Aua li'i kama lea. Le lava fo'i kagi. Gofo fa'alelei, ua iloa? Don't man. I'm tired of crying. Stay well, ok?

Sau loa iga alu, suga Sia. O ou mama ga. Come now Sia. It's time for you to go. Go with my blessings.

Ia ua lelei oe lea. Kai le alofa. Good. Thank you for your well wishes.

E iai la gi popcorn a le kou aiga? Ua uma le ka aka, li'i keige. So does your family have any popcorn? It looks like our movie has come to an end, aye girl?

Hahaha! Se ga'o ia oe! Fa la'ia! Hahaha! O you shit you! Goodbye then!

BOOK TWO
AO MA LE PO/
DAY AND NIGHT

Fai Se Tatalo
Say A Prayer

Poʻo ua lata ona ʻe moe
Pele ea, ou te tatalo mo oe
la ʻe manuia
seʻia oʻu foʻi atu

As you are about to go to sleep
Dearest, I shall pray for you
That you be blessed
Until my return

Fai se tatalo mo aʻu
O aʻu foʻi mo oe
Pele, i aso uma
Ta te vava mamao
E tagi loʻu fatu
Ma alu pea
Ou te manatua
Pea oe i loʻu fatu

Pray for me, dear
And I will pray for you
Every day I will
That we are separated
My heart cries
But it continues
I'll always remember
You in my heart

A mafatia oe ma mamao
Pele, i loʻu fatu, e le afaina
Leai se tasi o le a ia faʻaluaina

Ui ina le tau o la'u va'ai
A e manatua pea oe ia ita
Ia e manuia se'ia ou fo'i atu

No one will come between us
When you should suffer while you're so far away
Dear in my heart, it should not matter
While I can't see you
I will always remember you
Be blessed until my return

Dear Night, *(America is so strange. There is no place for solitude. I can't even see the stars. I can't see you, Ioage. You are fading. Fading. Fading. The only way for me to see you is to leave the mirror uncovered at twilight which puzzles my American cousins who don't know that you grow in me . . . you grow, Ioage, you grow . . .)*

The Day is so long. Much too long. Twelve hours is unbearable. I long for the Sun to disappear from the Sky and for the Clouds to be extinguished by the Moon. Every waking hour finds me yearning for you. Like a nocturnal flower I am dying a silent death at the thought of you away from me.

When you are near, I am exhausted. Exhausted from the very thought of you near me. The thought of your hands holding mine. Caressing my fingers between yours. Tracing your name in the middle of my palm, over and over as I close my eyes and imagine your breath on the nape of my neck.

O Benevolent Moon!
O Merciful Constellations!
O Sagacious Galaxies!

O Bountiful Stars!

You hold my anguish in your cosmic memory exploding in the distance, illuminating the sky with your chaotic, stellar pulse.

I am Inosia Alofafua Afatasi. I am the Despised, Freelove, Unprecedented Descendant of the Sun. I am standing on the shores of the Is- Land of Dreams with a melancholic Wind, heavy on my back and a secret song of despair in the palm of my hand, calling out to the shadows at twilight.

Come to me Night! Come to me my dark, aging warrior with the long memory, the scarred body and hair the color of clouds. Look at me! Show me your Owl eyes. Press your once warring hands into mine. Cup my mountainous feet in your palms. Hold my oceanic face close to yours. Exhale into my lifeless nostrils and revive me with your mana. Ravish me with your riddles of existence that question the widths and depths of the Vast Expanse and Wo-Man's quest for immortality. Enthrall me with tall tales of how you received each scar across your face, each battle you've had to fight, each river you've had to cross, each mountain you've had to climb, each monster you've had to slay, each fear you've had to overcome and the men and women embedded in the memory of your skin.

Dear Day, *(I drove by the lake the other day and guess what? Old man Lamaga asked me about you. Whether you were eating fruit and driking sea water. The baby should be able to taste both the land and the sea, he said. I blushed when he said that and wished him well while my thoughts wondered towards your garden, your lake, your scent, your womanly scent which I press to my lips in the middle of the afternoon).*

Ravish me Day!

Ravish me with tales of your youth.

Take me back to when you were a girl. How your mother spied on you with horror when you caught your first pigeon at the star mound, (an activity reserved only for boys and men) only to release it back into the forest because that's how you understood the nature of the wild which meant you understood your own nature at such a young age. Even then you knew that wild things were not meant to be tamed or to be held captive.

Or when your grandfather first took you out to the deep and showed you how to speak the language of octopus, eels and flying fish and how you lost two fingers to an anxious White Shark who was offended by the audacity of someone female and so young who stared at him unafraid. Yet, despite your missing fingers you grew into one of the most powerful warriors, Goddess of War, turning your opponents into stones, one by one.

And it all started then.

Or is it when you held your first spear in the middle of the malae while all the other girls and boys were still in the land of sleep, and the dead body of a wild boar laid at your bloodied feet. Fearlessly, you called out to the ancestors who inhabit that sacred circle, center of all that is seen and unseen.

I come to Honor you!

Grant me your strength! You had said.

An eerie silence fell upon that place where you stood. As if nature itself was astounded by the sight of you, seeking the brotherhood of warriors. Only your head did not possess the long dark hair of a boy or a man but was shaved instead like the head of a woman's with a curl behind your left ear, signifying your virginal taupou status. Generations since have called it Taeaoligoligoa, Morning of the Eerie Silence. The day Nu'uolemanusa was confronted with the limitless nature of possibilities outside the realm of what it had always known and understood as their way of doing things. And right when you thought no one was listening, that the silence would stretch into the rest of the Day and into the Twilight of Eternity, The Great One, The Owl, flew across the circle and broke the silence with the sound of its wings, hovering above you, looking you directly in the eye, as if to say, You have done well Girl. But you are no warrior. Not yet. Not until you walk into a green battlefield leaving it red will you know what it's like to bear the responsibility of duty and the ethics of becoming a warrior. And with that, (S)He shed three feathers on your feet, the feathers of victory which you carried and carried and carried on the end of your spear, each time you walked into war. Undefeated. Yet in all my dreams, my love, I've never seen you smile.

✧✦✧

Dear Night, *(I can't wait to cut my hair. You know? But your seed grows. And I can feel every movement of it growing like a beanstalk to heaven. Or pulotu. Or beyond the Milky Way galaxy. And into the outer or parallel universe of the unknown. But like they say, e manino lava le mata o le vai... the eye of the water will be clear sooner or later....)*

With secret delight I watch the stars that sleep in your oceanic eyes. How they twinkle each time your insatiable mouth covers the geography of my body. How your lips press themselves on the mountain that is my face as I feel the wetness of your tongue in the crevices of my ears, the valleys of my collarbone, my ribcage, my stomach, as you arch towards the summit of my breasts, circling my lifeless nipples that come alive under your breath while I stroke your long long hair, watching it curl around my fingers. Your mouth moves towards my belly-button, circling it over and over as if you're seeking another entrance into my body until you become weakened and your head drops and falls into the garden that grows and blooms between the forest of my thighs where you quench your thirst in the lake that springs there. Like an abandoned animal that has been deprived of food and water for days, weeks, months, you devour me with such force that I break apart into a million pieces that float like cosmic dust at the birth of a star and I am lost. Lost in a universe that has no words for shame, guilt, fear, pain. Where the Light makes space for the Dark and the Dark gives birth to the Light. Like waves caressing the lips of the land I am suspended between the Vast Expanse and Infinity.

Dear Day, (*Today I was in Apia, sweating at the Public Library. I couldn't read. Couldn't concentrate. Thinking you'd burst into the Pacific Collection anytime. I look for you everywhere, Sia. Everywhere. My pain is deeper than the lake. I ache so much sometimes I think I'm going to throw up everything I ate, which is not a lot lately. I mean, I don't eat. Food is tasteless. I've been fasting lately. I tell myself that if Ghandi could do it for more than 60 days then I could surely do it for the rest of my natural life. Where are you? Where?*)

They say each season has its own lou, its own pole to pluck and gather breadfruit, its own warrior to fight its wars but that a time comes when even the greatest of warriors needs to lay down His or Her weapons and pass the torch to the next generation and just be. Still. Malie tau! Malie toa! Is what I call out to you now. You have fought a good fight. They've already composed epic poems and songs and dances and stories after you. As long as these islands are peopled you will continue to live on and on and on and I will smile whenever I hear them call out your name as they recount your conquests in legendary accounts that magnify your fearlessness, your courage, your valor. And I will hum along to their tune. Hum until I can hum no more. But for now, come to me Day! Let us be still together. Let us hold each other and listen to breadfruit leaves fall and fall and fall. Or to the sounds of waves lashing at the shore in that violent, tender dance. Come to me Day. Bring me an Owl egg with you as your oso, your gift when you visit an old friend. So I can look at you and see you and listen to you and laugh with you and love you and love you and love you and remember the time when there was no time.

Dear Night, *(I'm wet just thinking about you. Again. Just watching people on the boardwalk stroll by hand in hand and I wished so much that our love was not the secret that it was and that we could have done the same, walking hand in hand in the middle of the government road, can you even conceive us doing that? It's funny how Americans express their love. Everything is so out in the open. They say I love you at the drop of a hat. It's so impersonal. They don't know the language of love that we know. You know? I'm thinking of the lake and suddenly, a gentle wind from the ocean caresses my cheek and I'm blushing in the middle of the afternoon at the thought of you whispering, Suga!).*

Watching you in such a famished state causes my moa, my center, to stir. Stirred by your ravenous hunger that moves me to tears. Tears that flow down my mountainous face as I listen to you drink, making forbidden sounds that awaken all my senses in a most frightening way that reminds me of what my mother and the aunties and the pastor's wife (your mother, our mother together), used to say whenever they warned us about girls and women of the night. And now, I too have become such a girl. You have turned me into a woman who seeks nourishment in coconuts that fall at midnight. Husking them with my teeth. Drinking their forbidden juice. Devouring their soft flesh that leaves me yearning so that my hunger expands at the thought of you away from me and I die a thousand little deaths at the thought of you near.

Dear Day, *(Sometimes I think being away from you is like dying. A slow and horrible death. A death unlike the Death I've come to know with you. As I find absolutely no joy whatsoever in this death. Unlike the Death I came to know with you. The delicious and sinfully delectable Death at your bosom or in the garden between your thighs. Oi aue!).*

Tell me the story of how your grandmother used to shave your head with bamboo when you were a girl, to make you more desirable towards the many chiefs who sought your hand in marriage, despite the fact that your physical beauty had little to do with your prospects; status being the main determinant of who was to eventually take your hand and bear his children. Something you never experienced. A warrior's children are the children of the village one protects.

You already knew that.

Poor grandmother!

Did she know she was shaving the head of a warrior?

A girl who was to grow up to walk into a battlefield of mighty male warriors alone and leave it with the silence of a pool of blood at twilight?

It was Grandmother Aveolemasina who named you Alofafua. Freelove. One who loves freely. But history remembers you at times as Sina, lover of Eels or Nafanua, Forest Woman, a clot of blood, hidden in the Land from your incestuous birth, and War Goddess. Leaving that one lock of curl which she lovingly tucked behind your left ear as she oiled your body and told you to stay out of the sun, even though you knew you were not meant to be shielded, still, you bit your lip and obeyed. The first lesson of a warrior is to obey one's elders. Those who have walked the path. Remind me again of how you kept eels as pets. Defying an entire village while you ran with him into the forest. Only to later realize that he was teaching you the most painful lesson a warrior should ever learn. And while your very soul died along with Him as his head rolled onto the dirt reddened by the flow of his blood, which he had instructed you to do, you picked it up and buried it. Such an act took all the strength you had and you became weakened and fell onto the grave and slept a restless sleep of nightmares. Until the first rooster woke you with His excitement.

And there it was!

The first coconut tree!

Food and drink as promised by the Eel!

Sealing Him to you each time you pressed a coconut to your lips. But before that, your grandmother, Alofafua, the nurturer of you, the caregiver of you would tell you to lay your head on the ali and listen to her hands on your skin as she combed your pubic hair and you giggled because it tickled. And as she did, you had visions of weapons which you later designed with stark precision and the secret tears you shed as you held them in your hands, knowing how much blood they would shed. Why do you cry? Alofafua would ask. And you wouldn't answer. Your silence a premonition of the color of the life you were meant to live, the color of a crimson Horizon at sunset after a victory.

Your memories have become my memories Day.

Your wounds have become my wounds.

Your pains have become my pains.

The terror that once lived in your eyes is now reflected in my own eyes. I hold your anguish in the palm of my hand, pressing it to my mouth, swallowing it so that no one else will ever know.

I am possessive that way Day.

No one else will have you.

No other man or other woman or fa'afafige. (Are you smiling?)

No one will have you Day.

No one but me.

Dear Night, (*I can't eat also. I can't sleep also. I can't taste salt also. I can't taste sugar also. I am indifferent to the world around me. Tell me, Ioage. Where are you? Where? Even the spaceman misses you. I mean, spacegirl. Ha. Even my laugh is laughable. I can't laugh without a shot of melancholy like an invisible blanket of loss that covers every word that escapes my lips. I long for your hands to be on my hands, my hair, my mouth, Ioage. I'm longing that I'll never. I'll never. Be. With anyone. Else. But you!*).

I'm not listening to the Moon as it sings star songs of the constellations and the meteors that travel light years from Jupiter or Mars, orbiting the Sun for millions of years before they collide with Earth. Instead, I'm listening to your moans as you draw the fragrance from the flower with the thousand petals that live there. And bloom there. Wildly in the dark there. The dark that has become y(our) alter of worship. So that after what seems an eternity you surface finally with an intoxicated smirk on your face to offer me petals. The taste of which lingers in your mouth as it covers mine, sending me floating on the Sea of Tranquility while you continue to devour me with kisses. Light and violent kisses, marking my body with your tongue. I have no shame, Night. Your touch has erased all concepts of original sin from my very Christian memory, replacing it with the magnificent darkness that is you: savage and gentle, fierce and gentle, wild and gentle. Bold. Your strength has become my strength. Your weaknesses have become my own and I am powerless at your touch. You ravish every pore of my skin while your whisper causes my heart to flutter like a school of butterflies seeking the nectar of wild flowers. Approach me from the South and I will coo. Approach me from the East and I will shiver.

✧✦✧

Dear Night, *(I find myself talking to myself, reciting word for word all the conversations we ever had from the time we said hello to the last time I saw you. I am like a mad woman walking in the shadow of your memory, of our memory together before the moto ka took me to the airport and flew me away from you, so far, far away).*

I can no longer wait for your response because there's an urgency in what I need to tell you. Your touch has transformed me. Turned me. Turned me from a good girl instructed from birth to be selfless. To always think of others first. To be modest. To be meek. To be humble. To dissolve and disappear into the group. The family. The village. The community at large. The girl who is the first to be called by the pastor's wife (your mother, my mother, our mother together), to serve tea to matai after the evening service. To say tulou when she passes anyone older or whenever she passes a grave or a cemetery. A girl whose been raised to memorize the chronology of the books that make up the Old and New Testaments. Kenese, Esoto, Levitiko, Numera, Teuterenome, Fa'amasino, Ruta....That girl is no longer a girl, Night. You've turned Her into a woman. A shameless woman, wandering headless without memory of other people. When I am with you, I have no family. No friends. No village. No district. No island. No country to shame. I am yours, dear Night. I belong only to you and your soft caresses. I am yours eternally. Yours forever and ever. Yours ad infinitum!

Dear Day, *(I'm not saying this to make you feel good. It's the truth. It's my truth. But I can't imagine sharing my body with another human being. Another woman. Another man. A fa'afafige even. They don't have your scent. Your musk. The smell of you on my fingers which I press to my nose when I am in a room full of people. Damn, this hurts. So much its unbearable. So this is what they mean by the unbearable lightness of being. Only I feel like I'm dying daily. There is no being in that. Only death. And it's not Our way of Dying. It's just deadly boring if you ask me. Living without you is like perpetual suicide. Over and over and over again. Are you still drowning like you said you were? Where are you? Where?).*

My head keeps turning behind every hibiscus, behind every raindrop, behind every shadow, wondering if you are there. In town, I search for your scent among strangers. In buses. In taxis. In Herr Retzlaff's store a.k.a Le Fale o Kelefogi. Herr von Reiche's Supreme Ice-Cream house. At the Tivoli. The Savalalo Grand. The Starlight. The Fale Kifaga o Saiga. Fale o Fong. The Gold Star Building. The courthouse. The Police Station. The Air New Zealand Counter. The SPIA counter. Le Fale o Nelesoni. a.k.a. Nelson's. Le Fale o Pakele a.k.a. Bartletts. Misimoa's. A.k.a. Mr. Moors. Le Fale o Evegi a.k.a Carruthers. Aggie Grey's. Even the Ioane Viliamu Building! The Pharmacy. Le Maota o Tina. The marketplace. Amau's. Under the town clock. Burn's Phillips of the South Pacific. Morris Headstrom's. Le Ele'ele Fou. CC's Stitches & Things. And The Nelson Public Library! But alas, you are not there! Where are you Day? Where?

Dear Day, *(Again...Are you also hurting like I am? Do you also feel like someone has gutted you? Unload your insides to the side of the street while you gaze and gaze and gaze at the government road, looking into the face of every man woman and child that exits Koma's bus. Wondering if you were one of the passengers. Wondering?)*

I look for you among faceless men and women, swimming in oceans of conventions. Surfing waves of the mundane where they hide from the terror of admitting the utter boredom, the pettiness, the straight lines that make up their lives. Men like my father (your father), and women like my mother (your mother), who play roles: social and cultural roles that maintain the status quo and uphold their so called ideas of dignity, of nobility and of good standing Christians who have sadly, forgotten. Forgotten what it's like to abandon one's self to dancing without fear that someone might be looking. To adore one's own body and that of the lover's. Not only in the privacy of one's own thoughts but in the very public exhibitions of poula nights that shocked the first missionaries out of their very Victorian minds and sent them back to England with reports of our savage ways. Ways that needed to be desperately reformed and erased all together from the social, religious and cultural imagination. Calling us godless because we worshiped no idols, no symbols like a cross for instance. Too quick to judge they saw only what they wanted to see. Or rather what could be seen through their spectacled eyes that could not penetrate the forest of you, O Great Owl! So they called us barbarians whose sins needed to be cleansed. And by blood, no less. But tell me this. What is sin, I ask? What is sin but the inherent belief that one's culture and way of life is superior to another's? That one's God is the only God? That you can deliberately annihilate a people's history and wipe it completely from memory, replacing it with guilt and shame and terror while you stand there at a podium dressed in white, telling them about the sins of the body while you offer them flesh to eat and blood to drink on Sundays. And they have the audacity to call us cannibals! To say that our ways of having sex are dirty and sinful. Sinful acts that have given birth to so many hang-ups. Not to mention a century of ethnographic psycho-analysis; of psychosis so deeply hidden under our very 'happy camper' smiles. We've forgotten how to love, freely. How to make love with any meaning. How to give what we can to a family who've lost a chief or a mother or a son. Here, take this. A string of fish. An octopus. And a small basket of taro that still has dirt and small worms attached to its roots. It's what we have. And we offer it to you. Not the circus that it is now. A fa'alavelave is no longer about what is given to ease someone's pain but rather it's become a competition to see who has the most wealth.

Dear Day, (...*are you avoiding me? Please don't. Ok? But if you've found someone else. Someone that gives you that thrill like I told you, then do what you think is best. But know that I will always be here for you. Always, keige lea. Ua iloa?*)

I flew into the future and this is what I saw.

A funeral procession.

And this is what I saw.

This is what I saw, Day. Oh the horror!

Cases upon cases of tinned fish, corned beef and mountains of food in white plastic foam. Rolls and rolls of the biggest fine mats. And a dollar stuck to a can of Pepsi to signify one's cultural generosity. Here, there's more where that came from! Forget the sorrow and loss of the grieving family. Forget their pain. Forget their cry. Forget the cry of your own family and the lengths they had to go to cough up your demands. Forget that the rent is due. That your own children need to be fed. That the loan sharks are already after you because you're still not done paying off the last fa'alavelave and your car is already on the list for repossession while your house is to be foreclosed at the end of the month. Instead, let's just show them our might. Our power as a collective. Just this once. And wait for them to reciprocate by returning everything we've given and more. How did it all come to this? How? Remember when love was intimate and genuine? When sugar and salt was shared? Along with shame and joy? When a beating was stopped by any adult who passed by and called out, Se ua lava loa! That's enough! When making love was the exchange of breaths with the beloved not only to experience ecstacy but as a sign of utmost respect for the sacredness mirrored in the lover and his or her ancestors who also danced that dance. The dance that is as ancient as when the Sun first looked upon Alofafua with cosmic desire so powerful it burned the river where she stood on its banks adoring herself and her reflection in its depths. So that when she turned towards the Sun and opened her legs, exposing the flower that lived between her thighs, the Sun became so aroused by her daring beauty that he removed his rays and fell upon her, sinking, sinking deeper into her as he danced with her and danced with her and he danced with her and danced with her and danced with her until his seed was firmly planted in her but not before he died a thousand deaths and returned to the Heavens while Alofafua returned to the land of her father, Nu'uolemanusa and gave birth to its first descendant; Nanamuolela or Fragrance of the Sun.

✧◆✧

Dear Day, (*I don't care where you are or what you're doing, I can't stop thinking about you, try as I might to distract myself with other thoughts, you envelope everything, Sia. EVERYTHING!!*)

Now you know why talking chiefs refer to the fallen Sun whenever a chief dies. It is in honor of the union between the celestial and mortals, sealing them and their descendants in the eternal dance of life and death. But I digress dear Day. I digress from the faceless men and women who are the face of authority. The eyes of the law. Of what is proper and right and dignified. In their eyes, we are nothing. Nothing but social deviants. Nothing but outcasts. Untouchables who have lost all considerations for family, village and country. They will spit on us if they were to ever discover us. Bark at our "waywardness". Snigger at our "perversity." Condemn our "irresponsibility." Our "selfishness," and our "promiscuous union" which they will refer to over and over with self-righteous ugliness as a meaningless and illicit and incestuous liaison unsanctioned by their institutions. An impossible union! Un-Samoan! Oh the irony! Tell them Nafanua! Tell them!

Dear Night, (*I am not ignoring you, Ioage. I just can't come to your every beck and call. I have a life you know!!! A life that I'm trying desperately to lead as close to all the principles and ethics that you had taught me. Do you think you're the only one hurting? A kama lea? / Man? Do you think your pain is more painful than mine? I can barely see the professor during lectures and I've missed the bus several times because my head is somewhere else. Somewhere sandwiched between your stomach and your thighs. So don't say hurtful things like that any more. You hear? Just because I don't respond, doesn't mean my heart*)

*and my soul and my mind is not on fire. Burning with desire
for you. And you alone. No one else but you. Don't you ever
question that. Ever! You hear?).*

I cannot help but close my eyes and fish the memory
of my ancestor Alofafua once more, daughter of the Great
Owl and Gau who was given to the Sun as a bride. The
desire of a celestial being for the secret petals between a
mortal woman's thighs and the tunnel that leads to her
sacred womb burn wildly in your eyes Night. One that will
shield us both from the stones they will throw at us and
the first stone will undoubtedly be, Who is her mother?

Dear Day,
Suga!..............Girl!

Dear Night,
Aua!..............Don't!

Dear Night, *(Everything is different here. For one, the cars drive so fast on roads that float above your head. Blows my mind, Ioage. I long for the silence of the forest. The buzz of bees. And the scent of moso'oi. The scent of vines. Of the earth. The land. Of you).*

Ahh . . . the Fragrance of the Sun. I can smell it from here. Through time and space. Remember when I left you I told you that it was a pity I hadn't tasted you? That I didn't have the time? Let me taste you now night. Let me kneel before your mountain and stroke your mountainsides with my Sun rays. Let me stroke and stroke and stroke you until your desire is so intense you erupt like a volcano. And I will drink your fires, Night. And drown in your craters. What a death you've given me. Oi aue!

Dear Day, *(Your letter arrived today and I nearly ate the paper! Suga! E! ka le lava pologa! Girl, eh! I'm tired of being a slave!)*

I can smell you in the Rain from here. Your frangipani. Your gardenia. Your tiare. Your pikake. Your Seaweed that I touch to the tip of my tongue. Oi aue! You're killing me Day! Oi aueeeeeeeeeeeeee!

Dear Night, *((I sat what's called the S. A. T which was a university entrance exam. I scored a perfect score for the Mathematics section. And I had 5 mistakes in the English. Apparently my score was so incredible they had me sit it all over again. With three administrators in the room. I felt special momentarily. And then it dawned on me that they didn't believe me that I could score that high a score. Funny enough, Night, when I retook the S.A.T, I scored a perfect score on both sections, Maths and English. Apparently this is unheard of. They don't think a Samoan or a Pacific Islander had the capacity to score such a score. Which is*

why I did that deliberately to piss them off. I'm now at U.C. L.A. Studying to be a physicist. There's a Samoan woman here married to a Micronesian who heads the Pacific Islands Student association. They are an amazing team. She's doing her Ph.D in Gender Studies and he is a full professor of Pacific History. Now I know what you meant. The world of ideas is like a floating world. Only I have access to it. And I have the propensity to become what you've always wanted me to become. Someone who walks the earth with the pearl of the world in the palm of her hands. Thank you, Ioage. The spacegirl and me thank you from the bottom of our hearts).

Don't resist Death, my Sweet. Dive into its depths and embrace everything it has to offer. But first, you need to empty your head of reason and empiricism before you could surrender to it's euphoria. You'll find its abyss deliciously sinful, if I may say so myself.

Dear Day, *(Today, I became closer to my father that ever in my entire life, Sia. Here's why. The nu'u fined Elisaia's family with 50 pigs, 200 good ie. 10 cows, in the discovery of his son Elisaia la'ikiki's affair with Koligi, the sa'o's wife. It was devastating. All I did was bow my head in silence and looked out at the sea. At one point I locked eyes with Kolilgi and I saw her pain. It was immeasurable. Like the one I too carry. She broke my heart, you know? Poor woman. The Elisaia family were to be banned from Gu'usa. But it was my father that stopped it. You know how he is not part of the fono a matai, the meetings of the high chiefs. But yesterday, he went before the chiefs. He bowed in utter humility, and begged them to please, have mercy on Elisaia and on Koligi. That we could massage this problem by ourselves. That it didn't need to be escalated so that other villages know of what had befallen us. It is unfortunate*

*that these things happen. But they had happened. And it
is up to us to mend it. To heal it. Ourselves. The matai at
first were hard. But my father's humility touched them. So
Elisaia and Koligi were brought before the fono. They were
scolded. Scolded with harsh words. Especially Koligi who as
you know is older than Elisaia. He could easily be her son.
A woman is the nurturer, the matai told her. She should
not be seen looking into her own house for a lover when
she has a husband! The highest chief in the village! Elisaia
started weeping until he was sobbing. Koligi had tears in
her eyes but she did not make a sound. There was no ifoga.
No need to bring attention to the matter. The matter was
solved by the matai. But still, the men of Elisaia's family
followed him wherever he went yesterday and didn't leave
him out of sight. They feared that he might commit suicide.
He looked determined in his shame. And so was Koligi in
hers. I just thank God you and the spacegirl are in America.
Away from the wrath of the village. I wanted to hug both
Elisaia and Koligi to me. To comfort them. To tell them that
it was ok. These things happen. Not by our own choice but
by divine intervention. They way our own love story beagn,
you know? But I don't want to bother you futher with what's
going on here. How are you feeling? It's nearly time, isn't
it? Remember, your waters. That when your waters break,
don't panic! Ua iloa? Apparently, the water will gush out of
you like a strong waterfall, with such force it would thrill
you at first until the inevitable pain that accompanies it.
Think of the lake and the moso'oi blossoms. And that wild
boar. And how my snore kept him at bay. Think of my big
toe when it happens, ok? I hope that brought a smile to
your face. Alofa aku).*

Is there a chance that we could witness an eclipse
together? Let me know.

Dear Night, *(I want you to know that I am about to do something that you might not agree with but I am doing it anyway. Not because I would ever deliberately disrespect or dishonor you but because I feel it in my gut to be the right thing to do. Fa'alogo ae se'i laku le fagogo. Listen as I tell you my story. I got kicked out of my sister's house the instant she found out about my pregnancy. She was so devastated by it, Ioage. Devastated! She kept calling me all sorts of names, trying to make me ashamed and guilty for your seed inside of me. Then she asked me who the father was. But as you might suspect, I was unrelenting in my resistance. We did not sleep. She kept threatening that she will revoke my visa. That I needed to go back to Samoa. Back to Gu'usa and face the consequences of my actions. Tell me, she kept saying. Who is this pua'a elo? This rotten pig that did this! That attacked out family's honor? She told me that I was shameless and that I had defeated our family's name. That she is absolutely ashamed of me! And to think she did everything so that I could come to America and soar like an eagle in the home of the brave and the free. And now, look at me! Who is he? Tell me! She kept yelling at me. But I just bowed my head and tuned her out. And focused on the scent of the moso'oi. And your scent Ioage. I just felt like I was in the forest again and I couldn't hear her at all. I didn't wish to alarm you. I am fine. I have decided to give the space girl to Kevin and Losa. They are good people who don't have children of their own. They have tried for the last 10 years but they discovered a cist in Losa's fallopian tube that prevents her from ever conceiving and successfully carrying a baby to full term. Ioage, I know you will understand. I feel it in my heart. That this is the right thing to do. As much as I love the thought of us in our baby, I know I am unable to*

care for it and give it the kind of life that Kevin and Losa will. They are amazing people who will care and love the spacegirl with all their hearts. I told them about you and your wishes for names. They say they will respect your wishes and are deeply grateful. They keep asking me if you are ok with giving them the baby. I tell them you are. That you are the kind of man who respects his woman's mind and that whatever decision I make, I will make on your behalf. They were impressed with that and thought that was very mature and thoughtful. I told them about you and they are in awe. I am too. And yes, when my waters broke, Kevin held my hand and told me I would be ok while Losa called the ambulance. They took care of all my expenses. I decided not to breastfeed Sa. That is her name. Taeao'oleaigalulusa. Roslyn Perez. She's beautiful, Ioage. She has your big nose and big ears and big feet. Ha!)

I haven't heard from you since the eclipse. There are limits even to the universe you know. Tell me, have I lost you? Have I? Look at me, Night! I demand you to look at me! Can't you see what you've done to me? You have single-handedly colonized me and my senses. Monopolized my every move. Erased the memory of anyone who has ever sought my attention so that my first waking thought is to be suspended between your thoughts. To be cradled by your reflections, your contemplations, your musings of a meaningless existence without my life and my existence.

And while you might be somewhere else. Somewhere, where the bed is soft and the music intoxicates and the food is exquisite and there's wine and other women and other men and fa'afafige and other delightful temptations of the flesh, I want you to know this: I will just as easily throw myself to a den of lions like Daniel did in the Bible or eat stones on demand or drown myself in this Big Blue Ocean rather than continue in this life without you. Don't

make me beg, Night. Make your Self known. Astound me
before the Sun comes up!

✧◆✧

Dear Day, *(That was a very wise thing you did, Sia. I
apologize for the pain and suffering I've brought upon you
and your still very young life. That being said, I wish I was
there to shield you from your sister and from anyone who
questions your integrity. That being said, I can understand
what she is going through, Sia. It is what I had known
was coming all along and I warned you about it but what
can we do? Like your Aunty Aimaʻa would have said, Ua
le aoga leaga ua masaʻa le ipu vai /It is of no use because
the cup of water has been spilled. I can feel Simeamativa's
disappointment. Her disbelief. Her loss. After all, her way
of looking at the world is shaped by the status quo, which
is not how we see the world Sia. But do you know what?
I have every confidence that this experience will give you
depth and perception into human nature in ways that will
turn you into a greater woman. A knowing woman. And
a woman of compassion. I know giving Sa up was not an
easy decision for you Sia. I can still hear your pleas in the
forest and I can feel your pulse from here, woman. It was
undoubtedly a painful but wise thing to do and I am proud
of you. Remember that always. Now that Sa is in good
hands, you can concentrate on school. Put everything you
have into it. Your heart, body and soul. Astound yourself
Sia. Never forget that, ua iloa?)*

I like it when you do that thing you do with your Sun
rays. My mountain rises again just thinking about it! How
you turn the horizon from blue to pink to red as rivers
empty themselves with urgency towards the ocean. It's
mind blowing! Tell me what you're going to do about it,
Day. About my mountain rising again at the very thought
of you. Tell me Day, tell me!

✧◆✧

Dear Night, (*Thank you for your encouragement, Ioage. I know it's always there but I still need to hear you say it, you know? I have now moved into an apartment in West Hollywood. My room-mate is a girl from Vietnam. She reminded me of Mei-Ling. She's a fashion model slash pharmacist major. As I had already told you, I had declared a double major two yeas ago and I've been studying Physics and Astronomy. I want to further understand how our ancestors were able to calculate everything in time before compasses and other technology. I met a Tongan-Fijian-Samoan woman. Her name is Kat Lobendahn. She is here studying astrology more specifically and wishes to some day sail the vast Pacific from Hawai'i to Tonga all the way down to New Zealand. But guess what? She wants to do this with an all female crew and has suggested that I join her. I think I might consider it, Ioage. It will be the culmination of everything you ever taught us! But we'll cross that bridge when we get there. As I know you have to be physically fit for such an undertaking. Besides, time has become more and more important to me lately and my radius is quite narrow. Apartment. Plasma Science Facilty. Supermarket. Apartment. It's sad. I know. But there's just so much to learn and discover and explore and so little time to do it all in.*

Space continues to fascinate me, Ioage. You know me, I'm a trekkie for loife! Ha. I am fascinated by it as I am by controlled thermonuclear fusion, my latest obsession. I don't wish to brag but my department awarded me with the Outstanding Undergraduate Poster Award, which is kind of a big deal here. Apparently, I'm the youngest student to ever receive the award since its creation thirty some years ago and I wished you were here to see me accept it. When I accepted the award, I spoke firstly in Samoan as you might suspect. 'Ia avea lenei avanoa e momoli atu ai la'u fa'afetai fa'alelava i o'u faiaoga uma. Ia avea lenei fa'ailoga e fai ma lu'itau i lo'u nei tagata vaivai aua a'u taumafaiga uma mo so tatou lumana'i manuia lautele. I take this opportunity to give my heartfelt thanks to all my teachers, past and present. May this award continue to challenge me and my humble person to always strive for the best for the good of mankind's future. Additionally, I have received a full scholarship from the MC sq Foundation for graduate school, which I will begin in the Fall semester, on the day I turn 21. Ehh! I have been associated mainly with the Basic Plasma Science Facility devoted to the study of the basic plasma phenomenon. As you know, plasma is from the Greek, and means 'anything formed' and is merely one of the four fundamental states of matter which as I know you also know to be solid, liquid and gas with the difference that plasma has properties unlike those of the other states. Think lightning and neon lights! I've been working mainly with Professor Philip Culbertson. He worked on Mauna Kea in Hawai'i and was adopted by a Samoan family there and considers me a daughter which is very comforting. He reminds me of Tama Esimoto, your father, our father together. And he's always asking me to teach him more Samoan as he wants to surprise his aiga in Hawai'i next time he visits.

Anyways, my research centers on the fundamental problem of controlled thermonuclear fusion which in Gu'usa lingo would be the process which generates energy in the Stars and the Sun. Ioage, if fusion energy is achieved, water could be used as fuel, providing an almost unlimited supply of energy. Imagine that, Ioage! Just imagine that! I mean, the potential pay-off is just mind blowing! And that's just one use of plasma! Another is to purify water and rid it of contaminates which will become more and more necessary as the world's population continues to explode at its current rate. Eh! But as your Uncle Va'apopo used to say, Fa'apu'upu'u lau kala suga, ua koeikiki ka le kaimi o pi'iga. A ea? But as your Uncle Va'apopo used to say, Make your story short as it's nearly time for Big Time Wrestling. Ha!

It all sounds complicated, Ioage, but it really isn't. It's all about working with these devices which momentarily are not large enough to produce the results in volume which we hope for but hey, we'll eventually get there, a ea?

I've just realized that I'm beginning to talk and sound like you! Ha! I am reminded of that beautiful day once more when you first told me about Euler's Equation! Remember? Ioage, whenever I'm lost, I think of the perpendicular line missing from your tattoo and how Mathematics has become such an intrinsic part of my life, like breathing, you know? At any rate, that missing line on your finger makes me smile. Ioage, I am in a world where everything you ever told me makes sense to me now. Thank you so much for preparing me, Ioage. I had no idea you were preparing me for this. But you know what? You were wrong about me loving another man. Admittedly, I have been able to turn some heads here. A chiropractor I saw in my last trimester asked me about you. Where you were. And when I told him, he said, Let me be here for you and the baby, Sia. I want to massage you and realign your senses. I thanked him for his generous offer but I told him that my senses had already been re-aligned and that I'm only here to fill my brain before I return home, to where my man awaits under the shade of the moso'oi. He smiled and as he held my hands and told me, He is one lucky sonofabitch. Cause I wouldn't have let you out of my sight. Not for one minute. I told him you didn't either. And that I was the lucky bitch. Not the other way around which made him roar as he held me and said, Eres una hermosa mujer guerrera. Puedo tener el honor de llamar amigo? I said yes. He can call me friend. And that you would do the same. He has a heart of gold, Ioage. Like Felicity and Mei-Ling. And it wasn't just Dr. Neruda. Even a linguistic professor, Lyons. Professor Paul Lyons, who is studying Pacific languages to understand the origins of our people's migratory patterns. He told me that he would gladly step in to take your place. That he will hold the baby to his heart as if it were his own. He is a beautiful man who is very humble and reminds me so much of you. I told him about you and he smiled and said, I don't expect anything less from you, Sia. Your loyalty to Ioage makes me wish I were him. But I understand. I will love you as a true friend. I held his hands and thanked him from you, Ioage, and simultaneously, I keep telling him that everyone else must have migrated from somewhere else but that Samoans or at least Gu'usa peeps originated in Gu'usa and nowhere else! But he has this theory that we all came from Taiwan. Leikioa sasaiga ou maka li'i, Ioage! Ha! No wonder why you have slanted eyes, Ioage! Ha! I just want you to know that I love you more now from this distance than ever before. I do, Ioage. I do. Before I go, I just want you to know that. Ok? I know mail takes forever to get here and there but I trust that you are well. And your letter that time about what happened to Elisaia and Koligi tore at my heart. Thank you for telling me. And thank you for your compassion towards Koligi. I am proud, so terribly proud of you. You make me want to do more. To become better. I hope one day to return home, to astound you, kama lea. Ok, I'm heading off to the post office. And for your information, Sa is Kevin's heart. When I see them together, my heart misses a beat. As they remind me of what I had originally wanted but couldn't have. And how you searched your soul to give it to me. I know no other man will do that for me, Ioage. Which is why I'm tied to you like a wolf, a swan, an albatross. I'm your albatross Ioage. We mate for life, bro! You better believe it! Say hello to your new students. The girls must just adore you! Ha ha! E, kala ula a! Just jokes. Fa la'ia. Bye then).

I prefer to keep these things to myself as you know Night, but since you insist. First of all, I'm going to gently caress the grass that surrounds your mountain. Cupping Owl eggs that might be in residence there. Taking them into my mouth one by one until I hear you moan and the sounds of your moan causes my rivers to flow to glide and cascade over ancient mossy rocks. Then I'm going to stroke your mountain, a little faster. Using the cave of my mouth to engulf you until your moans become my moans and your desires become my desires until we drown and drown and drown with wild abandon.

Dear Day,
Oi aueee!
Dear Night,
Ahhhh!
Dear Day,
Kiss me!
Dear Night.
Hmmmmmmmm.
Dear Day,
Oh Night! Oh Night! Oh! Oh! I'm....!
Dear Night,
Me too, Day! Ahhhhhh! What a death!
Dear Day.
Can we do it again?
Dear Night,
E, kauka'ikiki! Hey, Cheeky!
Dear Day,
Please Night, pleaseeee?
Dear Night,

But what about the stars? The constellations? The galaxies? The planets? The solar system? Not to mention the moons.

Dear Day,

Ahhhh, the Moons. I would die to see even one, Night.

Dear Night,

I'll see about that eclipse.

Dear Day,

You do that Night. But hurry. These inter-galactical torrential rains are killing me, if you know what I mean!

Dear Day,

My name is Night. You killed me and my aiga and my family and my nu'u and my village and my itumalo and my district and my atunu'u and my country. Prepare to die!

Dear Night,

Like I said before Night, I will not die for your family or for your aiga or for your village or for your nu'u or for your itumalo or for your district or for your atunu'u or for your country even. Only for you Night! I die only for you and you alone. No one else but youuuuuuuuu!

Dear Night,

Ahhh Day!

Dear Day,

Nighttt!

Dear Night,

Day!

Dear Day,

Night!

Dear Night,

Dayyyyyyyy!

Dear Day,

You look so stunning in Death, Night.

Dear Night,

You make me blush.

Dear Day,
Ahhhhh, I am sighing at the thought of you blushing.
Dear Night,
Suga!........ Girl!
Dear Day,
Se aua se!.......... Don't, please!
Dear Night,
Sweet dreams, k?
Dear Day,
K.
Dear Night,
Good night, my Heart.
Dear Day,
Ia manuia fo'i le po/Good night to you too.

ACKNOWLEDGEMENT OF SOURCES

I am grateful for the insight and wisdom I received from the following authors and books and articles and plays and poems and songs that became important to me during the writing of *Freelove*. I don't quite know or have the words to express just how valuable the knowledge I received from their works. It is a tremendous debt that I know I cannot possibly repay. All I have, and I say it wholeheartedly, is thank you. Fa'afetai, fa'afetai, fa'afetai tele lava. O la outou pule lea!

O si Manu a Ali'i by Aumua Mata'itusi Simanu Papali'i, Tama'ita'i Samoa; *Their Stories* by Peggy Fairbarn-Dunlop; *Raising Research Consciousness, The Fa'asamoa Way* by Anne Marie Tupuola; *Aspects of Samoan Spirituality and Christian Spirituality and Spiritual Direction* by Sr. Emanuela Betham (SMSM); John Kneubuhl's *"Polynesian" Theater at the Crossroads*; *At Play in the Fields of Cultural Identity* by Caroline Sinavaiana-Gabbard; *The Last Virgin in Paradise, A Serious Comedy* by Teresia Teaiwa & Vilsoni Hereniko; *Gender Status and Power in Samoa* by Penelope Schoeffel; *Fa'afafine Notes* by Dan Taulapapa McMullin; *E pele i 'upu, pele i ai, pele i aga, pele i foliga* by Atua Tupua Tamasese Ta'isi Efi; *Ola* by Albert Wendt; *Lagaga: A Short History of Western Samoa* by Malama Meleisea; *Samoan Custom and Human Rights* by Unasa L.F Va'a; *The Ifoga, The Exchange Value of Social Honor in Samoa* by Cluny Macpherson & La'avasa Macpherson; *Fa'a'aloalo: A Theological Reinterpretation of the Doctrine of the Trinity from a Samoan Perspective* by Rev Dr. Luma Va'ai, Ua motu mai le taula; *'Va' Oration Epilogue* by Fa'amatuainu Tino Pereira; *Whiteness, Smoothing and the Origin of Samoan Architecture* by Albert L. Refiti; *Finding and Forgetting the Way, Navigation and Knowledge in Polynesia* by Damon Salesa; *Stop Being Cowards*, Eliota Fuimaono-Sapolu, interview in the Samoa Observer; *Our Sea of Islands* by

Epeli Hauʻofa; *Psychoanalysis and Tongan Poetry: Reflection on 'The Song of Flowers'* by ʻOkusitino Mahina; *Some Use of Chants in Samoan Prose* by John Charlot; *A Grammar and Dictionary of the Samoan Language with English and Samoan Vocabulary* by George Pratt; *Traditional Samoan Music* by Richard Moyle; *First Contact in Polynesia, the Samoa Case, 1722-1848* by Serge Tcherkezoff; *Oceanic Encounters, exchange, desire, violence* edited by Margaret Jolly, Serge Tcherkézoff & Darrell Tryon; *Quest for the Real Samoa* by Lowell D. Holmes; *Not Even Wrong: Margaret Mead, Derek Freeman and the Samoans* by Martin Orans; *Sex, Lies, and Anthropologists: Margaret Mead, Derek Freeman and Samoa* by Paul Shankman; *Food, Power and Globalization in Samoa* by Jim Bindon; *The Rare Plants of Samoa* by Art Whistler, *Coming of Age in Samoa* by Margaret Mead, *The Making and Unmaking of an Anthropological Myth* by Derek Freeman; *The Fateful Hoaxing of Margaret Mead* by Derek Freeman; *"Heaven and Earth" Samoan Indigenous Religion, Christianity, and the Relationship Between the Samoan People and the Environment* by Grace Wildermuth; *Contesting Development, The Experience of Female Headed Households in Samoa* by Rochelle R. Steward-Withers; *Theorizing Self in Samoa* by Jeanette Marie Mageo; *Aitu: Eine Untersuchung zur autochthonen Religion der Samoaner* by Horst Cain; *Die Samoa-Inseln, Entwurf einer Monographie mit besonderer Brucksichtigung Deutsch-Samoas* by Dr. Augustin Kraemer; *Penina Uliuli: Contemporary Challenges in Mental Health for Pacific Peoples* by Philip Culbertson; *The Tragedy of Julius Caesar and The Merry Wives of Windsor* by William Shakespeare; *The Daffodils* by William Wordsworth, Star Trek, CBS and Paramount Television Series; *Oka, Oka Laʻu Honey* and *O Oe o Laʻu Uo Moni*, lyrics by Le Fetu Lima/The Five Stars; *Fai Se Tatalo*, lyrics by Le Punialavaʻa; and Madonna's *Like A Virgin* by Billy Steinberg & Tom Kelly, 1983.

AN INTERVIEW WITH SIA FIGIEL
BY VILSONI HERENIKO

1. If someone were to ask you what Freelove *is about, what would you say to them?*

The short answer would be that it's a love story. But it's also a story of the sexual and intellectual awakening and coming of age of a 17 ½ year old girl. A very bright, brilliant and bold girl named Inosia Alofafua Afatasi, whose thirst and curiosity for knowledge leads her into a forbidden relationship with her teacher who becomes her lover. That would be it in a coconut. A more extended description of the book would be that, *Freelove* explores so much more in its very minimalist structure and style which is basically the pre-colonial and colonial history of Samoa as told by star-crossed lovers whose love exceeds the boundaries of time and space which I hope readers would find engaging in ways that it engaged me while writing it.

2. What are your reasons for giving this novel a title that is more transparent (and less literary or metaphorical) than the titles of your earlier novels? Was it difficult making a decision or did the title come to you before you wrote the novel? (My preferred title would be Coconuts that Fall at Midnight, *a line in your novel.)*

The concept of 'free love' had been floating in my world of ideas for the last three decades since I left undergraduate studies where I first came in contact with it in a history class that talked about manifest destiny and how it justified the acquisition of the U.S territories of Puerto Rico, Guam and American Samoa. It was in this context that Margaret Mead and Derek Freeman's names popped up again on my radar, only this time, instead of merely hearing about them, the way I had heard of them back in high school when a peace corps teacher excitedly told us that Samoa was featured on the cover of Time magazine and the perplexed look on her face when none of us showed any interest, I remember the professor asking me, specifically because he knew I was Samoan, Mead or Freeman? Who got it right? And then he giggled and smiled in a way I hadn't recognized him doing before. It was strange. I remember smiling back awkwardly but not knowing exactly why because I hadn't read either Mead or Freeman's works. All I remember from that day was a sense of defeat at my own ignorance of what appeared to be a punchline ('free love') that supposedly represented where I was from.

That is the background to how *Freelove* got its title. It's a book I wish to give to anyone who has been asked that question, the one the professor asked me three decades ago. I feel that I've devoted a fair amount of time researching and getting to know that cultural anthropological 'controversy' that lead to Samoa being called a sexual paradise for 'free love' which is vastly different from the highly regimented Samoa I grew up in.

And it's because of that, that the protagonist's middle name is Alofafua or Freelove; the unconditional love that Samoans are taught to have for anyone who seeks one's help. I wanted the protagonist's name to convey an indigenous concept and its implications both personally and communally for Samoans which in essence means a reclaiming of a concept that is gravely misunderstood by outsiders. By the way, *Coconuts that Fall at Midnight* is an excellent suggestion metaphorically and a perfect title for the book, but I knew that if I were to ever lay to rest outsiders claims on 'free love', then I would have to reclaim it not only for Samoans but for Pacific peoples across Oceania, hence the title as it is.

3. How is this novel similar or different from your earlier work? And would you agree with me that

your observations about gender relations and your insights into Samoan life are more nuanced and complex (even positive for the most part) in **Freelove** *than in your earlier writing?*

where we once belonged was written by a 27 year old woman slash history buff who was living in Berlin, Germany at the time and had newly discovered the works of Women Writers, while still digesting the canon of (dead white) male narratives.

It was while I was living in Berlin that I came in contact with African, Chinese, Carribean, European writers who showed me other ways of being, and in particular, I found myself vis a vis one of the world's greatest living writer, (although I didn't know that at the time), Nobel Prize winner, Toni Morrison who came to Berlin on a reading tour of her then recently released novel Jazz which basically turned my world upside down.

At the time, there was an urgency in my pen to break the silences of sexual violence and to form a space for a female voice, not only my own but for others who needed to be heard. Morrison's *The Bluest Eye* became fundamental in asserting that urgency on the Pacific landscape where it was basically non-existent.

And so, I created Filiga Filiga, as the ultimate disciplinarian along with Iosua Iosua who mirrored Cholly Breedlove's sexual frustration that lead to the rape of his own 10 year old flesh and blood. This vision of men was thus tied up with my own understanding of patriarchy at the time and how Samoa's social hierarchy cemented the fate of the girl as an entity that was only seen but not heard.

Fast forward twenty years later to the writing of *Freelove*. I understand now what it's like to be a mother. I am someone who has experienced my share of wounds, both physical and emotional. And granted men were responsible for some of the pains in my life, I was also equally responsible. And that's what made me change the way I viewed the literary narrative.

I wanted specifically to express a broader view of men, based on the different types of men I grew up with. I basically wanted to create a male character that was the antithesis of what I had previously written. That took a bit of growing up on my part.

I'm very excited with Mr. Ioane Viliamu's presence on the Samoan and Pacific literary scene. He is my version of Braithwaite's Mark Thackeray as immortalized by Sidney Poitier in the movie version of *To Sir, With Love*. But unlike Filiga Filiga and Iosua Iosua, Mr. Ioane Viliamu is a righteous dude. And I hope readers of *Freelove* find him just as intriguing.

4. The early works are quite bold in that they venture into taboo areas (such as sexual awakening and experimentation) that most Pacific writers avoid like the plague. With Freelove, you write about sex and lovemaking (some passages are as good as the "Song of Solomon"!), as though you "don't give a damn" what your conservative readers think of you or the novel. What gave you the courage to be so free?

There was an urgency and a strong conviction in the first books to address what I myself was experiencing then, as I was closer in age to Alofa Filiga, Samoana Pili and Malu. The silences surrounding female sexuality not only in our lives but especially in literature compelled me to find a way where conversations about this very culturally sensitive subject could take place. The role of literature as I understood it then and still do now, is to break silences from the inside/out which is not only a form of liberating the self but of decolonizing the mind simultaneously.

I knew after reading Toni Morrison that I was going to have to learn how to write. That is, to pay attention to the tools of writing and words and how they're linked to other words became important to me then.

My early memory of the sensuality of language came from reading the bible which I did in Samoan. It's interesting that you mentioned Song of Solomon, whether you meant Morrison's masterpiece or the bible itself, either way, they're both texts that influenced me tremendously.

The freedom you speak of came to me when I was living in Berlin. There, I discovered pre-colonial texts and found that sexual vulgarity in the Samoan language is almost sacred as documented in the work of German ethnographer, Augustin Kramer. For instance, some of the songs were so 'vulgar' that it's like cerebral gymnastics trying to imagine how that could ever come about physically...I mean its' quite stunning the metaphysical dynamics of old Samoan in comparison to the saccharine Samoan we now speak. The Samoan language itself has undergone such a traumatic transition . . . the Samoan we speak now is a colonized Samoan that has woven out all that is intimate and 'vulgar' and impure so as to fit a Christian aesthetic that is sanitary, safe, and deadly dull and boring if you ask me. And that's where my freedom came from. It came from an awareness of how sexuality was viewed by Samoans themselves before the missionaries arrived and it is my firm respect for the ways of old Samoa that pushed me towards sexual metaphors (the octopus in *where we once belonged* or the moon in *The Girl in the Moon Circle* or the tattoo in *They Who Do Not Grieve*).

In fact, *Freelove* was conceived immediately after *where we once belonged*...but I didn't realize that it would take me this long to finally write it, almost a 20 year break between the 2 books. I wanted Freelove to be exactly what it is; a movable feast that is pleasurable to all the senses and celebrates the power of sex and indigenous sexual practices and doing so unapologetically and yes, freely, the way Albert Wendt did in Sons for the Return Home or John Pule in The Shark that Ate the Sun only it would be from a very female place of origin, which explores sensuality and sexuality with tenderness, passion and compassion. And quite honestly, I was more concerned about the poetics of Freelove than about fear of reprisal from conservative readers. Besides, diabetes has taken my teeth. What else is there to be afraid of?

5. The novel's structure is minimalist and yet its concerns are many (culture, colonialism, materialism, religion etc.). You also tap into a myth pool that gives your novel a resonance and timelessness that transcend Samoan culture. For example, you weave in the myth of "Sina and Tuna" into the love story of Ioage and Sia and in doing so, imbue their love with a mythical quality. (And as I read it, I am also reminded of the biblical story of "Adam and Eve" in the Garden of Eden.) Could you elaborate on your intentions here and your creative process?

For the last 20 years I have wanted to write a book that is stylistically minimalist in nature with a focus on a smaller cast of characters than my earlier work which as you know is peopled with all sorts of colorful characters that reflect the vibrancy of our Pacific communities. Freelove is the internal monologue that occurs within Sia's character as well as a devotion to poetry and sexual realism, a critique of the status quo and society's indulgence or rather over-indulgence in the material.

These large themes had to come together in this narrative as I knew that this would be the last time I base a story in Samoa. As a writer who has lived more than half her life away from 'the source' I felt pushed towards writing this all out of me.

Fagogo or Samoan storytelling is at the root of my work, along with the Holy Bible which is how I learned how to read; in Samoan before I learned how to read English. I guess because of this, my idea of God and the Divine is Samoan and I find that even after all these years of speaking English, my thoughts and thought process is Samoan. That is the power of the mother tongue.

I've found in my creative process that it is very closely linked to those two traditions which surprisingly are not that different from each other. In Samoan for instance, the story of the origins of the coconut talks of Tuna or the Eel as the ultimate martyr who sacrificed his life for his lover, Sina, in similar ways that Jesus sacrificed himself for the sins of the world. I don't believe in the concept of original sin as it is not indigenous to Samoan thought. But I do however understand the concept of sacrifice, which finds its way into my books subliminally or more blatant as it does in *Freelove*.

In *Freelove*, I was very aware that I wanted the lovers to be in movement, in similar ways that Marguerite Duras's characters in The Lover, find love on a ferry crossing the Mekong River. The idea of the red pick-up truck was thus born. Instead of the ocean, I saw Inosia and Ioage in the forest. I guess this takes me back to my readings of Nathaniel Hawthorne's *The Scarlet Letter* and that scene in the Forest between Hester Prynne and Minister Dimmesdale where they confess their love for each other, after 7 years of silence for Hester and hell and torment for Arthur.

It is also in the forest that Ioage finally tells Sia what happened to him in New Zealand. The Forest is also symbolic of The Garden of Eden where Adam and Eve learned that they had "sinned." These associations with world literature and with the bible more specifically are all part of the colonial imagination and how it got filtered into my own consciousness.

Although in the back of my mind, I always associate the forest with Nafanua, the War Goddess whose name means hidden in the land as she was born a clot of blood as a result of the incestuous relationship between her mother Tilafaiga (the Siamese twin that brought the art of tattoo with her sister Taema from Fiji) and her half-Man/half Eel Uncle Saveasi'uleo, who ruled Pulotu, the Samoan underworld and Hades equivalent. *Freelove*, is an expression of the reluctant marriage of the indigenous with the West, the native with the West, the Samoan language with the English language, etcetera, etcetera.

6. Some of your readers might see your novel as quite critical of certain aspects of Samoan culture (its materialistic tendencies or religious hypocrisy, for example). I view your criticisms as arising out of a deep love and compassion for the culture and its people. How would you respond to anyone who accuses you of "biting the hand that feeds you"?

I don't necessarily see myself "biting the hand that feeds". If anything, I see my work as a perpetual meditation on ways to restore the integrity of agency, like those writers who did before us. Albert Wendt, Epeli Hau'ofa, Vincent Eri, Konai Helu Thaman, Subramani, Pio Manoa, Sano Malifa, Ruperake Petaia et al.

My critique of my society is rooted in a deep love and respect for her. Most importantly, I was and continue to be determined to empower girls and women and strive always to clear the path for future voices to be heard. I feel I have done that and I refuse to indulge anyone who demands that I apologize for it.

7. Ioage and Sia are two of the most interesting characters I have ever come across in Pacific or world literature. They are the kinds of people I would love to invite to dinner: intelligent, open-minded, witty, honest, free of hang-ups, and they love to laugh! Are these two characters based on or inspired by people you know or are they purely works of fiction?

Both Inosia and Ioage were conceived over time. I was pregnant with them for nearly five decades and it took me six weeks to give birth to them. Six weeks locked up in a warehouse in Tampa, Florida, writing day and night! They are an expression of people I've known not only growing up in Samoa but during my travels around the world several times both physically and metaphysically in the books I've read and the authors I've known.

But more specifically, Inosia and Ioage were created to fill an ache and a need that I had as a reader. To create characters that were absent from the literary scene. Characters rooted in their own culture and language and values. Who were smart and sensitive and loving and deep. Characters I'd like to know and invite to dinner myself.

8. One can't help but wonder if the Sia in your novel is based on Sia the writer when she was seventeen and a half years old. Do you want your readers to make this association between your female protagonist and yourself? And how much of the novel is autobiographical?

They're not really that different. Only Sia in the novel is smarter but she basically has the same values as me. I grew up in a rather typical and conservative household (our aiga's homestead in Matautu Tai) and I contributed vastly to our bible collection since I always placed first in Sunday and Pastor's school which was no easy feat and is how I am remembered by the elders whenever I return home.

I am a trekkie for life. That's another thing we have in common. We are similar in every way except Math. I hate Math but love Science and I know that had a lot to do with my Math teachers who always made things more complicated that they actually are. One of my very close friends is an Engineer and she was so excited when I read her excerpts of *Freelove*. I wish she were my Math teacher growing up. I would have loved the subject more.

I really wanted to create a protagonist that was smart. Smarter than me. That has been my focus over the last 20 years. To create characters of depth whose intelligence and perception supersede my own which of course meant that I had to do a lot of research to ensure this was so. I chose Math for Mr. Ioane Viliamu because it is a precise and universal science which connected him to his first love, Mei-ling while I chose Physics for Sia to show how her initial love of Math which was nurtured by her teacher, Mr. Ioane Viliamu had developed into a love for another subject that is equally compelling and mind-blowing, one she discovers on her own while away from him. And not only does she discover it, she completely owns it in a way that astounds Mr. Ioane Viliamu and makes Ioage proud.

Concurrently, I want young Samoans and Pacific Islanders who would read the book to know that the characters are them. Sia and Ioage are all about the empowerment of the reader and thrusting her or him into the realm of possibilities, which as Inosia reminds us all are multitudinous, amaranthine and endless.

9. Sia and Ioage are into Mathematics and Science. Ioage has a university degree and Sia is pursuing one at novel's end. Both are also steeped and well-versed in traditional Samoan culture. In real life today, if the love affair between them (a "brother" and his "sister") is discovered, what is most likely to happen to the lovers?

There is a scene from Book Two, a letter from Ioage in Samoa to Sia at U.C.L.A. that details what happened when Koligi the sa'o or high chief's wife was caught in a forbidden love affair with Elisaia, a much younger man that could possibly be her son. The lovers were confronted by the chiefs and it was Father Esimoto, Ioage's father who contained the wrath of the village from the severe punishment they had prepared which was banishment from Nu'uolemanusa which would be the same for Sia and Ioage.

I could easily see Ioage's father Esimoto being removed as pastor and their family being banished from the village. The same would go for Sia's family. Banishment is severe in Samoa. It is one of the worst forms of punishment. It's being ripped away from the land where your placenta is buried which essentially means that you are dead. It's a death sentence, really. One that could only be reversed through a ifoga, or a ceremonial apology but even that is not guaranteed. Especially if the ifoga were unacceptable, as in the case of rape or murder.

But in this case, the breaking of sexual taboo that involves the pastor's son, it would most definitely be severe. Because it means the breaking of the covenant between the messenger of God (the pastor) and the village.

10. Unlike Sia's experience with her father and mother who do not express love for her or each other verbally, Ioage and Sia are quite expressive verbally (physically, they are off the charts!) about their feelings for each other. Your novel provides an alternative approach to expressing love that is idealized rather than actualized in real life. Of course fiction is an excellent medium for providing alternative ways of being. Could you comment on the ideal and the real in Samoan society and what you are trying to achieve in your novel?

When I was growing up, you couldn't even be seen together with a boy you liked. Let alone hold hands with him. The laws that governed intimacy were quite strict. All eyes were always on you at all time; day and night. The expression of love in a family was not done with words but rather with actions. For instance, Ioage's decision not to go through with getting a tattoo. And his father's response to that act. That is love. Understanding how your actions impact the well being and happiness of others.

As for Sia and Ioage's language of love, I wanted those conversations to take place the way they did. In an honest and unpretentious way that illuminates the language of intimacy in ways not previously spoken or written in Samoan or Pacific literature. For instance, I wanted girls and women who would read *Freelove* to know that it's okay to speak up during sex when something hurts. Which is not often done in real life. People would much rather endure pain with a smile than admit that something is wrong. So much that needs to be said is not said. The important stuff. The things that are unsaid once spoken, can change the direction of someone's life. Those are the kinds of conversations I wanted to encourage with *Freelove*.

11. You have done a lot of research for this novel, judging by all the references that you list at the end. Why was this necessary and how did all this research influence your thinking about the issues or concerns in your novel? Give us an example in the way of illustration.

I'm a student of history so naturally, I'm curious about the past. The whole Mead/Freeman controversy and my feeling inadequate when first posed the question Who Got It Right? triggered and ignited an intense interest in the history of Samoa which became magnified during my time in Berlin when I found myself standing before material culture in Volkekunde Museums across Germany, specifically in Berlin, Leipzig and Hamburg.

I also met up with a German scholar on Samoan ancient Religion Dr. Horst Cain who became a mentor to me. His extensive knowledge pointed me to the works of Dr. Kramer and other European ethnographers and since he knew I was returning to Samoa, he brought me in contact with Dr. John Charlot at UH Hawaii, another specialist on ancient Polynesian religions who had written on Samoa. I met up with John and we had long talks on the concept of aitu which Horst specialized in.

I threw myself almost exclusively into reading as much as I could about first contact. The idea itself gives me chills even now. I wanted to know what life was before the whalers and the explorers and the missionaries and what life was during those early incidences of first contact. The most fascinating account is to be found in the logs of Captain La Perouse during what was to become known as Massacre Bay which is the French account of that first contact that lead unfortunately in violent outburst and the death of 12 Frenchmen (documented) and apparently 39 Samoans (French documentation).

One thing I remember from my history lectures was the professor saying over and over that history is written by the victors. I understood that concept in Samoan because of the many versions of stories in existence which swayed favorably to whoever won a war. But juxtapose that with a people who had a whole other mode of recording history, I found myself asking, what about people who didn't have a written language? How do we account for their victories and their losses in an English context?

Massacre Bay on the island of Tutuila, American Samoa for instance, is called Massacre Bay not because of the so called 39 Samoans whose lost lives outnumbered the 12 Frenchmen. But rather, it is Massacre Bay because 12 white men lost their lives there. After that encounter, Samoa became known as barbaric and savage and was avoided like the plague by captains of industry et. al for another three decades until the arrival in 1830 of missionary John Williams (Ioane Viliamu) of the London Missionary Society and his crew on Sapapali'i, Savaii and the conversion of Samoans to Christianity was initiated with High Chief Malietoa Vainu'upo, my ancestor and great, great,

great, grandfather, whose family God was most probably the Owl, (or so it is in my dreams).

The research I did over the last two decades was to further familiarize myself not only with the cultural anthropological controversy of the century which had Samoa merely as the background, but more specifically, as someone who is fascinated by language, I wanted to further know and to learn the Samoan language, its complex nuances and its meanings as well as Samoan indigenous beliefs and ways of looking at the world which are vastly different from the way we see things today due to our colonial past.

What makes me sad sometimes is how Samoans see current missionized ways of being as indigenous. It's quite incredible. Which is why I specifically decided to dive into research and to learn more about our pre-colonial past and to bring that to the surface the way Mr. Ioane Viliamu did with his re-telling of Samoan history.

12. Ioage and Sia often laugh uproariously after ribbing each other mercilessly. This is of course a common trait among Polynesians or Pacific Islanders, a means by which we bond with each other. Elaborate then on your view of laughter (or humor) and why it plays such an important role in Freelove. And do you think we should all laugh more often?

My earliest memory of laughing out loud came in the form of watching a faleaiku, or Samoan theater. The power the performers had to address just about any taboo subject one could think of in the presence of respectable folks fascinated me then and continues to do so to this very day. I learned very early on that faleaiku, which we all associate with pure comedy was actually a tool used not merely to make people laugh out loud but to raise awareness of issues in the village that were not spoken of easily.

Faleaiku of course are performed only by men and fa'afafige. Never or rarely with women. I secretly wanted to be a faleaiku performer. To be able to hold an audience's hearts in the palm of one's hands was something I found uber exciting not to mention sexy! And faleaiku as you might know is all about sex and innuendos, you know? Transforming one's self from man to woman to beast right before an audience is such a turn on that takes a special knowledge of people and human nature to be able to pull off successfully. I have the highest respect for its practitioners as the best of them are geniuses disguised as clowns. It is how I wrote my very first stories, ending them always with humor which is something my mentor, John Kneubuhl saw and discouraged me from doing. He said, Sia, stop this. Stop wanting to be liked. You're trying too hard. Stay away from shallow waters and venture out to the deep. I sort of knew what he was saying to me. We all have that need to be liked. And as a younger writer dealing with the issues of sexual and physical abuse, I wanted to be liked as it was just too intense and deep. So I left Samoa and went to Berlin and for a while, I was swimming in the deep. Even drowning in it in my attempts to learn how to swim and find my own voice.

But it wasn't until reading Epeli Hau'ofa's Tales of the Tikongs that opened my eyes to the possibilities of including humor in my own narratives. I don't know what 'where we once belonged' would have sounded like had I not read 'Tales' because I was swimming in the world of Toni Morrison which as you know is void of pure comedy and has very subtle humor. I understood the deliberate omission of humor in Morrison's novels as a tool she employs to talk back to those in power who expect her to write humorous characters in the same way blacks were depicted in early Hollywood as nothing but either entertainers or housemaids. And for a while, I was caught in that web and found it to be the surest path for me to follow as it is literature that in the words of John Kneubuhl, was deep and profound

'Tales' freed me from this trap. And I was half-way through writing 'where' which was 'too deep' as it focused squarely on sexual and physical abuse and turned when I first met Epeli in Hawaii during that Inside/Outside Conference in '94 and it was after that meeting that I decided to let it go. To embrace the pure comedy I was raised with alongside the painful stuff. So in many ways, 'Tales' allowed me to be myself. To tap into that powerhouse which I knew something of and I've tried to develop it with each novel, though I suspended it in They Who Do Not Grieve but felt it absolutely essential to *Freelove* as it sets the mood and the tone of Inosia and Ioage's relationship as it developed and matured throughout the book.

And lastly, the medicinal properties of laughter alone are numerous. And we should all be perpetually engaged in it or at least be very close to its healing embrace.

13. Who is the ideal reader of your novel? Since the novel is predominantly in English with a smattering of Samoan, I presume the ideal reader is a college or university-educated Samoan (from a university outside Samoa?) who is steeped in Samoan culture but is more comfortable speaking in English than in Samoan? But how many of these ideal readers are out there? I suspect you want non-Samoan speakers to read your novel, and I also suspect that most of your readers will not understand the Samoan in your novel. Could you explain your thinking here?

The instant the last line was written, I sent the first draft to friends across Oceania asking them to review it. We had a very tight deadline for the digital version on kindle and so, time was a factor. But the overwhelming response from 20+ readers at universities from Papua New

Guinea to Pohnpei to Hawaii to Tonga, Fiji, New Zealand, Tahiti, Australia and Samoa was affirmation that I was not singing alone.

That the issues raised in *Freelove* are common throughout the vast Pacific and I was merely the one holding the pen. And that's how I felt throughout the entire 6 weeks of writing it. That I was writing it not merely for myself or for Samoa but for the Pacific and Oceania at large. The almost instant response from academics and other writers and artists and critics across Oceania was indeed very comforting to me. As ideally, they are the first readers I had in mind.

This might give the impression that *Freelove* is for university folks only. It really isn't. *Freelove* is written in a language that is accessible to everyone and anyone who wishes to explore and discover new ways of looking at the world. Samoans will find it exciting. Especially because of its bilingual nature. Having said that, I really don't see the Samoan in *Freelove* as an obstacle for non-Samoan speakers since the Samoan is translated and included, side by side, right there on the page and not in a glossary which was how I conceived it originally. I had done what I needed to do as far as bilingualism is concerned in *where we once belonged* and the deliberate omission of a glossary, forcing the reader to become more active contextually.

In *Freelove*, I wanted the reader to be aware of my thought process as a bilingual writer which is why the Samoan is very present in the text but it is done not to intimidate anyone but rather to show how a bilingual mind works (my own) as it is expressed through Sia and Mr. Ioane Viliamu's use of language.

14. *How would you respond to critics who say that your novel is perpetuating stereotypical notions of young Samoan women being readily available for free*

love? Could you explain with reference to Margaret Mead's book Coming of Age in Samoa?

Saying that I perpetuate stereotypes of young Samoan women being readily available for free love is like saying Mr. Spock is a Neural Parasite or a Salt Vampire or some other inter-galactical monster. It is simply preposterous.

My work has been and continues to strive not only to challenge the colonial gaze but to empower and to increase the visibility of a female narrative that has been silenced not only because of that very gaze but by virtue of the Samoan social hierarchy which is for all practical purposes very patriarchal in scope.

I am very much aware of the connotation the word 'free love' has regarding the Pacific Islands as I've stated earlier, particularly in reference to Samoa. I'm talking of course about the image of the Pacific as a paradisiacal sexual haven which originated in the narratives of early Western whalers and sailors and explorers and artists like Paul Gauguin and other male writers like Pierre Loti and Herman Melville who did not understand our ways and our protocols and why we were dressed (or rather not dressed) a certain way and what we mean by alofafua or alofatunoa or free love.

Margaret Mead's very female narrative, *Coming of Age in Samoa. A Psychological Study of Primitive Youth for Western Civilization*, not only put Samoa on the world stage but cemented its reputation as the home of sexual promiscuity without consequences or punishment which got blown way out of proportion by Derek Freeman and his obsessive insistence on exposing Mead's paradisiacal free love as nothing but a fraudulent myth and offered instead an aggressive people with uber violent tendencies at every turn and we found ourselves smack in the middle of the cultural anthropological controversy of the century deemed to be so gargantuan in proportions it was going to dethrone it's matriarch who Time magazine had deemed 'Mother of the World' and cited as one of the most influential woman of the 20th century.

Meanwhile, back in the islands, the average 'primitive youth' and his or her friends were like, Mead who? Freeman who? What? And all this was played out on the world stage and promoted by U.S media particularly the New York Times that broke that story in September, 1983 with Samoa merely as background. Talk about the total hijacking of agency.

That is the background into which all my books were born. Each was born with the intention of further re-claiming that agency not only away from the colonial gaze but to own it, ourselves, so that we could tell our own stories, our way. And *Freelove*, is but a continuity of that idea of indigenous sovereignty, which has its origins in Albert Wendt's *Sons for the Return Home*, Vincent Eri's *The Crocodile*, Konai Helu Thaman's *You, The Choice of My Parents*, Epeli Hau'ofa's *Tales of the Tikongs*, Subramani's *The Fantasy Eaters*, Ruperake Petaia's *Blue Rain*, Sano Malifa's *Looking Down At Waves*, Satendra Nandan's *The Wounded Sea*, Jully Sipolo's *Civilized Girl*, Momoe Malietoa von Reiche's *Solaua, A Secret Embryo*, John Kneubuhl's *Think of a Garden*, John Pule's *The Shark that Ate the Sun* and other Samoan and Pacific writers who dared to create narratives that reflected their own experience while simultaneously striking back and refusing to be captured by what they've been traditionally confined to, which is a constant look at the seat of empire for affirmation and for definitions of 'literature.'

15. Out of all that you have published, this novel impresses me the most. Your talents as an artist/writer soar and hover above us like the wise owl you write about. Like the owl, you warn us about the dangers of materialism and individualism as well as cultural

intolerance (to name a few) and you're not afraid to shit on the giant white threads intended for White Sunday clothes. Tell us about how you see your role as a writer among conservative folks (young and old). And to end on a humorous note, do you wish you had a Mr. Viliamu in real life that carries a bottle of vinegar (or stain-remover) in his backpack for emergencies?

Immediately after I returned from the celebrations in London of *where we once belonged* after it had won the Commonwealth Writer's Prize Best First Book for the South East Asia-South Pacific region, I went and lived on the island of Savai'i where I taught English at a Catholic school for boys and girls.

It was while I was in Savai'i that I discovered for myself the dichotomous nature of the older men and women I came to know there. On the one hand, they appeared to be very respectful with their white hair and grace. And then on the other hand, I've never heard such vulgarity in my entire life during storytelling nights, called Po Poka when I spend the nights with my very outwardly conservative aunties in the village of XYZ when the idea of hoaxing or tausua was introduced to my not so innocent ears and yet, I found myself in a dimension I had never experienced before in that it shocked me to listen to these unassuming women and the almost incredible way they talked about sex and metaphor and innuendos. It was the best year of my life! Like finding the pot of gold at the end of a rainbow!

And in response to part 2 of your question, please indulge me in a question of my own. So what makes you think I don't have a Mr. Viliamu? Um, excuse me, Dr. Hereniko. That's highly presumptuous of you.

You've basically fried my brain, man.

Fa'afetai tele. Thank you.

And as Sia and Mr. Ioane Viliamu would say, Ia manuia!

ABOUT THE AUTHOR

Sia Figiel is an award-winning, internationally acclaimed poet, writer and painter from Matautu Tai, Samoa. Her first novel, *where we once belonged,* won the 1997 Commonwealth Writer's Prize, Best First Book for the South East Asia - South Pacific region, the first Pacific Islander to win the prize. Her work has been translated to French, Catalan, German, Spanish and Danish. Sia has represented Samoa and the Pacific Islands at international literary festivals and conferences and has performed her poetry at the Shakespeare Globe Theater, London. Sia is also an ODDe Warrior and fights obesity and diabetes with diet and exercise. She is an amateur athlete and has completed several 5k's to raise diabetes and cancer awareness, the 2015 Irongirl, the Clearwater Florida half Marathon, the 2014 Nautica Malibu Triathlon, and the 2015 Honolulu Marathon. Sia is a tandem-mom to two teenage sons. Freelove is her fourth novel.